CLASSIC CASE

Out of the trees came a runaway horse, complete with maiden in distress. This happens often in romances and sometimes even in the true tales I tell. The cure is well known: Hero leaps for the bridle and hauls the brute to a halt. Maiden falls swooning into hero's arms, hand in marriage and half the kingdom to follow in due course.

That's in the romances. In real life, that prescription is more likely to cause disaster than stop the horse. The cheekstrap-grabbing maneuver is horribly dangerous; I have seen men maimed trying it, and riders killed. The prudent course is to yell at the stupid girl to hang on and let the beast run itself to a standstill, which it will in a few minutes. If she can keep her head out of the branches, she will come to no great harm.

Having said that, I confess that on this occasion, I jumped to my feet and ran to intercept. Call it a reflex ...

By Dave Duncan
Published by Ballantine Books

The Seventh Sword
THE RELUCTANT SWORDSMAN
THE COMING OF WISDOM
THE DESTINY OF THE SWORD

STRINGS

REAVER ROAD
HUNTERS' HAUNT

A Man of His Word
MAGIC CASEMENT
FAERY LANDS FORLORN
PERILOUS SEAS
EMPEROR AND CLOWN

A Handful of Men
THE CUTTING EDGE
UPLAND OUTLAWS
THE STRICKEN FIELD
THE LIVING GOD

THE CURSED

THE
HUNTERS'
HAUNT

Dave Duncan

A Del Rey® Book
BALLANTINE BOOKS • NEW YORK

A Del Rey® Book
Published by Ballantine Books

Copyright © 1995 by D. J. Duncan

Library of Congress Catalog Card Number: 94-74137

ISBN 0-345-38459-8

Printed in Canada

First Edition: April 1995

10 9 8 7 6 5 4 3 2 1

To my daughter Judy, who has never had a whole book dedicated to her alone but has merely shared one (because we did not then realize how many books there were going to be!), this book is belatedly and lovingly dedicated.

WARNING

This is the second extract from the memoirs of Omar the Trader of Tales to be offered to the public in vernacular translation. Certain passages herein may seem to contradict statements Omar made in the first book. Those who have not read the first book will not be troubled by this. Those who have will not be surprised.

1: The Traveler Returns

Some harsh words had been spoken the previous summer, the first time I lodged at the inn. Nothing serious, milords, just a minor misunderstanding—a small imbalance on the slate. A trivial sum, truly!

I admit that appearances were against me. My taste for shortcuts has been misinterpreted before. When the hour for my departure dawned—it was slightly before dawn actually, but I am by nature an early riser—I chose the swiftest route. I was in a hurry, being bound that day for Gilderburg, a city many hard leagues away. Moreover, I feared I might disturb the other guests if I went clattering down the stairs. Only when I was halfway across the vegetable patch did I realize I had forgotten to pay my bill. The house door would still be locked, so I resolved to leave the money on the hostler's desk in the stable.

That was the only reason I approached the stable. Why else would I do so? I had no horse lodged there!

The trouble arose because the innkeeper, Fritz, motivated by unseemly greed, had rented out even his own quarters the previous night. He had chosen to sleep in the hayloft overhead, from which he had a clear view of my window.

The stable door gave me a little trouble. Then it swung open, freely and quietly on well-oiled hinges. I stooped to lift my bundle, and when I straightened up I was exceedingly surprised to discover myself facing what appeared to be a haystack.

I have often been complimented on my expertise in animal husbandry. I am well aware that general practice is to put the livestock on the ground floor and the fodder in the loft. It is a technical matter of getting them up ladders. In this case I could not see why Mine Host Fritz might have reversed the normal filing system. Then I realized that what I was seeing in the chill pre-dawn light was Mine Host Fritz himself. He had no shirt on, which is what had confused me. When I tilted my head back, I discovered his face, higher up.

There can be something very unwholesome about blue eyes. Jaws of that magnitude are better left un-clenched.

Instinct warned me that there could be a misunderstanding brewing. I explained carefully, using short sentences and speaking distinctly.

Another problem then arose, concerning the house tariff. I do not deny that it was posted in large letters on the taproom wall, a list very detailed and well lit. No one could claim that the inventory of services offered was incomplete or the scale of charges ambiguous. The Hunters' Haunt was an inn of the highest standards. Though small, it offered quality personal service most welcome to experienced and sophisticated travelers such as myself. Within its range, it was one of the finest hostels I had ever graced with my custom, and one I fully intended to recommend heartily to the numerous fellow wayfarers I meet upon my travels—as I repeat-edly assured the innkeeper. However, being a stranger in the Grimm Ranges, I had mistakenly assumed that his prices were posted in Nurgic dinars.

To my astonishment, Fritz informed me that Gilder-burg thalers were specified at the bottom of the notice. I explained that every time I had been looking in that direction the previous evening, Fritz himself had been drawing ale from the left-hand barrel, directly under-neath. The vital postscript must have been obscured by his shoulders. True, that was a remarkable coincidence, and most men would not have blocked my view, but Fritz was not most men—only about three of them, hammered into one.

Of course I had funds enough to cover my tab, had the amount been calculated in Nurgic dinars.

That was the truth of the matter, milords. Alas, the oaf chose to disbelieve me!

Do not be too hard on him! Large as he was, Fritz was young for his responsibilities. Even an older, more experienced man might have misconstrued a situation of such manifest ambiguity. He was perhaps a little coarse in his language. He might have used more tact in the way he disassembled my bundle, pronouncing my spare garments to be useless rags and strewing them in the mire of the stable yard. Finesse is not to be expected in the young. But he resisted overt violence, which must have been a great temptation for one of his size.

Pretty much resisted it, that is. He carried me by my right ear over to some distant outbuildings, and there presented me with a monstrous ax, more fittingly sized to his thews than mine. He indicated ten or eleven tree trunks and where they should be stowed when cut into hearth lengths. And then he whistled up an animal I had seen the previous day and at first assumed to be a full-grown bear. It was a dog.

Its name was Tiny, but even by Fritz's standards that was inappropriate. Tiny, Fritz assured me, would keep me from leaving—ever, under any circumstances—until its master gave it the correct password to release me. Tiny was an excellent guard dog, the innkeeper added, its only fault being the killer frenzy that came upon it when it tasted blood.

While I mulled the implications of that subtle innuendo, Mine Ex-Host stalked away to prepare breakfast for his guests. Tiny ran a tongue like a black doormat over a picket fence of white teeth and lay down to plan my dismemberment.

The sun rose about then, promising a hard day, or

perhaps several hard days. I began with a few lusty blows of the ax, continuing until I judged young Fritz would be engrossed in other pursuits and hopefully out of earshot.

I think I mentioned that I am not without knowledge in the ways of our four-legged brethren? Pausing to catch my breath, I edged closer to the corner of the woodshed. Tiny raised a forest of hair down the entire length of its back, rumbling a growl I found strikingly reminiscent of the earthquake that threw down the walls of Atlambaron. Clearly the beast was expressing a warning that I should not progress any farther. Fortunately I was already close enough for my purposes.

To be explicit about my next actions might bring a blush to sensitive cheeks, so I shall wash over the details. Suffice it to say that I rendered said corner of the aforementioned woodshed of immediate interest to the dog. When I had finished, Tiny rose and came across to inspect my labors, its manner indicating a clear belief that it might not know much about firewood, but it did know about *that.* Tiny came, in short, within reach. When it turned away to initial my signature, I stunned the brute with the back of the ax.

I missed breakfast and lost my bundle, but I sold the ax for six Gilderburg thalers in the next village, so I came out well ahead on the exchange.

That, as I said earlier, had been in the summer. Now winter was setting in.

I had come to the Volkslander in search of the ending of a certain story and had failed to find it. The experienced collector of tales learns to accept disappointment and will not let it discourage him. Somewhere, someday, I would pick up the trail again—in bazaar gossip, a chance remark upon the highway, a tale heard in an alehouse, or perchance a legend recounted in a monastery. Meanwhile, warmer climes called me, for my way of life can be arduous in cold weather.

Three possible routes south were available. I could take ship, although the season was late. I might seek out a caravan following the amber road and accompany it as far as the salt rivers, but the wild children of the steppes were being gruesome again. All in all, it seemed safest and easiest just to venture a recrossing of the Grimm Ranges. The way is strenuous, but extremely scenic.

My sojourn in the northern marches had not been entirely fruitless. My repertoire of stories had been well rewarded. I left Luzfraul on a sunny, frosty morning, mounted on a sprightly bay mare, journeying in the company of a convivial band of merchants bound for the misty valleys of the Winelands. Our conversation sparkled like the ice crystals on the grass of the verge while we climbed through the foothills. I gathered some trivial tales for my collection, granting others in return, as is my wont.

We lunched well, seated on the bank of a joyous cataract, resting our mounts and making the crags ring with our laughter. The peaks above us wore their winter finery, white and pure in the sunlight. Scenery can be overdone, of course.

By afternoon the sky was taking on a menacing leaden hue, an unfriendly wind was tugging at our cloaks, and we had entered into the forest's dark domain. We passed few habitations, only the lonely cottages of woodsmen or charcoal-burners. We debated stopping and taking shelter at one of these, but rasher counsels prevailed. We decided to push on in the hope of crossing the pass before the weather turned on us—or turned at all, because nothing is more fickle than mountain weather.

Alas, it was not the elements that brought disaster upon us! We were set upon by one of the many bands of brigands that too often haunt such wild places. They were ragged, hairy, and ferocious—desperate, ruthless men who would have been more than a match for my genteel companions even had we not been outnumbered, which we were, hugely.

Although I am not without skill at swordplay, I was without sword that day. In any case, I have always preferred subtle stratagem to bludgeon brutality. Ambush may succeed where mere impetuous resistance will not. As my horse reared in terror, I reached up and caught hold of an oak branch fortuitously overhanging the road. I hauled myself up, drew my dagger, and waited to drop on the first marauder who came within my range.

I did not expect to escape attention for long, because the trees were bare of leaves. But I did.

I watched in silent horror as my companions were odiously murdered, their goods sequestered, their corpses stripped. Soon it was too late for me to achieve anything other than gallant suicide. In short order the outlaws drove off the baggage train, leaving only naked bodies behind.

Now I was in a difficult situation. The brigands had headed south, deeper into the ranges. They would go no faster than I, for many of them were still on foot. I had no desire to catch up with them to explain that they had overlooked me in their massacre.

My only logical course of action was to retrace my steps northward in the hope of finding one of those woodcutters' cottages. Already the first flakes of a winter storm danced amid the boughs.

Having waited awhile to make sure the desperadoes would not return, I scrambled cautiously to the ground, said a sad farewell to my erstwhile friends—together with a heartfelt apology that I lacked the means to grant them decent burial—and set off alone through the forest, whistling to keep up my spirits.

There are numerous tales of trolls and evil spirits preying on wayfarers in the Grimm Ranges. I have never spoken with a man who had met any himself, although that does not prove that the stories are false. I encountered none that evening. What I did meet was a mountain blizzard, the likes of which have killed more travelers than all the trolls ever spawned. In pitch darkness, flying snow is not white, it is black. It insinuates into every crevice of a man's clothing, it weighs down his cloak and shoulders, soaks his skin, fills his boots; trickles, freezes, and blinds. I should certainly have wandered off the road had it not been flanked by dense woods. I followed the path by bumping into trees.

But where were the cottages? Gradually I was forced to conclude that either I had staggered right by them without noticing, or else I had lost my way. Several routes lead up to the pass, and I might easily have taken a wrong fork. I had no guarantee that there would be any shelter at all on this road.

The night grew colder, the wind stronger, the drifts deeper. I never plague the gods with prayer, since omnipotence requires no advice, but that night I fully expected to greet them in person. I reached the last stage of endurance, the stage of promising myself a rest after fifty more paces and then fifty more, knowing that if I ever stopped, I should never rise again.

Suddenly, to my great relief and astonishment, a light blazed up ahead of me. A moment later it shrank and vanished, but I was not discouraged, knowing that a shutter blown open in the wind would not be allowed to remain open for long. What mattered was that there was a dwelling within reach, and it was inhabited. Surely no one would refuse hospitality to an honest traveler on a night like that?

I plowed through waist-deep drifts, guided eventually by chinks of light. I stumbled at last to the door and fell against the handle. The latch lifted. The door flew open and I through it. I reeled into a crowded room, accompanied by a hurricane of wind and blowing snow. Thus, not exactly unobtrusively, I returned to the Hunters' Haunt inn.

2: A Challenge Accepted

As inns go, milords, the Hunters' Haunt is not large. Being the only habitation of any sort for many leagues along the Gilderburg route, it rarely lacks for custom. Curiously, the fickle weather is more its ally than its enemy. In winter, wayfarers may be forced to remain in residence for days at a stretch.

The previous owners had died less than two years before, of pestilence—a professional hazard for those who associate with travelers. The business was now owned and run by their two children. Fritz I have already mentioned. He may best be described as an ill-tempered blond brute of unnecessary size.

His sister, though—almost do words fail me! Few women have ever bewitched me as Frieda had, upon our very brief acquaintance the previous summer . . .

I hear you sigh, miladies? You roll your eyes at my masculine ways? Ah, but hear me out.

Yes, of course Frieda had youth and beauty. One word from her would turn men's heads, and two their wits. She was as blond as her brother, tall for a woman, as tall as I. Her golden hair hung in two long braids. Her eyes were shining fragments of summer sky, her cheeks ripe peaches, her lips promises of Paradise. She was slim and light on her feet, and although her heavy homespun country dresses and voluminous aprons fought hard to hide all evidence of the figure they concealed, no man would doubt that beneath them further excellence would match the perfection of her face.

I will admit before you ask that she was accomplished in feminine skills—the house was sweet-scented and clean, the fare mouthwatering. A few weeks of her cooking would have induced obesity in grass snakes.

I do not deny that men too often judge women by such trivia, but I insist that in this case they were merely seasoning. Believe me, miladies, in my life upon the road I have met beauties by the thousand and good cooks by the hundred. One or two who were both, even. It was neither her physical charms nor her rabbit Wellington that endeared her to me, truly!

Frieda was not merely attractive and accomplished, she was also a wit. There is a rare combination indeed, in woman or man. How many humorists do you know who are truly likable?

She could return jest for jest, quote for quote, pun for pun, quip for banter, and the melody of her laughter lingered long in the memory. That first evening she bested me in barroom jocularity, greatly delighting the other guests and much surprising me. Yes, it does happen, milords, but rarely without my connivance. In Frieda's case I did not submit; I was outclassed. Nay, I was conquered! Alas, my flirtation was its own reward. I am certain no other man in the tavern fared better.

Mayhap I came closer than most did, for Fritz's evident animosity toward me waxed steadily stronger throughout the evening, long before the next morning's misunderstanding about Nurgic dinars. When Frieda came to sit beside me on the bench, the knuckles of his gargoyle fists whitened like hens' eggs. Unlike his sister, Fritz had no sense of humor at all. He consistently failed to appreciate my efforts to include him in the conversation, although everyone else did.

This may be an opportune moment, milords, to describe the taproom of the inn, for it features largely in the course of my narrative.

It occupies most of the ground floor. Visualize, if you will, four sturdy walls of fieldstone, their thickness ex-

posed in the deep embrasures of the windows—all of
which were then firmly shuttered, of course. The front
door is of ancient, massive oak, studded with nails. An
open plank stairway against the opposite wall leads up
to four poky guest chambers, and the owners' attics
above them. A third wall is largely occupied by a great
stone fireplace, and the fourth contains the way through
to the kitchen, partially blocked off by a bar counter of
solid timbers.

At the time of which I speak, three hogsheads of beer
stood in back of the counter, only the middle one being
truly potable. Shelves over the barrels were laden with
the coarse brown pottery of the region: cups, dishes,
steins. Alongside those hung the tariff board I have already mentioned. Its stylish black letters had doubtless
been painted by some wandering scribe in years gone
by, in return for a night's lodging, or perhaps just a slab
of venison and a flagon of ale.

The decor was simple. Heads of elk, mule deer, and
mountain sheep mounted on the walls testified to the
inn's hunting clientele. A battle-ax and two-handed
sword hung on the chimney were somewhat less ex-
plicable. Below them, a mantelshelf held bric-a-brac: a
battered military helmet of antique design, a nodule of
rock crystal, a small brass vase, a few clay figurines, an
hourglass, a hand-carved music box. Tasteful oil paint-
ings and elegant sculptures were absent.

Dry fern fronds covered the flags of the floor. The
high beams were smoke-stained, and the communal
board table in the center of the room was shiny black
with the grease of generations. By day, two long
benches flanked it and two high chairs stood by the
hearth. That bitter night the benches had been pulled
close to the fire, also. The copper ewer on the hob emit-
ted tantalizing odors of yeast and spices. The evening
meal had been tidied away, the spit and its succulent
burden removed, although a scent of roast meat still
hung in the smoky air. A single lantern swayed over the

counter, but the roaring pine-log fire provided more light.

The occupants clustered near the heat while their shadows danced in the cold corners. Storm winds wailed in the eaves and rippled the ferns on the floor. The atmosphere was creepy; yet on such a night, deep in the heart of the unfriendly ranges, this was a very welcome haven.

More! A haven not merely welcome but necessary, for Death waited outside in the forest.

The absence of a dog was ominous.

As might be expected, my dramatic entrance provoked consternation. I was lifted bodily and borne to the fireplace. Once it had been established that I had no companions left in adversity outside, the door was forced closed and latched again. In a babble of sympathetic chatter, my snow-laden cloak and hat were hauled off, my jerkin and singlet and boots, also. Stripped down to my shift and trews, I was quickly enveloped in a rough blanket.

I caught a glimpse of the person doing the enveloping and yanked a corner over my head. I was not quick enough. Her limpid blue eyes widened as she recognized me.

"Idiot!" she whispered.

I have known more affectionate greetings, but in this case the word was a warning and therefore probably well intended. I hunched down to warm myself before the blaze, and the company resumed its places around me, all jabbering at once.

"Innkeeper!" The voice was male, hearty and boisterous. "Surely your new guest will welcome a stein of mulled ale?" I thought I knew the speaker, but I did not look up.

"He is no guest of mine!" replied a voice I had no trouble identifying. "And I prefer not to have my blanket soiled."

My cover was yanked away, leaving me crouching in wet undergarments in the brightest part of the room. My eyes streamed as warmth began to penetrate my hands and feet and face. I shivered with such intensity that I could barely twist my head around to squint up at the barely-haired giant.

"Ho!" the first voice boomed. "Do you not realize that your tavern is honored to shelter the renowned Omar, the celebrated trader of tales?"

I knew him then, a merchant I had met more than once upon the road. His name escaped me for the moment—and when I did hear it, it was not the name I had known him by before. Indeed, several of the persons present in the Hunters' Haunt that night were already known to me, and not all of them by the names or stations they were then professing.

"The celebrated thief," young Fritz replied. "He is a freeloader. He tried to steal a horse. He killed my dog. He gains no shelter here, my lord."

Voices rose in protest and were drowned out by the merchant's booming laughter. "Hold! Curb your impatience, mine host, while we clarify the legal aspects of the matter. To drive out a supplicant upon such a night as this is to send him to his death."

"My pillow will remain dry," the young monster retorted.

I confess that discomfort made me testy. "Boy," I snapped. "I notice that your attempts at a mustache remain largely theoretical, but if you continue to grow at your present rate until you reach manhood, then you will have to acquire a kennel with greater headroom."

Fritz growled and reached down with hands like plowshares, intent on evicting me from the premises.

"Hold, I say!" the merchant roared. "There need be no haste, for we are all confined here until morning at the earliest—with the possible exception of Omar, that is. State your grievance, innkeeper."

The giant released me and straightened. "Theft, my

lord! He departed without paying his reckoning. He stole my ax. He killed my dog."

"Specifics?" the merchant said, hefting a foaming tankard. "What is the exact amount he owes you?"

"Fifteen thalers."

"Twelve," Frieda said in the background.

"Plus three for the ax!" her brother roared.

"Twelve?" the merchant repeated. "Why, he must have treated the entire house, all evening long!"

"He did," Fritz said grimly.

That was a vile exaggeration! Three or four rounds, no more.

The merchant beamed. He was a corpulent man of middle years, swathed in soft furs and shiny leathers. He glittered: rings on his fingers, jeweled buckles on his boots, and a gold chain looped across his breast. His face glowed red in the firelight, lit from within by good food and much ale. The fact that he occupied one of the two chairs by the fire showed that he outranked or outriched the rest of the company. Even the pouches under his eyes might be stuffed with gold. He was the sort of man who enjoyed life hugely, especially if the enjoyment did not come at his own expense.

"But perchance he has returned tonight repentant, intending to settle his debt? If he does so, and pays in advance for whatever else he now requires—plus a small compensation for insult, perchance—then you can hardly refuse to accept, can you?"

"I can, sir! We have no empty rooms and the table is cleared. In any case, this vagrant has no gold."

A few voices twittered in alarm. The storm wailed angrily in the eaves and chimney. Door and shutters rattled.

"Well, Omar?"

I sighed and went back to studying the glowing logs in the fire. That morning I had left Luzfraul with five or six thalers concealed in my saddlebags. I still had a few coppers in my pocket. The robbers had taken everything else. I did not think my sad story would influence the innkeeper even if he believed it, which he wouldn't.

"The entire business was an unfortunate misunderstanding," I said.

The background chorus murmured disapproval.

The merchant chortled, almost choking on his mirth, as if this were no more than he had expected. "Well then, that cloak? With a sable collar! Those boots, the dagger, the hat ... not everyone's choice of style, perhaps, but good stuff nevertheless. I should say that fifteen thalers might be a fair estimate of their worth. Take those, mine host, and call the former matter settled."

"It is a good cloak," Frieda's voice said.

"Stolen, doubtless. Who would want such a hat?"

"You would turn him out in his shirt?" a scandalized female voice demanded. "On such a night?"

Right on cue, the wind rattled the door again and blew smoke from the fireplace.

"Ah!" the merchant said. "The future has yet to be debated, my lady. We are still trying to settle the past."

I have talked myself out of tight spots in the past. Tonight I should need to talk myself *into* one, and I was still too muddled by the aftereffects of the cold to concentrate my mind.

"The affair of the dog is a matter of blood!" Fritz proclaimed.

He was still standing directly behind me. I mused on the possibility of grabbing his belt and tipping him over my head into the fireplace. I have known warriors who could have done that. I did not think I could, though. He would probably crush me. Even if I succeeded in bouncing his skull on the hearth, I would just make him cross.

"Wergild?" the merchant mused. "It is time for a legal ruling on this matter. Advocate?"

Everyone turned to peer at someone on one of the benches. I twisted around also and observed a mousy man in a clerk's black robe and biretta. As he was about as far from the fire as it was possible to be, he obviously lacked status. His complexion was sallow, but little of it was visible within his collar, which he had turned up against the chill.

He squeaked. "Oh, I am not qualified—"

"You are more qualified than anyone else present," the merchant boomed, his fat hands clasped on his paunch. "I am sure you can cite some legal precept on the topic. Now, how can Omar settle the matter of the dog?"

"Wergild is hardly . . . Although I do believe that dogs have been classed as companions in some instances." The notary chewed his lip for a moment, wrung his hands, screwed up his eyes and then muttered, "I recall a precedent where the plaintiff attested that the defendant had maliciously and with prejudice—"

"God of my fathers preserve me! Spring will be here before we know it. How much for the dog?"

"If memory serves me, the total judgment in that instance came to thirty thalers, being comprised of—"

"Making a total of forty-five," the merchant said with satisfaction. "And let us assume another five for tonight's board and room. Friend Omar, we judge that you need to tender fifty thalers to our host, or he will be entitled to confiscate your outer garments and toss you out in the storm in your present apparel. How do you plan to settle the bill?"

He handed up his empty stein to the landlord, who hastened off to refill it. I was relieved not to have him looming at my back, for I had been half expecting a boot in the kidneys. The merchant leaned back and beamed at me, ruddier than ever, wiggling thick black eyebrows like signal flags.

My own face felt hot from the fire, and my thighs were steaming. I turned around to warm my back. Still on my knees, I surveyed the congregation. As I said, several of the faces were familiar to me, but few of the names that later emerged. For simplicity, therefore, I shall list the spectators by the stations they professed that night.

The portly merchant occupied the chair to the left of the fireplace. On the bench at his side sat a striking young lady who claimed to be his wife. Her apparel was almost as rich as his: a green satin gown, hat and cloak of ermine, assorted jewels and precious metal. When I had last seen her she had been dancing on a table—wearing earrings, only earrings and nothing but earrings. As she was so obviously talented at playing diverse roles, I shall refer to her here as the actress.

She was trying to keep her distance from her other neighbor, a hunched, miserable, undernourished young man in threadbare doublet and hose. His hair was lank, his expression woebegone, and his nose a boiling furnace. Every few minutes he would wipe it on his sleeve. He sneezed repeatedly. I knew him for a second-rate minstrel, but I obviously need not worry about him singing tonight.

The end position on that bench was occupied by the majestic Frieda, staying well back from the fire as a good hostess should. Recalling our innocent flirtation and merrymaking on my previous visit, I wondered if she would stand up for me against her brother. It seemed unlikely, unless she was a dog-hater.

On the other side, the fireside chair was occupied by an elderly dowager, almost invisible inside a full-length cloak of lush sable and an elaborate hat that descended in folds to her collar, mercifully concealing her hair and neck. Her hands were tucked away in a matching muff. Hideous patches of rouge on her cheekbones merely drew attention to their angularity and the crumpled parchment of her face, speckled with age spots.

Next to her sat a tall, spare man. Observing the scuff marks of chain mail on his brown leather jerkin and the way his silver hair was cut short for comfort below a helmet, I deduced him to be a soldier. Besides, he wore a broadsword. He had the eyes of a hungry eagle. Whether he was traveling alone or was the dowager's escort I could not immediately determine. He was past his prime, but still a man to be taken seriously.

At his side sat a younger woman, whose coat was of faded cloth, too light for the climate. Her face was hidden from me by her bonnet. Her downcast gaze and simple attire suggested that she was the dowager's maidservant. The moth-eaten clerk was next to her.

So there was the court assembled: merchant, actress, minstrel, Frieda on one side; dowager, soldier, maid, and notary on the other.

Giant-boy Fritz returned, squeezing through between the benches to deliver the merchant's stein. Then he stood back a pace, looking huge in the firelight and glowering at me. My mouth watered at the thought of a draft of ale, or even some food, but I was not about to beg.

Not openly, anyway.

"My honorable friend," I said—meaning the merchant, although my sarcasm might not have been appreciated by all my listeners—"has been quick to judge a case on the basis of inadequate information. As I tried to explain, my disagreement with our host was due to a misunderstanding. The true facts must be determined by a proper tribunal of law. Until such time as that can be arranged, the universal dictates of hospitality and the edicts of the gods require that a benighted wayfarer be granted shelter from the storm. I shall be quite content with a place by the fire and the chance to roll up in my cloak, once it has had a chance to dry. Of course, a crust or two of bread and—"

"Out!" Fritz roared, who was standing in the background with his arms folded like tree trunks felled by a hurricane. "You may roll up on the doorstep if you wish. I have taken precautions to improve the locks on the stable and sheds."

"One admires a man who knows what he wants," the

merchant observed, complacently wiping foam from his fat lips.

"Surely on such a night this would be murder?" the dowager rasped.

"It would indeed, milady," I agreed, smiling gratefully at her. "And I fear you would all share complicity in the misdeed."

"Would we, though?" the soldier sharply asked, speaking for the first time. "What lord would judge us? In whose domain is this inn located, innkeeper?" Trust a soldier to worry about such trivia! "To whom do you pay your taxes?"

"Taxes, Captain?" Fritz's eyes widened in disbelief. *"Taxes?"* Being the only one on his feet, he dominated the group like a bull in a chicken run.

The leather of the old campaigner's face wrinkled in something resembling a smile. "Then who gives you protection?"

Fritz raised a fist like a stonemason's mallet.

"Long may you trust it, lad," the soldier muttered. "Notary? Whose writ runs in this land?"

The clerk twitched nervously. "An excellent question, Captain! The free city of Gilderburg does not claim jurisdiction this far into the Ranges, and I doubt that the cantons to the south do."

"No-man's-land, then?"

"I do believe that the principle of *terra nullius* would apply, yes."

"If no lord rules," the merchant murmured, "then we ourselves must be the law?"

The clerk mumbled, unwilling to commit himself aloud to such an outrageous idea, but then he nodded.

"Out, scum!" Fritz said. Yet he made no move from his place at the back of the group. He was enjoying the charade—and he was certainly not alone in that.

"The situation is tragic," the merchant proclaimed. "Has no one any helpful suggestions?"

The actress frowned at me, creasing her pretty brow.

She probably remembered our previous meeting. She was certainly not going to mention it, and she would not prejudice whatever influence she had on her paramour by pleading my case.

"Well," the soldier mused, "I do feel that thirty thalers seems excessive for a mere hound. With respect, innkeeper, a silver crown would replace the beast."

"I was exceedingly fond of the dog, Captain," Fritz said narrowly.

"Oh, I daresay! I have felt affection for animals myself. But if it is your feelings that are wounded, rather than your money pouch, then how can gold compensate you?"

"What are you suggesting, sir?" A sinister gleam lit the pale eyes; his lip curled menacingly.

"Were it me," the old warrior said reflectively, "I should rather seek satisfaction with a horsewhip. The exercise would assuage my grief better than money would."

"Oh, an excellent suggestion!" the merchant said heartily. "Do you not agree, Goodman Fritz?"

"The idea has merit, Your Honor. You think, then, that I should flog him before I throw him out?"

"I strongly recommend you proceed in that order. See, Omar, how your situation improves? We are now down to a mere twenty thalers."

"Nay!" Fritz was leering again. "You added five for tonight's lodging, and he is not going to get that. So just the original fifteen. Settle now, thief, and then leave."

"Just fifteen!" the merchant marveled. "Such a trivial amount. Why, my darling fritters that much away in a morning's shopping! Don't you, dear?"

The actress simpered. "You are so generous to me, my love." She leaned over to cuddle him and place a kiss.

My back was well roasted now, but I feared to move farther from the fire, lest once I began I might find myself continuing indefinitely. The howling of the storm was even louder than before. The entire building seemed to tremble beneath it, the shadows around the walls gibbered at me. I needed a brilliant preserving inspiration, but my normally quick wits remained stubbornly torpid.

"And we agreed that fifteen was the value of his cloak and boots," the merchant mused. "So our host can go fetch his horsewhip directly to settle the remaining matter of the dog . . . Have I overlooked anything, Trader of Tales?"

"Entertainment," I suggested. "I normally expect compensation when I regale a noble company, and you have certainly been enjoying yourself at my expense."

His eyes seemed to darken. He pursed his thick lips like slabs of raw steak. "Indeed. Perhaps the price of a stein of ale before you depart would be only fair."

"I have a suggestion," the dowager announced in her croaky voice. Everyone looked respectfully in her direction.

"My lady?" the soldier murmured.

"Is not this Omar reputed to be the finest storyteller in the world?"

"Others have made that claim, ma'am," I said hurriedly, "but never I."

The eyes peering at me were like amber in milk. "Do you deny it?"

"I cannot venture an opinion!" I shifted to ease my back farther from the heat. "I cannot listen to myself narrate in the way I can others. I have no basis for comparison."

"Surely audience reaction provides such a comparison? But no matter. I shall certainly not venture up those stairs to an ice-cellar bedroom while this storm lasts. I shall remain here! I expect many of us feel that way."

"Indeed!" the merchant said thoughtfully, but his hand slid to his companion's thigh. "I suppose this is the warmest place. You propose that Omar be allowed to spin us one of his yarns, milady?"

She chuckled, a noise like snakes moving in dry leaves. "I propose a contest! After all, we have another professional here with us this evening." The crone pulled a bundle of bony fingers from her muff and aimed one at the minstrel.

He flinched. "I am in no condition to sing for you tonight, my lady, much as I . . ." He doubled over in a massive sneeze.

"No, we do not expect you to sing, troubadour. But if I permit our host to add a stein of mulled ale to my account, could you manage to tell us a story, do you think?"

He brightened greatly. "Most kind of you, ma'am!"

She smiled, covering her paucity of teeth with the same shriveled hand. "And then Omar can try to top your tale! The rest of us shall be judges."

The old hag knew how to brandish rank and authority; no one was going to oppose her very seriously. I decided that perhaps she was not quite as poisonous as she looked. My life expectancy had just increased by a half hour or more.

"This is a most promising proposition, ma'am," the soldier said. "But the night is young yet. Why do we not extend the contest?"

She eyed him suspiciously. "What have you in mind, Captain?" I decided that they were acquainted and thus he must be in her hire. I had trouble visualizing a woman of her antiquity on horseback; of the men present, only he could be her coachman.

"Subject to our host's agreement, ma'am, I suggest that all seven of us tell a story. After each one, the Omar man will be required to better it. We shall vote on each pair."

"Ah! Spoken like a strategist! And if he fails?"

"As soon as he fails, then the contest is over. The rest of us can repair to bed, leaving our host free to work out his grief over the dead dog and thereafter evict Omar from the house, as is his right."

The dowager nodded graciously. "Is that agreeable to you, innkeeper?"

Only in the crocodile swamps of Darkest Arinba have I ever seen a grin to match the one the big lummox now wore as he thought of all the food and drink he was going to sell that night. "Whether he leaves now or at dawn will matter little, ma'am. These storms often last for days. As long as it is agreed that he must leave."

"And you accept these terms, Omar?" asked the soldier.

I could not read the message in his eye, if there was one.

"Certainly not," I said.

The shutters wailed. Nine frowns looked down at me.

Ah, the impetuosity of youth! Fritz was the first to speak. "I think I will dispense with the horsewhip, Captain. Bare hands would be more fitting. I am always reminded of poor Tiny when I hear the crunch of breaking bones." The oaf had no native humor at all; he was just playing up to his betters.

"Your choice, lad. Omar, have you a counterproposal?"

I was unworried by the prospect of seven story duels, but I could think of several improvements to the rules, the most obvious being that I should be allowed to depart safely and with a whole skin if I succeeded in besting all of my opponents. However, this happy ending would require that Fritz abandon his blood feud, which meant someone would have to buy him off. Only the merchant and the dowager had that kind of wealth, and neither seemed likely to make such a commitment.

But the festival surely could be spun out till dawn, and who knew what the gods might send with a new day?

"I have no quarrel with the contest," I said, "but my journey was hard. I am hungry and thirsty. More important, I am inadequately dressed. To expect me to tell a convincing tale in my present costume is manifestly absurd."

"Beggars cannot be choosers," Fritz said.

"And honest men do not gloat!" Frieda declaimed, jumping up at his side.

He turned to look at her, first in astonishment and then with a flush of anger. She gave him no chance to speak, wagging a finger under his nose. Big woman though she was, she seemed small alongside him.

"You have very little cause to strut, brother! You were the one who set your dog to guard a man and then armed the man with an ax! I suppose you think it was your cleverness that brought him back here and threw him on your mercy? I say it was the gods' justice. And I say that I will not see a man exhibited undressed. This is a decent house. You go straightaway upstairs and fetch some clothes for him!"

I had an ally. Indeed, I probably had at least two, for the old soldier had contrived to postpone my execution by several hours.

Fritz began a protest, but his sister planted both hands on his chest and pushed. She could not have moved him an inch had he put up any serious resistance, but he let himself be urged in the direction of the stair. With an angry growl, he went thumping up the steps.

Frieda ran around the counter, snatching the lantern from its hook as she went by and disappearing into the kitchen.

From my lowly place on the floor, I surveyed the audience. The dowager was inscrutable, the soldier quietly amused, the little lady's maid shocked, the mousy notary disapproving. The stringy minstrel had apparently failed to notice the byplay, lost in thought as he worried over the story he would tell. The actress flickered me a hint of a wink and the merchant raised his woolly caterpillar eyebrows in cynical admiration.

Frieda was the first to return. She came bustling over to me, bearing a wooden platter loaded with white cheese, yellow butter, fat onions, and two thick slabs of her own rye bread, which I remembered well from my previous visit. I sprang up. I did not accept the offering, although my mouth ached at the sight of it.

"The gods will repay your kindness, friend," I said, "but I cannot. Nor will I risk being the cause of dissension in this house."

"Why this sudden repentance? Here—eat fast!"

But already heavy steps overhead announced that Fritz had begun descending the ladder from the attic. I glanced meaningfully at the dowager. "Her ladyship proposed this encounter and undertook to fortify her champion in advance ... were she also to accept responsibility for this wonderful gesture of yours, so that I might enter the lists similarly prepared, then trouble could be averted."

The old harridan glowered at me. Fritz's legs were coming into view on the stairs before she nodded agreement.

He reacted with a bull roar of rage when he saw my repast, but was cut short by explanations. He scowled at his sister to show he could guess whose idea it had been. He went off to amend the dowager's bill.

I donned the serviceable trousers and padded doublet he had brought. Of course they were grotesquely large for me, but the pant legs covered my toes and would keep my feet warm—I could see no chance of having to run anywhere that evening. I turned back the sleeves in cuffs that reached almost to my elbows. I was cumbersome as a turtle, my face disappearing into my collar whenever I tried to sup.

What matter? Aromatic mulled ale was distributed from the jug on the hob, and several of the others chose to refill their tankards at the same time, which somewhat restored our host's temper. I found a place on the bench next the notary, and proceeded to enjoy my meal

as I have rarely enjoyed anything. Frieda resumed her
previous place opposite, with Fritz squeezing in beside
her. This meant that the two of us were unpleasantly
close, our knees almost touching across the gap, but he
seemed able to contain his desire for violence. Vengeance is always sweetest in anticipation.

At last we were all ready and naught could be heard
but the banshee wailing of the storm and possibly my
immodest crunching of onions.

"You may begin, minstrel," the dowager said graciously. "And begin by introducing yourself, so we
know who you are."

The minstrel sneezed four times in quick succession
and dragged a slimy sleeve across his nose. "My lady,"
he said in a painful croak, "my name is Gwill, son of
the Gwill who was troubadour to the Count of Laila.
My father, may the gods cherish his soul, apprenticed
me to Rolfo, a minstrel of renown in the Winelands. My
master treated me with kindness and schooled me in his
craft according to the oath he had sworn my father. He
trained me to perform upon the lute and cithern, taught
me diverse lays, romances, and ballads. At his behest, I
was accepted into the troubadours' guild in Faima.
Storytelling is not my usual—"

"What are you doing in the northern marches?" the
crone demanded sharply. From the way she was peering, I realized that her eyesight must be poor. In that
light, she would be almost blind.

The youth's face twisted in a wry smile. "I ventured
to the Volkslander in the hope of taking service with
some noble lord."

"And why didn't you?"

"Alas, ma'am, I was not quite so ready for the big,
wide world as I had hoped. The day I reached the free
city of Gilderburg, when I was still walking around with
my head back, marveling at the fine buildings, I was
hailed by an elderly lady. She was bent over on her staff

and heavy laden with a bundle. She timorously asked if I would be so kind as to carry it upstairs for her.

"In the Winelands, young men are expected to extend such courtesies to the elderly, and indeed to all the gentler sex. I shouldered her load gladly and proceeded into the dark alley she indicated. I took about three steps before I awoke lying in the filth with a lump on my head. My assailants had taken my lute, which was most precious to me, having been my father's, and had stripped me of all my money and even my garments, except the few I had left behind at my lodgings. There was no sign of the old woman. I have heard it suggested that her disappearance shows she was one of the gang, and I had fallen into a trap, although even now I find that hard to believe.

"All my subsequent efforts have failed to recoup my fortunes. Discouraged, and loath to face the winter in these colder climes, I am making my way home again to the Winelands."

He paused, but no one commented.

"If it please you, I shall tell you now the Tale of the Land of Many Gods."

I almost choked on my feast in my efforts not to laugh. He could hardly have made a poorer choice. I did not then realize what had moved him to choose that story, nor where it would lead me that night.

3: The Minstrel's Tale

Gentle lords, fair ladies, may my tale please you. Tonight you have requested a story of me and your whims are my command, but her ladyship did not specify whether my narrative be sad or merry, frivolous or edifying, romantic or bloody. Having regard to my own plaintive health, the inclement disposition of the elements, and the pending sad demise of one of our number, I am moved to relate a tragedy.

Music is the keel of my craft, yet tonight I must strive to move you without its aid. My voice must walk, not dance. Bear with me, I pray you, as I seek in stumbling fashion to follow the footsteps of a great tale-teller of yore. His name, curiously, was the same as that of one of our present company. Omar, he was called, or Homer in other dialects. The name is common enough, and it may well be that sundry poets and narrators have borne it through the ages, in many lands, among many peoples.

The particular Omar of whom I speak was renowned as court storyteller for a certain king of Hilgamthar, a land far to the east, and served him well in that capacity for long years.

It is said that one day, when this Omar was very old and near to death, a certain princess, a granddaughter of the king, came to him as he sat in a garden. With vestments of snowy silk floating about her, with golden tresses shining around her head, she flitted through the trees like a butterfly borne on the summer wind. She

was young and beautiful and merry, and her retinue of
maidens trooping behind her in a sparkle of rainbow
hues were young and merry as herself and many nigh as
beautiful.

Omar was seated on a low wall by a pool of golden
carp, under the shade of a willow, in the late afternoon.
His beard was white, his countenance sad, and he spoke
no word of greeting to the princess, but merely continued to study the play of sunlight on the scales of the
fish in the deep waters.

"Omar!" the royal maid said. "We are bored. We
wish you to tell us a story." So saying, she sat down eagerly, cross-legged upon the grass, and all her retinue
sat down around her, whispering excitedly at the prospect of hearing a tale from the great teller.

Omar sighed. "Highness! If you are bored in your
youth and the clear light of summer, then how ever will
you bear life when you are aged, when the wind is cold
and frost blights the bloom? Come not to an old man
for tales of what may have been, Princess, but go
straightly and enjoy life as it should be—immediate and
passionate and precious. Seek out joy and love and mer-
riment, and do not trouble one who can barely remember those." So saying, he returned to contemplation of
the golden fish.

"Omar!" the princess retorted, in a voice she had
learned from her mother. "You flaunt a royal command!
Tell us a tale, a wondrous tale. Tell us a tale that you
have never told before."

Again the old man sighed. "There is only one tale
that I have never told, sweet princess, and it is one I
never wish to tell."

Alas! Now the princess and all her maidens became
most exceeding eager to hear the untold tale of Omar,
chiding him for letting himself grow so old with yet a
tale untold, lest it should be lost forever upon his death.
With much importuning, with tears and tantrums and
teasing, they at last persuaded the bard to tell them the

story. Having extracted their promise that they would then depart and trouble him no more, he began, and he told them the Tale of the Land of Many Gods.

Far away to the west and long ago lay the Land of Seven Cities. It was known also as the Land Between the Seas, or the Smiling Land, or the Land of Many Gods. Warm oceans washed its shores to east and west. Dense jungle flanked it on the south and stark white ranges on the north. Three great cities stood along the western coast of the land: Kylam, Jombina, and Lambor. Three lined the east: Damvin, Ilmairg, and Myto. There was also Uthom in the Middle.

The people of the land were a cheerful and industrious folk, much given to music, dancing, and argument. Their women were skilled at spinning and dyeing and weaving, but spurned tailoring. Both sexes delighted in draping their bodies and limbs in sashes of contrasting hues and patterns. The resulting motley might be as demure or immodest as the wearer chose, and could be swiftly shifted from one to the other as circumstances required.

Rich and poor, men and women, town and country, the people of the land were renowned for their stubborn self-reliance.

The sons of cities were doughty sailors, trading to far countries. The sea, they said, made men hardy and tenacious.

The peasants drew obstinacy from the land itself. It was everywhere hilly. Villages of red-tiled, white-walled cottages nestled within little valleys among orchards and olive groves and smallholdings. Men who work their own humble plots of earth develop ways of thinking that seem quite foreign to the hired laborers of great ranches or paddy fields. Furthermore, the fertile soil was watered by copious rains. Rivers and canals obey the miserly whims of kings, but the gods bestow rain equally on all men. Such profligacy may have helped incite the people of the land to their peculiar notions of equality.

Obstinate . . . but the people were frugal and obedient to their gods. Thereby they flourished. Surprisingly, by and large, they flourished in peace. The why of this was long pondered but too late understood.

A lack of horses was one reason. Sheep grazed the sunlit uplands, mules and bullock flourished on the flats. Horses did poorly. Having few horses, the land had no knights, no cavalry, no castles. Warfare, when it happened, was a clumsy affair of farm boys on foot throwing spears and then walking home to tend the crops again. It brought no profit and little glory, and was generally regarded as very foolish.

From time to time two cities might draw into dispute and others take sides in the argument, but because the seven were roughly equal in size, they tended to divide into evenly matched alliances. The larger group was rarely strong enough or stable enough to oppress the smaller.

Furthermore, the ruling families of the seven cities exchanged daughters in marriage as readily as they exchanged birthday greetings. Every ruler was related to all of the others. Any hotheaded young king who stepped beyond the bounds of family decorum would find legions of fearsome aunts and uncles descending on him and admonishing him severely.

But the real reason for the long peace of the Land Between the Seas was that it had so very many gods. Every family cherished its own god. Families might rise and fall, but none ever turned away from its household deity, and the gods in turn looked after their children.

The gods' names were very ancient, so that whatever meanings they might once have had were now lost: Voxkan and Graim and Dralminth, for example. The people were named after them. Merchants from other lands might smirk in their beards when they traded with Upright-tree of Voxkan, Shining-helmet of Graim, or

Fair-pearl of Dralminth, but the natives of the land saw nothing amusing in the practice, for that was how it had always been done.

Had the Land of Many Gods continued to prosper as it did in those days of yore, then I should have no tale to tell except directions on how to reach it. Alas, this was not to be.

Karzvan was the god of the ruling family of Uthom in the Middle. Old tradition claimed that Karzvan meant "mighty," but there was no written evidence to support this belief. Perchance he was not as mighty as he had been, or perchance the burden of centuries had made him inattentive to his duties, but it came to pass that a certain king of Uthom in the Middle grew old without heir.

His name was Brazen-horn of Karzvan, and one day he came to the tastefully appointed shrine in the palace where the image of the royal god abode. The image was very ancient, cunningly carved from a jade of the deepest green in the form of a grasshopper some two hands high. It stood on an altar of fretted marble, surrounded by jewels and precious trinkets that members of the family had donated over the years. This day Brazen-horn knelt and made offering in proper style of a pearl of unusual pink hue, one he had hoarded many years for just such a need. Then the king lamented in this wise:

"Most Holy Father Karzvan, hear my prayer! I am weary of years and my strength flags. My dear wife is barren and like to remain so. I have spoken to you on this matter oftentimes before, and you have chosen not to send us a miracle, so I accept that this be your will. I am loath to put her aside and take another wife, and I fear now that the substitution would be equally fruitless—barring miracles, that is. So it would seem that I must die without issue. My city will be left without a ruler, Most Holy Father, and you without worshippers to praise you and bring offerings.

"I have examined most carefully the lineages of my family and the ruling families of the other six cities. I have nephews and great-nephews uncountable, yea, aunts innumerable; uncles, nieces, and cousins to the farthest remove, but I can find no stripling whom I could adopt as my successor without stirring up serious dispute among his relatives and the other five cities. Grant me your divine wisdom upon this matter, I pray you."

After due consideration, the god replied. "My son, you have appraised the situation precisely. Loud-thunder of Maith is a malleable young man, but his brothers-in-law are jealous of him, and notoriously impetuous. Sweet-waters of Jang is a hothead, Pillared-virtue of Colim a libertine. And so it goes. Harken, therefore, and do as I say. Summon the people of our city to an assembly, and bid them choose eight persons of wisdom and integrity, who shall be your ministers for the next twelve months. Then let them rule in your name. Whatever edicts they lay before you, no matter how ill-considered, sign without demur."

"I hear, Most Holy Father," quoth the king, "but I fail to understand. I have reigned with your blessing for nigh on threescore years; my skill and sagacity are widely praised, although of course I make no such claims myself, attributing all goodness to your guidance. My wits, at least, continue to function. Surely eight amateurs—lesser nobles or perchance even commoners may be selected, for you know how folly flourishes when folk flock in large numbers—surely these eight will make a truly festering cacophony of running the government?"

Of course the god did not answer, for gods never explain. So Brazen-horn arose and went and did as he was bid. The people were surprised, but obedient. They elected eight representatives and he appointed them his ministers. As he had predicted, they squabbled and blundered and raised taxes, but all in all they did not do as badly as he had feared they might.

At the end of the year, Brazen-horn returned to his god and again made sumptuous offering in proper form. He said a prayer or two concerning certain medical matters and then got around to asking what he should do next about the government.

"Same again," the god said. "Have the people elect another eight, or the same eight if they prefer. They will learn, and their delegates will learn, also."

Although Brazen-horn was now convinced that God Karzvan had taken leave of his senses, he again carried out his orders, and the second year things went a little better. The people learned that they could grumble without being disloyal, because the ministers were not beloved kings above reproach, but only rather stupid people like themselves, probably even more stupid. The ministers discovered that office had undoubted advantages, but they knew they would not be reelected unless they governed well, so mostly they tried their best. Each kept watch that none of the others got away with more than he did, and this kept corruption within limits.

Several years went by. Brazen-horn of Karzvan died. He was mourned, but not greatly missed, for the government now ran without him. The people continued to elect their magistrates; the magistrates continued to want to be reelected. There was grumbling and argument, but the unsatisfied knew they had only to wait another year until they could throw the rascals out, and even if they did not throw the rascals out, they felt better for having had a chance to try. Merchants and farmers and artisans were raised to high office, and the laws they made naturally tended to favor merchants and farmers and artisans. Trade flourished. Great buildings transformed the city.

With his dying words, Brazen-horn had begged his ministers to take care of his family god, for now Karzvan had no surviving children to bring him offerings and speak his praise. Of course each of the magistrates had a household god of his own. To take home another would certainly provoke trouble, so after some debate the eight decided that the whole city should adopt the orphaned god—after all, it was he who had made it possible for them to hold office and enjoy the perquisites they were enjoying, although none of them put the matter quite so crudely as that.

Thus Karzvan became civic god of Uthom in the Middle and accepted its people as his family.

Soon the people of the other cities began to take notice. They wondered why the inhabitants of Uthom in the Middle were citizens while they were only subjects. They wondered why they were being taxed to install marble bathtubs in the palace when Uthom in the Middle was building public toilets. They wondered why they had to guard their tongues while the citizens of Uthom in the Middle were free to utter any slander imaginable, and often did, especially at election time.

The royal families noticed, also. The aunts and uncles met and agreed that they ought to impose a king again on Uthom in the Middle to end to such dangerous experimentation. The vote on that was unanimous. There remained only the question of which prince should be the one imposed. Years of discussion failed to reduce the number of candidates to less than six.

Even the gods noticed. They observed that Karzvan resided in a grand public temple instead of a poky little shrine somewhere in the back of a palace. They observed also that he had thousands of people bringing him offerings and speaking his praise.

City after city demanded the right to elect magistrates. King after king discovered to his astonishment that his family god supported the idea. Some kings resisted. Alas, struck down by public violence or sudden fever, they all died young and childless. Others complied, but thereafter they sank rapidly to the status of ceremonial puppets, allowed to do nothing more significant than cut ribbons and read speeches written by their ministers.

Soon all the cities were functioning democracies and each had a magnificent temple. Sometimes now the land was referred to as the Land of Seven Gods.

The new regime worked well for a while—not an especially long while or an especially short while . . . a while that might seem long to men and short to gods, perhaps. When the grandsons of the grandsons of the first magistrates were selflessly serving their respective cities, trouble arose on both shores of the Land Between the Seas.

To the west, Kylam had been growing steadily larger and richer, taking trade away from its neighbors, Jombina and Lambor.

To the east, the harbor at Damvin was silting up. Business fell off, year by year, going instead to Ilmairg and Myto.

The magistrates of Damvin consulted their god Oliant, but the god was singularly noncommittal about silt. The magistrates ordered a new and larger temple built, to house a new and larger image of Oliant, who was always portrayed as a seated, potbellied man with a bear's head. The harbor continued to silt up. Other magistrates were elected. They ordered special offerings to the god, more frequent festivals in his honor, continuous chanting to entertain him, fresh wreaths hung about his neck daily. There was no visible improvement in the state of the harbor.

As the next elections grew closer and the magistrates of Damvin more worried, they were visited by a man who gave his name as Black-hair of Lusitair. He wore odd-colored motley and spoke with a funny western accent. There was something furtive about him; he insisted that the meeting be held in a private house, after dark. Even then, he seemed strangely reluctant to get down to business.

"Your Honors," he said eventually, glancing over his shoulder and edging forward in his chair, "here in the east, one city grows poor and two grow rich. On the other coast, the reverse applies. Two dwindle and one waxes."

"What of it?" demanded the current chairman, Honest-servant of Girb.

"Not so loud!" Black-hair whispered. "Now we all know that magistrates come and go. Some are good, some bad. Some are clever, some honest. By and large, though, it seems likely that all cities must have about the same run of luck in their officials, does it not? Over the long term, that is?"

His audience exchanged worried glances. Then they all leaned a little closer. Honest-servant murmured, "Continue!"

"So just possibly the varied fortunes of a city may depend upon the competence of its god? Over the long term, I mean."

"Well . . ."

"Yes?"

"Carry on."

Black-hair squirmed, then drew a deep breath. "It has come to my attention, Your Honors, that the cities of Jombina and Lambor are seriously considering taking action against the puffed-up, degenerate, greedy hyenas of Kylam!"

"What sort of action?" asked Shining-morning of Haun, who was not quite as bright as the other seven, although his honesty was never questioned.

"Oh . . . stealing its ships, throwing down its docks, burning its warehouses, looting its treasury, possibly abducting its leading merchants and seamen. I speak figuratively, of course."

"Of course," the eight agreed quickly.

"Now the brave citizens of Lambor and Jombina are confident that their righteous cause will prevail, if the two of them act together—and act soon, before the rapacious carrion-eaters of Kylam grow any fatter. However, the assistance of a third ally would certainly be advantageous in maintaining investor confidence."

"But how would that help us?" Shining-morning inquired.

"What he means is," Honest-servant said, and paused to consider the matter. "What we need to know is, how would a theoretical third ally, if there were such a party, benefit from the humbling of Kylam?"

"Well," Black-hair muttered, shifting even farther forward and glancing over his other shoulder, "while most of the, ah, compensation could be divided equitably between the two principals, there is one asset in Kylam that is indivisible. Neither would want the other to have it, you understand, and yet neither would wish to leave it where it is, if you follow me. But both might be willing to see it removed to some distant location where its potentially beneficial influence could not prejudice their respective interests."

Seven magistrates just pursed their lips thoughtfully, but Shining-morning said, "Huh?"

So it came to pass, a few weeks after this conversation, that three hurriedly gathered armies converged upon the unfortunate city of Kylam. Its ships were stolen, its docks thrown down, its warehouses burned, its treasury looted, and its leading merchants and seamen were carried off into slavery in a far country across the western ocean. The panther image of Jang, its god, was borne in triumph to Damvin and installed in the great temple. Oliant was removed to a very small temple on a back street and forgotten.

The other cities of the Land Between the Seas were shocked by this outrage. They waited to see what would happen.

What happened was that a series of heavy storms caused a certain tributary to burst its banks and permanently change its course. The flow of water in the

Damvin River was increased and the silt washed from the harbor.

Then all the cities began building walls, training armies, importing weapons and horses, and generally preparing for war.

Preparing for war, as was well known in other lands but perhaps not then in that one, is usually a self-fulfilling precaution. Soon the people of the Land of Seven Cities were learning the joys and sorrows of sieges, looting, crop-burning, slavery, slaughter, and wholesale rape. Famine, pestilence, and excessive taxation followed.

The surviving population of Kylam, feeling bereft, made a daring midnight raid on Jombina and bore its god Colim home in triumph. The army of Jombina advanced on Myto, demanding that it deliver Holy Maith into its hands.

How long this might continue, only the gods knew, and perhaps not even they.

One god who did not approve was Karzvan of Uthom in the Middle.

"This," he told the assembled magistrates of his city one day, "has got to stop!"

The eight bowed their heads to the floor in consent. They were already on their knees, so even the oldest were able to participate in the maneuver. Karzvan's temple was one of the more splendid, if not the most splendid, in the whole Land Between the Seas. It had marble pillars and a very impressive granite floor. Karzvan himself was now almost as tall as a man, although the greenstone from which he was now carved was not as lustrous as pure jade, nor the artistry as subtle as before. His left mandible was slightly shorter than his right, for example. But the offerings heaped around him were beyond reproach.

"Half the revenues are being wasted on weaponry," the grasshopper said petulantly. "My new east portico is taking forever. I have no desire to find myself removed by force to a damp maritime climate. Is it not obvious that someone will have to take charge?" He did not wait for an answer. "Is it not obvious that Uthom in the Middle is destined by its unique location to be the premier city of all the land? And I to be its premier god?" he added, in case the magistrates were lagging behind his revelation.

"Verily it is so," the current chairman said.

"Then we need to take charge," the god continued. "As we cannot trust any of the other gods, I mean cities, to cooperate in realizing our grandeur, we shall have to look farther afield."

Woe, woe! My tale has grown dark, and now it grows darker. Instructed by their civic god, the magistrates of Uthom in the Middle sent out emissaries to the Horsefolk.

Beyond the ice-clad peaks, through perilous passes, lay a land of grassy steppes, where dwelt a savage race of nomad herders. I would have mentioned them sooner had there been any need. Since the world was young they had wandered in small tribes, savage and barbaric and much too intent on their own blood feuds to bother with the civilized lands of the south.

Now it chanced that a leader had arisen among them, and his name was Hannail, who was later to be Hannail the Terrible.

Even as a young man, barely bearded, he became known as a fierce fighter, one whom the Horsefolk termed a drinker of blood. One day he rode alone far into the mountains. He was being pursued, his shaggy pony was lame, and he was near to death from hunger and cold, for he wore only the leather trousers of his people, inadequate garb for the high country.

He came at last to a stony slope, below a high cliff, and observed above him the mouth of a great cave. He dismounted and led his horse up the scree to inspect the opening, hoping it would provide safe refuge for the night. The wind was in the north.

Before he could enter, a great voice spoke to him out of the cave, saying, "WHOO ARE YOU?"

His mount shied. He struggled to hold it, and the two of them slid some way down the slope. When he had brought the beast under control again, he led it once more up to the cave, although every hair on his carcass had risen in fear.

"I am Hannail!" he proclaimed.

"Hannail of WHOM?"

"Hannail of no god," the young man replied. "I slew my father and uncles and their god cast me out. Now my brothers and cousins pursue me to kill me."

"I am HOOL," the voice said. "Bow down and worship MEEE and take MEEE for your god, and I shall make YOU ruler over AAALL the Horsefolk."

Hannail laughed joyously and fell on his face, worshipping Hool and taking him to be his god evermore.

"It is GOOD," the god replied. "Now sacrifice your mount to MEEE."

Hannail was benighted in a barren land, without food or water, or any transportation other than his faithful pony, but he drew his sword and cut its throat, offering it to Hool and smearing blood on his forehead in the way of his people.

Shortly thereafter his brothers and cousins rode up and surrounded him as he stood defiantly before the cave, making no move to take up his sword or bow.

"Prepare to die," they said, and some of the less subtle among them added, "painfully."

"Harken to me first!" Hannail replied, and he told them of his new god and how Hool had promised to make him ruler over all the Horsefolk, and he praised the power and cruelty of Hool.

His brothers and cousins scoffed and demanded that the god confirm these events, else they would proceed to flay the outlaw as custom demanded.

So Hannail called on the god to witness. At first there was no response, but he did not waver in his faith, continuing to call out the praises of Hool, even when his captors threw him down and began to rip the skin from his body. Then the wind shifted back to the north and the god spoke again from the cave.

"Behold Hannail, my chosen one," the god said, "WHO I SEE is steadfast. GO where he leads. Slay WHOM HEEE DOOMS. Destroy AAALL other gods and worship only HOOL."

Then all the brothers and cousins fell on their faces and swore to worship Hool and obey Hannail, his chosen one. They took out the little images that all the men of their people carried with them; they smashed their previous gods. They knelt to Hannail and demanded that he lead them wherever he chose.

All that Hool had promised came to pass. None could stand against Hannail. Before his first sons took wives, he ruled all the Horsefolk and there was no other god among them but Hool. Then Hannail was yet a man in his strength, a drinker of blood, and he could find no enemy on the steppes.

Then it was that the emissaries of Uthom in the Middle came through the passes and sought audience with the leader of the Horsefolk.

"Hear the words of Holy Karzvan," they said. " 'My city is destined to be premier city of the seven, and yet the six defy me. Send your fierce young men on their horses to chastise the upstarts in my name. My messengers bring gold, and you may also take home with you all the loot you can carry from the six. Their youths will be your slaves, their maidens your pleasure, without limit or mercy. Spare only Uthom in the Middle.' "

When the messengers had spoken and Hannail had seen them put to death—that being his custom—he rode off alone, up into the mountains, to the sacred cave. There was no temple there, no priests, no image, for

Hool was a stern god, requiring his people to worship him without the help of such frippery. Only a gravel of white bones upon the slope showed that this was the home of a god.

Hannail waited on the barren slope for several days, until the wind was in the north, for by now he knew that his god preferred it so. Then he knelt and told the words of the emissaries to Hool.

"It is GOOD!" Hool replied, louder than Hannail had ever heard him. "Take your fierce young men and GO into the Land Between the Seas and despoil it. THROW down the seven gods of the seven cities and let the people raise NO other gods in their place. Start with the one in the middle, whatever it was. BEEE terrible."

Overjoyed at these commands, Hannail hurled himself prostrate on the cold sharp stones. "Holy Father, I shall make the dogs worship you by night and by day forever!"

"No!" Hool said. "If YOU make them worship MEEE, then they also will be my people. Torment them in my name if you like, make them fear ME by all means, but do not let them make me their god. YOU are my chosen one. I give my solemn promise that your SEED shall RULE the Land Between the Seas as long as the sun MOVES."

And so it was.

Hannail of Hool became Hannail the Terrible. He led the Horsefolk through the passes. He came first to Uthom in the Middle and laid it waste, smashing Karzvan himself to green gravel, which he scattered in the cesspits. Then he worked his way around the coast, razing Kylam, Jombina, Lambor, Damvin, Ilmairg, and Myto, also, although not necessarily in that order. The Land of Seven Cities became a land of no cities. The Land Between the Seas was filled with lamentation from coast to coast, and the Smiling Land smiled no more. The Land of Many Gods became at last a land of no gods at all.

* * *

Thus spoke the Omar of old, Omar of Hilgamthar, of whom I told you.

When Omar had done, the princess sprang up in a terrible rage and said that that was the worst story she had ever heard, and subversive.

"That is why I have never told it before," Omar replied patiently.

But the princess was not comforted. She ran weeping to her grandfather the king, with her retinue of maidens weeping behind her. All trying to speak at once, they told the king of the terrible tale that Omar had related. The king agreed that it was a wicked story, casting aspersions upon the motives of gods. He banished Omar from the court and the old man was seen in Hilgamthar no more.

Gentle lords, fair ladies, may my words have pleased you!

4: Interlude

The minstrel's tale was followed by a thin and bewildered silence within the taproom. The wind howled mockingly in the eaves and the forest beyond. Smoke puffed from the fireplace.

The dowager was nodding in her chair. On the other side the hearth, the actress had her head on the merchant's shoulder. She was probably very uncomfortable, but that was her business. Of course it was.

Nearer to hand, Frieda's head rested on Fritz's shoulder. It was a larger shoulder, although doubtless much firmer, and regrettably she seemed quite content, with her eyes closed. He caught me looking at her and scowled dangerously.

The note I had discovered in the rye bread was now in my doublet pocket. I had not yet had a chance to read it.

The red-eyed, red-nosed minstrel tilted his stein in the hope that there might be a drop left in it, or that someone would notice that there wasn't. His voice had failed almost completely by the end. He looked ready for early burial. If a fever cart happened by, it would accept him as he was, without argument.

I gave him a smile of thanks, although it was an effort for me. Had he really thought I needed help like that? I noted a cynical glint in the soldier's eye and knew he was thinking the same.

"If you believe you can better that tale, Master Omar,

then I suppose you may begin," he said cheerfully. The company stirred.

"It was certainly a curious choice," the notary murmured at my side. "Interminable exposition with a regrettable absence of uplifting moral."

The dowager's old eyes opened in a flurry of wrinkles. "We should not prejudge!" she snapped. "Refrain from comment until we have heard the response. You may proceed, Master Omar."

"The fire needs stoking, my lady. Innkeeper, give the minstrel a stein of spiced ale and put it on my bill."

Fritz glared at me and his knuckles whitened. Then he rose to attend to the hearth.

"Put it on mine," the merchant said. "The poor devil surely needs it."

Good for old Moneybags-Under-the-Eyes! The minstrel croaked his gratitude.

"Perhaps a cup of your herbal tea, hostess?" the dowager said. "You, child?"

"Oh, yes, thank you, my lady." Had the maid no name of her own, or had her mistress never bothered to learn it? Her coat was thin and coarse-woven. I had not heard her speak before, and had rarely glimpsed her face, for the brim of her bonnet concealed it. I suspected she was cold. Perhaps she just did not get enough to eat.

The merchant ordered ale for himself and his wife, or supposed wife. The notary fumbled unobtrusively in his pouch and then said perhaps half a flagon of the small beer—a thought to make me shudder.

Frieda had gone to make the tea, her hand brushing my shoulder as she went by. Fritz was keeping careful watch on us, even as he tended to his duties. I fingered the note in my pocket—his pocket, actually, as it was his doublet I wore. What message had his sister passed to me? The gaiety and humor she had displayed on my last visit were sadly absent. Could a few more months of living with the boor have depressed her spirits so, or was she merely worried about my chances of surviving the night?

I wished I could do something to brighten her life. As my old friend the Blessed Osmosis of Sooth used to teach the Faithful, the devil you know may be a lot less fun than some of the others. There was more to it than that, I think, but I forget what.

"Hannail the Terrible begat Nonnil," I remarked. "Nonnil begat Grosail the Gruesome. Grosail—"

"We are not ready!" the dowager snapped. She was obviously in a very snappish mood, and understandably so after the minstrel's performance.

"I wasn't actually starting," I said. "Just laying a base. The Land Between the Seas made a sort of recovery. The cities were sad wraiths of their former glory, of course."

"Cannot we have a tale set in a more salubrious environment?" the notary whined.

I beamed at him. "A tragedy must be met with a tragedy, or how will you judge between them? Kylam, fifty years later ... Can you imagine fifty years of rule by the Horsefolk barbarians? Horrible, pale-haired monsters!"

Fritz happened to be going by at that moment with the big copper jug. For a moment I thought he was going to stun me with it. Frieda shot me a warning glance, as if to tell me that he was serious in his threats to kill me—but I knew that already.

When all was settled again, with wood on the fire and my audience waiting, I began.

"I am Omar the Trader of Tales, but you know that. What was the Gwill's formula?—'Gentle lords, fair ladies, may my tale please you'? Hear, then, the Tale of White-thorn of Verl."

5: Omar's Response to the Minstrel's Tale

All night long, White-thorn had been helping tend the wounded, the bereaved, the lost children. At dawn she slipped away and went home through the empty streets and the dim, cold light. As she climbed the stairs to her room, every creaking tread seemed to cry out in the silent house. She had sent the servants away the previous evening, for the home of Morning-star would certainly be burned before this day was out, and anyone found in it would die.

It was a modest house in a modest street, not far from the docks. For half a century no citizen of Kylam had dared display wealth. The Horsefolk overlords ruled by terror. Any native who raised his head higher than other heads lost it; his goods were confiscated, his womenfolk despoiled and likely murdered, also.

She went first to her father's room. The bed was tidily made, his favorite clothes still hung in the closet, his brushes lay on the dresser, and yet already the chamber seemed abandoned and haunted.

From the secret panel above the bed, White-thorn took out the least loved of the family heirlooms, a small and thin stiletto, razor sharp, crafted in some far-off land. It had belonged to her great-grandmother, so her father had told her, but he know no more of its history. He did not know if it had ever been used. The faint encrustation on its blade might or might not be poison. Today she might discover if that family legend was true.

She crossed to her mother's portrait. Golden-bough smiled down at her daughter as she had always smiled at her, for as long as White-thorn could remember. She looked very little older than White-thorn herself now. She had not lived long after that picture was painted, just until the afternoon she had run afoul of a band of Horsefolk thugs in the street. They had raped her on the cobbles and then killed her, while the people of Kylam hurried by unseeing. The atrocity had been a political statement, a demonstration of superiority. Golden-bough had merely been the first attractive woman the brutes had encountered after receiving their orders.

Faint childhood memories twisted in White-thorn's heart like skewers. "Good-bye, Mother," she whispered. "You understand. I hope I shall be worthy of your memory."

She rose on tiptoe to kiss the portrait. She had done that only once before, the night Sea-breaker had asked how she would feel if his father came to call on her father to negotiate a marriage union between their two houses. The betrothal had followed, but the wedding had been delayed by the revolution. Where now was Sea-breaker of Kraw? Facedown in the red pools of Mill Creek? Or buried on the field alongside Morning-star of Verl and so many, many others?

Back in her own room, White-thorn washed and brushed out her hair. Shivering, not entirely from cold, she took thought to the clothes she would wear. Under the rule of the Horsefolk, the people of the Land Between the Seas—especially the women—had learned to dress in public both modestly and unobtrusively. Only in the privacy of their homes had they dared sport the traditional styles of their ancestors, brilliant motleys leaving limbs exposed. In the last few weeks they had joyfully returned to the old ways, and the streets had flowered again with color and beauty. Now the brief spring of the revolution had withered and barbarian winter returned.

She began with one of her favorites, a swatch she had woven herself from the finest wool obtainable, a cloth as sheer and light as thin cotton, in scarlet and emerald. She draped it over her left shoulder. The hems fell below her knees. She spread it out on the bed and ripped a third from its length.

For her right shoulder she chose a silk that had belonged to her grandmother, copper blossoms on a ground of peacock blue. She discarded half of it, then wound a golden sash around her waist, spreading the hanging ends of the other cloths to form skirts.

She donned her silver slippers, her great-grandmother's onyx earrings, the pearl necklace Sea-breaker had given her to mark their betrothal. She must not think of Sea-breaker. She knew her father was dead. She would not abandon hope for her love. There had to be some reason to go on living, and a highly speculative vengeance was not enough.

Only then did she dare look in the mirror. Her heart pounded, her breath came in nervous gasps. Bare arms, bare legs, breasts barely covered—she would not have appeared before her father like this, and certainly not before Sea-breaker, not until their wedding night. Even by her own standards she was flaunting herself shamelessly, and barbarians would react with fury. So be it, shame was the least of her worries now. She would bait the trap with her own body.

One thing more—she concealed the stiletto in her waistband.

White-thorn descended the stairs and entered the hall, striving to hold her head high and walk calmly. Some of her remote ancestors had owned proper halls, great halls, halls capable of seating dozens. This one had been crowded when the eight leaders of the resistance had met in it.

The little alcove above the hearth was occupied. Every home in Kylam and the whole Land Between the Seas had an alcove above its central hearth. Once the household gods had lived in those niches. Then the Horsefolk had come and smashed all the gods they could find. Only the empty spaces had remained as memories of lost freedoms. That niche had been empty all White-thorn's life, except on special occasions when her father had banished the servants, locked the doors, and brought Verl out from his secret place to worship him. When his daughter had reached the end of her childhood, he had presented her to the god, and thereafter they had worshipped Verl together.

A month ago the gods of the Land Between the Seas had returned to their places again. Verl stood in his now, the niche that was his by ancient right, a small white dove. He was not very lifelike or beautiful, just a pottery image of a bird. One eye was a small black stone and the other an empty hole. His legs and feet were fashioned of twisted wire and he had lost a couple of toes. He was very old, a thousand years old or more. He was White-thorn's family god and she loved him.

She sank to her knees and bowed her head. On the fireplace before her lay a sword and a golden chain, both encrusted with black bloodstains.

"Most Holy Father, hear my prayer. I have no offering to give you—"

"You offer your life," a whisper said. "Can any god ask more? You always called me 'Mother' before."

White-thorn smiled through sudden tears. "I am head of the family now. I thought that 'Father' was more apt."

"Whichever you prefer," the dove murmured, her voice soft as a distant purr among rocks. "You are the last of my chicks, at least for now, and that is all that matters. Anyway, who can tell a father pigeon from a mother pigeon except another pigeon?"

"Holy Mother, then," White-thorn said gratefully. "Give me courage to do what I must do."

"I cannot give you courage, my child. You already have as much and more as any of your ancestors, and I have known your family for nigh threescore score summers and winters. I am proud of you, as I am proud of Morning-star, who came to me two days ago in honor. None in your line ever stood higher than he."

White-thorn fought back a sob. "I have no offering, Most Holy Mother. I ask leave to remove this one." She laid her hand upon the odious chain.

The god sighed. "It will increase your danger mightily."

"And my chance of success?"

"That, also, yes. So take it with my blessings."

White-thorn lifted the chain. It was heavier than it looked. It chinked and was odiously cold in her fingers. She laid it beside her on the rug. "And your sacred person, Lady? Shall I return you to your hiding place?"

There was a silence. Then the god sighed. "I am only a very small divinity, dear one. I can see but a very little way into the future. I know not if you will live or die today, but I do know this house will not stand tomorrow. Even your scullery maids know that. So wrap me in a plain rag and take me with you. Give me to a stranger and bid him keep me safe until the time is ripe. He will understand."

"Stranger?" White-thorn cried, looking up in shock at the little image. "To guard our household god? And which stranger?"

"It must be so. A foreigner. You will know him when you meet him. Hurry, child! The time for sacrifice draws nigh. The barbarians are dousing their fires upon the hills."

White-thorn shivered convulsively. She felt her bones melt with fear. She thought of the smiling picture on the wall upstairs.

"Courage, last of my chicks!" the dove purred softly. "Be brave and you may not be the last. Be brave and we may have vengeance."

* * *

Draped in a drab cloak of heavy wool, clutching her two small bundles, White-thorn hurried to the palace. The sky was blue already; sunlight glinted on the chimney pots and the tiled roofs of Kylam. The wind wafted a tang of the sea along streets still shadowed. Dogs wandered aimlessly, seeming puzzled by the silence, the absence of people. The docks would be different. There would be crowds at the docks, crazy, panic-ridden multitudes. Children weeping, adults screaming.

Two days ago, the battle at Mill Creek.

Last night, the fires of the victorious Horsefolk upon the hills.

Today began the vengeance.

Kylam would die first, because it was closest and because a magistrate of Kylam had raised the banner of revolution. Uthom would be last. There was nowhere to run to from Uthom. So the vengeance would begin in the ports: Kylam, then Jombina, and all the others in their turn. Quite possibly Vandok would divide his forces, sending half to ravage the east while he dealt with the west. Why should he not? There was no opposing army left in the field. The land lay helpless before his wrath. Naked and defenseless and spread-eagled on the ground . . .

White-thorn came into the plaza and still saw almost no one. One ancient beggar was huddled in a corner of the steps, at his usual post. He had always been there, for as long as she could remember, a beggar so blind as to be invisible to everyone else. Was he puzzled by the silence? Had nobody told him? Or was he just aware that, with no one's chances much good, a blind beggar's must be hopeless? She wished she had brought some money. It would do no good lying at home, and it might have let the old man die happy in his sudden wealth.

She did not approach the beggar. She hurried up the steps to the shining pillars.

There was no doubt where the fury would begin. This

was the only truly notable building in the city. Vandok would start here, where his father had died.

Once it had been the temple of Jang, in the days before the Damvinians had stolen him away to be their god. For a short while it had been the temple of Colim, when Kylam had managed to steal the baby god from Jombina. Then the barbarians had come and there had been no more gods. The temple had served as the governor's palace ever since. On the dread occasions when the king came over the mountains to enjoy the sport in his southern domain, it had sometimes served as royal palace, also.

"If they would only stay!" Morning-star had mourned to his daughter many times. "If they would just settle down and reside among us, then we could civilize them! A generation, perhaps two, and the Horsefolk dwelling amongst us would be indistinguishable from the natives. Hannail was too clever, or his god was. One or other of them saw the danger. So they send their sons to torment us, but then they call them back to marry within the tribes, dispatching a new contingent to afflict us afresh. The Land is not a vassal state, it is a deer forest!"

Climbing the great stairs, White-thorn realized that she had lost her fear. It would return later, probably much greater. Fear of death, fear of pain. Fear and pain were certain, death probable. Do not think of it! Think of vengeance. Think of Father, dying bravely on the field of battle. Many people had told her he had died gloriously, but she did not believe that death could ever be glorious, or anything but horrible, no matter how it came. So he had not died gloriously, and she could not imagine him dying any way but bravely.

She strode through the portico and into the basilica itself. It was a high, cold, sterile place, although there were fine carvings on the ceiling still. The Horsefolk had long since smashed all the ornamentation they could reach, and any soul or majesty the hall might once have possessed they had banished with their atrocities. Men and women had starved to death in cages in this hall, been burned in this hall, been mutilated, humiliated, butchered. Raped.

The throne had gone—it had been dragged out less than an hour after the rebels had declared it a chopping block, and Morning-star himself had cut off King Grosail's head on it. An oaken council table had been installed instead, and the magistrates had met there every day, while the people had trooped in by the hundred, to stand around in silence and watch, marveling at the restoration of their liberties, the freedoms their grandparents had described.

She stopped in surprise. She had expected the hall to be as empty as the streets, or at least she would have expected to hear voices. But there were many people present. Four or five sat at the table. A score of attendants waited on them. A hundred or more stood around among the pillars in somber silence. They were watching the sun set, the brief flame gutter.

She saw bandaged stumps, men on crutches. Even children had been brought to witness the end of the momentary dream. So not all the citizens had fled to the hills or the ships.

She hesitated, studying the group at the table and identifying the surviving leaders of the resistance. Old Pure-valor of Farn was there, bent and white-haired. High-endeavor of Kalint, his arm in a sling and his head bandaged . . . He was one who had told her that Morning-star had died gloriously. Even a couple of new widows she recognized in the background. Defeated, bereaved, wounded. A lump rose in her throat. The human rubble of Kylam.

Those men would certainly stop her carrying out her intent.

Suddenly her knees began to shake. The fear came rushing back. As long as her ordeal had been inevitable . . . But now perhaps it might be avoided . . .

Was hope harder to bear than doom? ... Ridiculous! She straightened her shoulders. But how could she manage to evade these ghouls, these watchers over a corpse?

Whatever were they doing here?

"Waiting for terms," said a voice at her side.

Realizing that she must have spoke aloud, she glanced at the speaker. Then she took another look.

He was a man of middle height, of middle years— slim, confident, neatly groomed. His short beard was striped with gray. His hair was curly, flecked with silver, also, and cut oddly short. There was nothing special about his face, and yet ...

"They expect Vandok to demand the surrender of the city," he said, regarding her intently.

"Will he?" she asked.

"I don't think so. I think he'll come and take it."

"And burn it."

"Certainly."

What was it she sensed about him? His eyes were grayish, which was rare in the Land Between the Seas. He was the only man she had seen in weeks without a sword or at least a quarterstaff. There was an unfamiliar timbre to his voice, and a faint odor of the sea clung to him. He wore salt-stained sailors' breeches and a open-fronted shirt that had once been fancy. Now it was faded and threadbare; half the embroidery had fallen out. A bundle wrapped in a grubby blanket lay at his feet.

"Who are you?" she demanded.

"A wanderer, my lady." He seemed puzzled by her, or just very curious. He had the same alert confidence that her father had ... had had.

"You come at an evil time, traveler. You should not linger here."

He shook his head and smiled. There was something reassuring about his smile, and yet something unfathomably sad in it, too. "I am by way of being a connoisseur of bad times, milady. There was a battle, I hear. I missed the battle." He frowned. "Most odd!"

"Why so?" She wondered why she was wasting time talking.

"Oh, my timing is usually better. The gods arrange . . . No matter. Who are you?"

"A woman of the city."

He raised his eyebrows. "A lady of the city. Pray tell me."

If he could see how she was dressed under her cloak, he would not think her a lady. "White-thorn of Verl."

His eyebrows rose higher. "Morning-star's daughter?" He bowed low. "You, especially, should not linger!"

"I have a duty." Why mention that to a complete stranger?

A stranger! Who else but this man?

She held out one of her bundles, awkwardly clutching her cloak tight with her other hand. "I was told to give you this."

He cocked his head in surprise, but not with the astonishment she would have expected. "Told by whom?"

"Verl."

"Ah!" The man accepted the wrapped form of the god with care. "And what is in it?"

"Verl. She . . . He said to tell you to return her when the time was ripe."

"No time? No place?"

"No." It sounded so crazy that she wondered if the stranger would think her unhinged.

He did not seem to. He looked down at the tiny package, clutching it with both hands. A group of men came running into the hall and hurried over to the table. Other people were trooping out. The stranger stood like a pillar in the midst of the confusion and ignored it totally, as if the little bundle he held was the only thing of interest in the whole city. "He or she?"

"Whichever you prefer."

"She will not speak to me, though?"

"Only to members of her family."

The stranger frowned. "Offerings? How do I care for her?"

"She would not accept offerings, either, I think. Not from a stranger. Perhaps sprinkle a few grains of corn once in a while . . . to show her that she is not forgotten?"

The stranger nodded solemnly and tucked the god away in his shirt. It hardly made a bulge. "Next my heart," he said. "I will return her when the time is ripe. You have my word." He studied White-thorn with gray eyes strangely bright. "And what road do you travel now, my lady?"

A fit of shivering convulsed her. She pulled her cloak tighter yet. "Please go, sir! Take care of Verl."

"White-thorn!" a familiar voice shouted.

She cried out, spun around. *Sea-breaker!* He came hobbling toward her, leaning on a staff, swinging it urgently. There was a blood-caked bandage around his head and black stubble on his face, but he was Sea-breaker, and he was alive. The staff fell to the tiles as his arms went around her. Within his embrace she felt the stiffness of the stiletto in her sash.

"I never doubted," she lied, snuffling against his shoulder. That was the trouble with very tall men.

"Your father . . . you know? Of course you must know! Dearest, he died gloriously. I saw. The elite of the barbarian—"

"I heard. You're hurt." She was going to hurt him much, much more.

"I twisted my ankle running away. Oh, my darling! I went to your home—"

"You bandage your head because you have twisted your ankle?"

"Only a scratch. An arrow . . . my skull is armored, don't you know that? It bounced off. If only we'd had proper armor and weapons, things would have been so different! Come, my darling, there is little time."

"No," she said.

He relaxed his embrace so he could see her face. "No? What do you mean—*no*? There is a ship. The captain's an old friend of . . . He promised to wait an hour, and the hour must be almost up. The crowds at the dock . . . Quickly!"

"No." She resisted as he tried to move her, holding her cloak tight. "Beloved, this hurts, but I cannot come."

People were shouting. In some confused corner of her mind she had absorbed the message. The horde was coming. Vandok was advancing with his army. At the gates. No terms . . .

The crowd had begun streaming from the basilica, jostling past her. She saw terror-stricken faces, saw tears, heard the screams of panic. But mostly she just saw the pain and shock in Sea-breaker's eyes. He bent to recover his staff. Again he tried to urge her, and she fought free of his grasp. Bless that ankle! If he had the use of both hands, he would carry her off bodily.

He shouted at her. She backed away, eyes blurred with tears. She tried to explain that she loved him. He kept talking of the ship waiting. There was no way to explain. She urged him to go. Again and again she said that she would not.

Sea-breaker lost his temper eventually. Obviously his leg pained him more than he would admit and the blood on the bandage came from no slight scrape. He had found a ship for them, deliverance, he had found her, and now she was refusing him . . . Of course he lost his temper.

When the tears left her eyes, she was alone in the hall.

She dropped her cloak around her feet and felt naked. Worse than naked. Stepping out of her sandals, she walked forward along the deserted basilica to the paper-strewn table. Past it, to the dais at the end where the throne had stood. The dried blood there had never been cleaned away.

She unwrapped her second bundle and took out the chain. Grosail's blood was on that, too. She started to hang it around her neck and thought better. Vandok might just choke her with it.

Sounds drifted in from the plaza. She turned to face the door.

A movement in the shadows behind the pillars caught her eye. She was shocked to see the stranger standing there, watching, his bundle at his feet.

"Go!" she shouted.

He did not answer, for at that moment the Horsefolk rode in.

Vandok was younger than she had expected. He sat his great horse as if he were part of it, staring at this un-expected committee of one. His followers halted behind him, a score of armed horsemen. For an age nobody spoke.

Younger than she had expected, and certainly taller, broader. The golden chain dangling athwart his chest proclaimed his kingship, but even without it, there would have been no doubt who led this company. Other than the chain and a headband to hold back his flowing hair, he wore only the buckskin trousers of his race. His mustache was thick and curved down to the line of his jaw, but it was almost invisible now in golden stubble of beard. He looked altogether hard, as if graven out of oak. Sword and bow and quiver hung at his saddle.

"They say he is the worst of the brood," her father had told her when the news came. "But we should have expected that. They say he bears a striking resemblance to Hannail himself."

Morning-star had counted on half a year to prepare. Vandok had granted him less than a month. He had emerged clear victor from the blood storm that followed the death of any Horsefolk king, trampling over four older brothers. Like a whirlwind gathering leaves, he had swept up the tribes and rushed through the passes before the snows came. Less than a month after his father's death, he had burst upon the Land Between the Seas, very much as his great-grandfather had, fifty years ago.

Fury burned in his pale eyes as he observed the blackened chain in the woman's hand, the stains on the floor at her feet. He must know whose blood that was. He could probably guess who she was. She resisted an urge to feel for the hilt of the stiletto. He would come for her himself. He must! With his men all watching him, he must!

But Vandok did not.

He gestured. Four men sprang from their saddles and rushed to her. Fingers of iron gripped her so hard that she cried out. One man took the chain and carried it to the king. He stared down at it for a long moment before he accepted it and added it to the one he already wore. Only then did he slide from his horse, and at once the rest of his followers did so, also.

Still he did not come to White-thorn.

He gave orders. His voice was quiet, unhurried, and he used as many gestures as words. Men scattered to explore the building, to examine the refuse on the table, to lead the horses over to a corner, out of the way.

White-thorn stood helpless in the grip of three men. Amazingly, none of them had yet discovered the knife. There were fingers around her wrists—so tight that her hand was going numb—and more crushing her upper arm. Boots pinned her bare toes to the floor. There were fingers twisted in her hair, pulling her head back. But no one had yet found the knife.

There had been treachery, she saw. More Horsefolk warriors were bringing in captives: Pure-valor, High-endeavor, Oath-keeper. The resistance had been betrayed. Fair enough! The resistance had betrayed the

Land, by failing. It had promised freedom and delivered only greater suffering.

Finally, Vandok turned his attention to the woman. He strode toward the dais, but he stopped several paces away and studied her.

"Your name?"

She tried to speak, but her mouth was dry as salt. The men holding her arms twisted them almost out of their sockets. She gasped at the pain and managed to whisper, "White-thorn of Verl."

"Louder!"

She repeated her name.

Vandok smiled. "Strip her."

The cloths were torn from her body. The stiletto clattered to the floor.

Vandok laughed. One of the men kicked the weapon away and another removed the rags. A third snapped her necklace and then callously ripped away her earrings. She bit back a cry of pain.

Only then did the king himself step up on the dais and come to stand before her, very close, a killer beast reeking of horse, of woodsmoke and sweat, of weeks in the saddle. He looked down contemptuously at her as she stood naked and still held helpless in the warriors' cruel grasp. He was very tall, very broad, hard as furniture. She shivered at the hatred she saw in his eyes. Had she ever known what hatred was, what *ruthless* meant? Hope had died. *Oh, Mother!*

"Did you really think I would be so easy?" he said. "Your father killed my father—here? Right here?"

She nodded.

He fondled her left breast. Grinning, then, he squeezed it until he wrung a scream from her. He turned to survey the hall, the leering warriors, the prisoners. The place was filling up. He had a large audience.

"What should I do with the rebel's spawn?" he demanded.

The Horsefolk roared out the predictable answer.

"On the floor," Vandok said. "Right where those bloodstains are. Bring the captives close. The punishment begins now and they shall watch."

He looked down at White-thorn, smiling as he untied his belt.

6: The First Judgment

"**G**entle ladies, and ah . . . fair lords was it? Anyway, may my tale have pleased you."

No one was nodding this time. The dowager glared at me, the patches of rouge showing like wounds on her sallow cheeks, her eyes milky with age. The merchant and the old soldier were equally disapproving. The actress pursed her lips and shook her head reproachfully. The little lady's maid seemed to be weeping, hands clutched to her face, but I could not be sure, because of her bonnet.

"Tush, child!" the dowager said. "White-thorn did not die, Master Omar, did she?"

"Eventually, of course. Not that day."

"Then I think you should finish your tale more appropriately!"

"But I don't know how she did die! You surely do not expect me to make it up, do you? Vandok raped her in public. He probably intended to kill her, but then changed his mind and decided to make a statement by abusing Morning-star's daughter in all of the seven cities. I really cannot say what his thoughts were. I know he took her on to Jombina with him and on an apple cart in the marketpl—"

"Stop!" the old hag barked. "This is not a fit subject for genteel company."

"Then I take it you vote against me, milady?" I said sadly. "I wonder if anyone will grant a dying man a drink?" The fire was sinking again, and the shadows creeping in on us. Perhaps the storm was not quite as loud as before, but that was still killer weather out there.

The silence was pregnant, slightly.

The soldier coughed. His weathered face was scrolled with fine wrinkles, roads on a map. A map of a long and probably full life? Had I been at liberty to select a playmate from among the company in that beery taproom, then Frieda would have won hands down, with the actress a close second. But had I wanted a staunch companion at my side in a tight spot, that old campaigner would have been the only choice. Well, for real mayhem perhaps Fritz with a battle-ax . . .

"The stranger?" the soldier said. "The one who took the god? You did not tell us his name. Do you know who he was?"

"Yes, Captain. But that is another story."

The actress shrilled a girlish laugh. "Naughty Master Omar is playing a very old game with us!"

I flicked my brows in a short of shrug: We all know *that* story!

"Very well," the dowager said. "Let us decide whose tale was the better."

"If I have a vote, my lady," the minstrel muttered hoarsely, "then I cast it for Master Omar."

"I'm not sure that is quite proper. Let us go around the circle. Burgomaster?" She beamed her much-wrinkled lips at the merchant. The proposed procedure would give her the final voice.

The fat man pouted and glanced at his companion. "You are more conversant with the arts than I, my dear. You cast both our votes."

"Oh, Master Omar's tale was quite shocking, of course." The actress studied my expression blandly for a moment, knowing that I was well aware of the arts with which she was most conversant, and hence was capable of telling much more shocking tales than that one.

"But I do believe it was better told, so let us say he won the first round."

The minstrel had already voted. Frieda smiled faintly at me, Fritz scowled predictably.

"The decision is far from easy," I said, "but on the whole I vote for me."

The notary shifted on the bench, turning to frown at me. "How long ago was all this?"

Why in the world did that matter? "About two hundred years ago, I suppose. Perchance a little more."

"I found both tales inappropriate. I decline to vote."

The maid said nothing.

"I believe I shall vote for Master Omar," the soldier growled. "As the lady says, he is playing an old game with us, but I am not quite ready for bed yet. He may do better as the night goes on."

"Then I have a majority!" I had not been seriously worried. The minstrel had thrown that round. "Does *no one* wish to buy a flagon for the winner?"

No one duly volunteered.

Fritz rose and strode forward to throw more wood on the fire. I fingered the mysterious note in my pocket but left it there. The giant hefted the copper jug from the hob, looking around hopefully. Still no one wanted to buy. He returned to his seat, wearing a surly pout that would not endear him to anyone.

"So who shall be next to tell us a story?" The dowager crouched in her chair like a long, furry, black caterpillar. Or a spider, perhaps.

"Oo!" The actress clutched her hands together excitedly and looked to her benefactor for support. "Do you think, dearest? . . . Do you think that little me could dare? . . . Will you let me try, beloved?"

"Go ahead, my sweet dove."

"Oh, very well!" she said, letting him talk her into it.

I gathered up my flagging wits. Fritz had started to smile, which was very bad news, but he could count as well as I could.

With her cute rosebud lips and her feather-duster eye-lashes, the actress could collect all the men's votes merely by reciting a recipe for borscht—not that she was likely to have set eyes on a recipe in her life. I could not imagine anyone voting against the minx, except perhaps the dowager. And hence her maid, of course. Moreover, the company was growing sleepy. Regardless of the merits of the tales, the contest might terminate without malice, just through inattention. The instant the tally went against me, Fritz would demand his due.

I had not meant to kill his accursed dog! Had I known he was so fond of it, I would have dragged its body off into the forest before I left. That way he would never have known what happened and would have been saved distress.

"Let me see," our new narrator began in her childlike tones. She adjusted her snowy ermine cloak over the green of her gown. "I have to start by saying who I am, right? Well, my name is Marla. I was a foundling, aban-doned one bitter winter night nineteen years ago on the doorstep of the convent of the Goddess of Purity in Luzfraul, so I can tell you nothing about my family, ex-cept that they must have been of noble blood, because the blanket in which I was wrapped had a crest em-broidered in one corner in silver and gold thread. Alas, the blanket was later stolen, and by the time I grew up no one could remember what the insignia had been.

"I was raised in the convent, of course. I was just about to take my final vows, when—goodness, it must be four or five months ago now!—poor Sister Zauch re-ceived really terrible, terrible news! Her dear brother, the only relative she had left in the world, was dying! Well, Sister Zauch was very old herself, so Mother de-cided to send me along with her on the journey, to care for her. And so I came out into the big world like a frightened little chick peering out of its nest for the first time."

If this was just her introduction, then her story was going to be spectacular.

"And there in Schlosbelsh, I met dear Johein and we fell in love at first glance, didn't we, my beloved?" She turned to the merchant.

"We did indeed, light of my life."

The fevered minstrel on her other side stared at me with a very odd expression: eyes bulging within their red rims, lips pressed white. Fists clenched? Was he about to have a fit? Ah, but then I recalled that the entertainments provided in the establishment where I had first encountered the lady also included music. Young Gwill might very well have performed there, at the Velvet Stable. Not for gold, of course—he would have been given his pay in trade. Such houses usually reward their artists that way, singers, musicians, storytellers . . . so I have been told. Gwill might know the lady more intimately than I did, but he had certainly not met her in a nunnery.

The self-named Marla was gathering self-confidence like an avalanche entering adolescence. "I'm going to tell you a much nicer, more romantic tale than Omar's! Gentle lords, fair ladies, may my tale please you! Did I get that bit right, dearest?"

"You're doing wonderfully, rosebud."

Nineteen? She was twenty-five if she was a day. Her name was not Marla, she had never been near a nunnery in her life, and she had tattoos in unmentionable places.

7: The Actress's Tale

When King Vandok had shamed White-thorn before the city leaders and his own men, he had her taken away under guard to his camp. The rest of the day he spent in looting and despoiling Kylam. It was all horrible! Houses were burned and people killed all over the place! I shall spare you the dreadful, terrible details.

That night he had White-thorn brought to his tent, and again he lay with her. He made love to her several times against her will. He was so big and strong that her struggles were useless!

All the next day she was kept prisoner, although her guards were not cruel to her, because they knew she belonged to the king. In fact, they brought her lots of food to eat and nice clothes to wear. They told her how beautiful she was, even in adversity.

And the next night again, the king summoned her and took his pleasure of her. Again she struggled in vain against his terrible strength, but he did not deliberately hurt her. He was just irresistible!

The next day he led his army on to Jombina, and there he exhibited her in the marketplace in chains, to show that the daughter of the man who had led the revolution was now in his power. She wore a simple black dress and no jewelry, but she looked so beautiful that everyone who saw her wept!

Vandok sent her back to the camp and that afternoon he came himself to visit her, and brought her some beautiful clothes he had looted from the city, and some rich jewels. She knew they were stolen, but she decided to wear them because she feared that if she angered him, he would just be even nastier to the poor people of the city. She could smell the burning houses!

That night she was brought to his tent again, but she was very beautiful in her beautiful dress and all the lovely jewels. He told her so!

"I have known many beautiful women," he said, "but none more lovely than you."

She saw that he was clean and freshly shaved and much better dressed than before, in a silk robe, so he looked more like a king. He was a very handsome man, with his long shiny hair and his thick gold mustache and his bright blue eyes. He insisted she dine with him, and later he undressed her very gently and patiently and when he finally clasped her against his hard, muscular chest, all tickly with golden hair, she began to fear that she might start falling in love with him, because she had never lain with any man before him, and it is very difficult for a woman not to fall in love with the man who makes love to her for the first time, even if she hates him!

Of course, if she loves him to start with, it is quite impossible!

I don't mean that White-thorn had forgotten the man she truly loved, Sea-breaker, or how she had parted from him in anger, because she had not dared tell him that she was going to try to kill the king of the enemy. She hoped that Sea-breaker had escaped to a fair land across the ocean and that he would be happy always.

The next day the king led his army on to . . . to the next city. When they arrived, he rode up to the coach in which White-thorn was riding and said, "My lady, I am going to show you to the people here, also, but I want you to ride at my side on this beautiful white horse, and I want you to wear beautiful clothes and I have brought many even more beautiful jewels for you to wear, and they will all weep to see that you are helpless in my power, because you will be so beautiful."

"Oh, Your Majesty," White-thorn said, "I beg you not to shame me by making my people think that I have betrayed them. I beg you to put me back in chains, so that they will know I am your helpless slave!"

The king frowned, but then he agreed to do as she asked, and he had a golden chain made and hung around her neck and he held the other end of it. So White-thorn rode on the beautiful white horse through the city, and she wept bitter tears to see their suffering! And all the people saw how beautiful she was, and how helpless in the king's power, and they all wept, too! And even some of the Horsefolk soldiers wept, she was so beautiful, and so helpless in the power of the strong king!

That night she came to his tent and he jumped up and kissed her. "Oh, beautiful Princess White-thorn," he said. "I have conquered all this land and everything in it belongs to me, and all the people must do whatever I say, but you are the most precious to me, because you are so beautiful and so brave. I want to bring peace to the land by making you my queen and uniting our two peoples."

Then White-thorn wept.

"Do not weep!" the king said. "I want to see you smile, because you have never smiled at me. Why do you weep when I offer to make you queen over all this land and the land of my savage people, also?"

White-thorn wanted to tell him that she could never love him, big and strong and so handsome though he was, because she loved another man and would always love him, even if she never saw him again, but she was afraid that the king would then be angry with her and take out his rage on the poor people.

"Your tears move me greatly," the king said. "I will not force you against your will ever again. Will you lie with me from choice, of your own free will?"

Then White-thorn dried her eyes. "Your Majesty," she proclaimed, "if it will bring peace to my land and stop my people suffering, then I will do whatever you ask of me."

"This is not enough," the king sternly said. "You must truly tell me that you love me as a man, because I love you as I have never loved any woman."

But White-thorn did not answer him, because we ladies cannot bear to tell lies.

So the king called for his guards and had White-thorn taken back to her own tent. And while she was lying there, all alone, staring at the darkness and wondering whether she should marry the king to bring peace to her people, she heard a strange noise. And then the flap of the tent opened and a man came in.

She opened her mouth to scream, and a voice in the darkness said, "Is that you, my beloved? Is that White-thorn, who is ever in my dreams?"

And White-thorn knew the voice and her heart almost leaped out of her breast with joy, and she said, "Yes, that's me. Truly are you Sea-breaker, my only love?"

"I am Sea-breaker," the man said, "and I have risked death to come and find you and rescue you."

Then White-thorn jumped up from her bed—I forgot to mention that she was still respectably dressed because she had been too unhappy to remove her beautiful gown and all her beautiful jewels—and she embraced Sea-breaker, and he was even taller and stronger than the king, and she loved him more than life itself and she thought how wonderful it would be to have Sea-breaker make love to her every night, well, *almost* every night, I mean, instead of Vandok.

"Tell me, my darling," she said, "how you came here in the middle of the camp of the fierce Horsefolk?"

"It is a sad story, my love," Sea-breaker answered. "When I left you, I went down to the docks to board the ship that would take me away to safety, and then I could not bear to go, for I knew that life without you would not be worth living. So I told the captain to sail without me, and I went back to look for you. But the fierce Horsefolk had taken you away before I got there, and they were burning houses and killing people. I fought several of them, killing them all, but I could not find you.

"Then the enemy army rode away to Jombina and I followed, with some loyal friends. We learned that you were the king's prisoner and we made plans to rescue you, but it has taken us all these long days to find a way. Now we have a ship waiting, which will bear us away across the seas to safety, so that you and I can be married and live happily ever after."

"Then let us go at once," White-thorn said, "because truly you are the only man I have ever loved, or will ever love, and King Vandok is a horrible man."

Then they went out of the tent, but the night was all bright with flaming torches, and King Vandok stood there with hundreds of his fierce warriors all around.

"Who is this intruder?" he cried.

"I am the White-thorn's true love," Sea-breaker shouted, and drew his sword.

"Then you must die," the king said, "because I also love her and I will let no other man have her!" And he drew his sword, also.

Then the two of them fought, Sea-breaker and King Vandok, while White-thorn watched in horror, praying to the gods that the man she hated would not kill the man she loved, and all the fierce warriors stood around and watched, also.

The king was a famous swordsman, who had slain many men and fought many battles, but Sea-breaker was more than a match for him. Their swords clashed and flashed in the torchlight, and they leaped about, while all the warriors watched, amazed at seeing such swordplay!

Then the king paused for a moment to catch his breath, panting with his exertions so that the sweat gleamed on his heaving chest. "Truly, Sea-breaker," he said, "I have fought many great swordsmen and killed them all, but never one like you!"

"That is because I am fighting for the woman I love!" Sea-breaker replied. And he was very cool, and not puffing hardly at all!

Then they fought again and at last Sea-breaker struck the sword from the king's hand and put the point of his own sword at the king's heart.

"Now I will kill you!" he said, "because you have shamed my beloved."

"Then all my fierce warriors will kill you in turn and her, also," said the king. "White-thorn, if you will tell me that you love me, then I will spare his life and let him go."

"I cannot tell such a lie," Princess White-thorn cried. "I love only Sea-breaker, and if you kill him, then I swear that I will kill myself, also. Maybe you can watch me now, but you will not be able to watch me always, and one day I will manage to kill myself, or else my heart will just break and I shall fade away and die." And she threw her arms around Sea-breaker.

"Alas!" the king said. "It is I whose heart is breaking! I love you, also, because you are so beautiful and because you are braver than any woman I have ever known. White-thorn, I can deny you nothing. Go, then, with this brave swordsman of yours, and may the gods make you happy."

So the king let White-thorn and Sea-breaker leave the camp, and they galloped away to the ship, and sailed off across the ocean together.

I hope I have pleased you, gentlemen? My tale, I mean. And ladies, of course.

8: Interlude

I felt sick to my stomach.

The merchant was beaming proudly. His wife sat with downcast eyes, smirking under her lashes.

Young Gwill was doubled over, face in hands. Judging by the heaving of his shoulders, he was being racked by some powerful emotion.

Frieda's face was expressionless, while the great oaf beside her grinned like a rabid timber wolf.

The dowager had arranged her web of wrinkles into an approving smile; the old soldier looked stunned, as if his sword had melted in the midst of a battle; the maid wept tears of joy. I had not seen her face properly before. She was surprisingly pretty and I might have believed that her fine-drawn features denoted sensitivity and intelligence, were she not now so obviously overwhelmed by all the romantic rubbish.

Vandok had been one of the bloodiest killers in the history of mankind. Compared with Vandok, even his great-grandfather Hannail had been a baby bunny. At least Hannail had sacrificed only animals to Hool.

"That is *absurd*!" I howled. "That is pigswill! You made that all up!"

The actress looked hurt. "You mean you will swear to the truth of every word you told us before, Master Omar? You really know what thoughts passed through the head of a woman two hundred years ago?"

"A little poetic license is one thing, but—"

"I do not recall," the dowager said, "that we specified anything about truth? Entertainment was all that we required. Thank you, Mistress Marla, for an inspiring tale. We all enjoyed your story . . . Didn't we?"

The minstrel raised his head. Tears streamed from his swollen eyes. "It was an unforgettable performance, my lady," he croaked.

"As I recall the legends," the soldier muttered, "White-thorn did gain her revenge in the end, so she must have escaped, surely?"

"Yes," I snarled. "But I never heard tell of *how* she escaped."

"Well, now you did," the actress said triumphantly.

"It demonstrates—" Gwill sneezed. "—how light may be shed on truth in the most ast—" He sneezed again. "—*on*ishing places."

"It does indeed," I said. "In time all veils of ignorance and deceit are stripped away."

The actress glared as she appraised our threat; her rosebud lips drew back to show sharp little teeth. I smiled, and Gwill tried to, but his nose and eyes were running too hard. There was no way she could ever explain away those tattoos. Quite literally, she must keep her husband in the dark, pleading the modesty of the nunnery, refusing to disrobe with the light on. He would not remain burgomaster of Schlosbelsh very long if it became known that he had married a whore.

Ignorant of our unspoken conversation, he hugged her with a fur-draped arm. "A wonderful story, and beautifully told, my cherub! How about some wine to celebrate your success, my little honeycake? Innkeeper, have you wine?"

Fritz was on his feet in an instant. "Indeed I do, my lord! I have some excellent red from the vineyards of the monks of Abaila, and white from the slopes above Poluppo. Sweet and new, my lord, stored in a cool place."

Ha! In those northern lands, and especially in remote rural taverns, wine tended to be both very old and very sour, long past its best. Down in Furthlin, the vintners had discovered a way of sealing wine in glass bottles so it would often stay fresh for years, but the secret had not yet found its way anywhere close to the Hunters' Haunt. The bulge of the merchant's belly suggested that he was more familiar with beer than wine.

Not to be upstaged, the dowager demanded some fruitcake. Frieda hurried out to attend to that, close on her brother's heels. I rose and shuffled over to the fireplace to refill my stein from the copper jug. I wanted to inspect the note in my pocket, but I was conscious of many disapproving eyes on me.

The notary favored me with a ferrety scowl as I wandered back to my place beside him. "You are compounding your felony!"

"If I am to die for a dog, then you may see I am suitably punished for this offense afterward."

"Don't blame me for your troubles!"

I took a long draught and wondered if I dared wipe my mouth on the sleeve of the doublet I was wearing, or whether I would catch rabies from it. Then I turned my attention to the pedant. He was not a type to excite admiration, the small man who wraps himself in the authority of the law and believes he has thereby achieved majesty. His eyes were restless as flies and as hard to catch, his nose long and coarse, peppered with pox and blackheads, his jowls ten years lower than they should be.

"Why not? You set yourself up as my judge."

He flushed all the way to his biretta. "I certainly did not! I merely gave my opinion that no secular authority claims jurisdiction here."

"And therefore the group of you appropriated that authority to yourselves." I took another gulp. The mulled ale was scalding, hot enough to raise a sweat from my scalp to my toes, but I was disinclined to linger over it.

"The gods judge all men and know all men," the

clerk said stiffly. After a moment he added, "But overt manifestation of their omniscience is rare."

I noted that the wind was not wailing so loud, that the ferns on the floor no long stirred, the shutters had almost ceased their rattling. Climate in the Grimm Ranges is a matter of hours more than years. The storm might have departed, but snow and cold were still waiting out there.

A heavy tread announced the return of our host, bearing a clay flagon and two small pewter mugs. While the merchant inspected the seal and all eyes were on him, I pulled out the note. *The stable key is on the beam above the door*, it said. I thrust it back out of sight and drained my stein while Fritz's back was still turned.

Fair enough. If I was still able to walk when he had done with me, the stable would be a warm sanctuary from the storm. But I would leave tracks. I could not replace the key without leaving the door unlocked behind me, so in the morning he would find me there. It would not work.

I decided I would do better worrying about how I could respond to Marla's malarkey. At least one person had dropped me a strong hint in the last few minutes.

The merchant pronounced the wine acceptable. The actress's face twisted when she tasted it, but she agreed it was delicious. The dowager graciously allowed her maid one piece of fruitcake. The fire was stoked again. The audience settled down to listen.

"Have we not had enough of the Land Between the Seas?" the old soldier suggested. "Can you tell us a tale of some other place, Master Omar?"

"Indeed I can, Captain, and I was planning to. Mistress Marla has told us of a gallant rescue. I shall recount a deliverance of another sort. Harken, gentle lords and fair ladies, as I unfold for you the strange Tale of the God Who Would Not Speak."

9: Omar's Response to the Actress's Tale

In the reign of the great Emir Mustaf II, the island city of Algazan flourished as it never had before, reaching a pinnacle of wealth that made it the envy of the world. Its ships reached out to lands previously known only in legend, trading in rich fabrics, scented woods, pearls and jade, slaves and spices, oils and perfumes, jewels, artifacts, and wondrously worked ivory. Kings flocked from the mainland to marvel at the glory of its many fine palaces and fabled gardens, merchants thronged from the ends of the earth to its bazaars. A hundred gods dwelt within its temples. Any who dared oppose it on the shores of three oceans, whether they be prince or pirate, were swiftly humbled by the might of its fleet and the armies hired by its gold.

But not all its avenues were paved with marble nor all its denizens dwellers in palaces. Men and women of a dozen races huddled in slums and tenements, in putrid alleys the rich never saw. For centuries, a human stream had trickled into the cesspits of Algazan: adventurers come to seek their fortunes, refugees from political oppression, malcontents yearning after their own gods. Few had prospered, most had sunk into dismal poverty. Their descendants congealed in lumps beneath the surface of society, enclaves of foreigners existing under uneasy tolerance—distinct from the natives, banned from the benefits of citizenship. The Algazanians discriminated but rarely persecuted. What the foreigners did to one another was worse.

One was a boy named Juss. He was Algazanian by birth but not by right. His skin and hair were a little lighter than those of the True, his accent faulty and thereby subject to ridicule. On the day of which I shall speak, he was approaching the threshold of manhood. He checked his height frequently against the doorpost, and on the rare occasions when he found himself both unobserved and close to a mirror, he would inspect his upper lip in it, although with more amusement at his own optimism than real hope of encouragement. He was wiry and unusually healthy for the neighborhood in which he lived. His dark eyes were quick and bright. He smiled more than his circumstances would seem to warrant, and the few adults aware of his existence tended to think well of him.

He was employed, after a fashion, by Gozspin the Purveyor of Fresh and Nutritious Vegetable Materials, meaning that Juss was allowed to stand with several other boys outside Gozspin's grubby little store from dawn until an hour before sunset. Whenever a customer departed, having purchased some of Gozspin's moldy roots and soggy leaves, Juss would try to outshout the others in offering to carry them home for her. Four or five times a day his offer would be accepted. He would then follow the lady around the bazaars until she had completed her acquisitions and he was so laden with packages that he resembled a walking bazaar all by himself. Upon arriving at her door, she would grant him whatever gratuity she deemed fitting. He was cheerful and respectful and had a sunny smile; many days he collected ten or even twelve copper mites.

He was expected to turn over half of them to Gozspin, and did. In return, Gozspin would allow him to buy some of the moldiest and soggiest wares at a sizable discount. If Juss had enough money left over, he would also purchase a stale loaf from the bakery next door. After that, he had the problem of conveying his supper, plus any remaining cash, safely home.

He lived in a very small room in a very high tenement in what was generally known as the Godless Quarter. To reach it, he had to pass through the territory of the Drazalians, the Jorkobians, the Alfoli, and the Children of Wuzz. Native Algazanians were another problem altogether.

On the evening of which I tell, Juss carried one loaf, two soft mangoes, and a bundle of almost edible spinach. Detouring up a particularly noisome alley to avoid some Jorkobian youths, he ran afoul of a gang of teenage Alfoli. When the brief encounter was over, he was bereft of his two remaining copper mites and had been kicked in various places for not having had more. Furthermore, his loincloth and sandals reposed in the sewer, and his supper lay in the mud.

It was a discouraging ending to a hard day, but not an unusual one. Juss gathered up his clothes and the food and walked on. His belly hurt, his right eye was swelling, and he had painful scrapes on his back. It could have been worse. He was later accosted by seven young Children of Wuzz. Concluding from his repugnant appearance that he was unworthy of their attentions, they let him past, promising to see him again the next day.

He felt relieved but very weary when he arrived at the Mansion of Many Gods. He plodded through a dark tunnel into the central courtyard that held the water trough and the toilets. The sun never shone there, except for a few minutes at noon. Those who lived on the outside of the Mansion despised those whose abodes overlooked the smelly court. The insiders retorted that the streets smelled worse. The two groups had separate stairs and walkways. Juss lived in an inside room on the seventh floor.

He washed himself, his supper, and his clothes in the communal trough, then headed for the stair. Not unexpectedly, a group of boys mostly older than he were sitting on the bottom step, barring his path. Several of them were chewing dream rope. Behind them sat Flower, their current leader. They all scowled at Juss.

"Let me by, please," he said.

"Who got you this time?" Flower demanded.

"The Emir's guards."

For a minute nothing more happened, but Juss was not worried. They all knew he was Ven's brother, and in the Mansion of Many Gods that was defense enough. They disliked him because he refused to join the gang and play his part in molesting Drazalians, Jorkobians, Alfoli, and the especially despicable Wuzzians.

Eventually Flower said, "Let him," and two boys wriggled aside to open a space. Juss climbed through, alert for hands grabbing his ankles, but today there was none of that.

He climbed one flight, went along the walkway, up the next flight . . .

Old folk sitting by their doors greeted him and he responded. He paused to talk with Moonlight, who was growing prettier and more interesting all the time. He had an even longer chat with Joyful and Intrepid, his closest buddies, and they commiserated with him on his new bruises. On the fourth floor ancient Fine-jade asked him if he would fill her water pail for him, so he left his supper in her care and trotted all the way back down with the bucket. On the sixth floor, Storm-blast, who was even older, asked Juss to take his slop bucket down and empty it, so down he went again . . . It took him a third of an hour to reach the room he shared with Ven.

Someone had been rummaging in his absence, but that was not unusual. A quick check of the secret place under the floorboards told him that it had not been discovered. That was where the treasures lived: the book, and the money, spare clothes, and of course the family god, who kept it safe. Nothing else in the room had any value: two thin sleeping rugs, a water pot, an old box that served as a table. None of those had been removed.

Having divided the loaf and the other victuals into

two unequal halves, Juss took the family god out of the secret place and set him on the box. Then he sat down wearily on his mat and waited until Ven arrived, a short while later. Ven had brought a bag of onions.

Ven was nine years older, and considerably larger than Juss would ever be. Like many large men, he moved with slow diffidence, as if constantly frightened of breaking something or hurting someone. His gray eyes and unusually light brown hair had caused him much grief in his younger days among the darker multitudes of Algazan, and he had learned then that his strength must be used with caution, even when righteously provoked. His stubbly reddish beard and crooked nose made him look much fiercer than he really was. In truth he was a stolid, deliberate young man, although he could be fierce when roused. He had been father and mother to Juss since their parents had died ten years earlier, and Juss worshipped him with all the fanatical zeal of a boy who has only one relative in the world to love and admire.

Ven worked as a porter at the docks, putting his great strength to good use. He frequently earned thirty mites or more in a day, although half of that went to the gang boss, of course, and another five to the porters' guild.

The brothers smiled at each other. They asked after each other's day, and each responded that it had not been too bad, nor especially exciting. Ven pretended not to notice Juss's swelling bruises. He remarked that the meal looked good, although he was a truthful man when truth was important. He knelt down before the god on his box, and Juss knelt beside him, taking comfort from his brother's nearness and strength.

"Most Holy Father Kraw," Juss said, "we thank you for keeping us safe this day and for giving us our food." It was the prayer he could remember their father speaking, and he said it every evening.

The god did not reply. The god never did.

The Godless had earned their name because they

never attended any of the hundred temples on the island. They had no need to, for every family owned its own god, like Kraw.

Kraw was a dragon's tooth, old and black and about the size of both of Ven's fists together—quite frightening if one thought about how big the dragon himself must have been.

But he never spoke. Other boys told Juss that their family god spoke to their fathers, or even to them sometimes, but Kraw did not speak. Still, a dragon's tooth was a much more impressive god than any mere figure of pottery or metal or stone, and Juss was proud of him.

They ate their meal in silence, Juss taking the smaller portion because he was the smaller brother. They chewed hungrily and did not take long. They did not experience the feeling of bloated satisfaction that a large repast will give. Never having known that sensation, Juss did not miss it. The light from the little window was fading already and soon it would be time to curl up on the mats. Most nights the brothers would talk for a while then, in the dark. Ven would tell Juss a story about their parents, whom Juss could barely remember. After that they would sleep, preparing for another day.

There being no dishes to wash, and neither of them feeling thirsty enough to run all the way down to the trough for a drink, Juss went to the secret place and brought out the book.

Next to Kraw himself, the book was their most precious possession. Ven had been taught to read by their mother, more or less. He had taught Juss, also, and in the evenings they would read the book together. Juss was a now a better reader than Ven was, although he concealed that fact from his brother as far as he could. Neither of them was truly expert. The book was difficult; it related the history of the land their parents had come from long ago, and it was written in the language of the Godless. Although they spoke that tongue with their friends and neighbors, in their daily lives they conversed in Algazanian, which was very different. Neither brother understood much of the book.

Ven smiled an apologetic smile and shook his head. "Not tonight," he said. "How much money do we have?"

Juss turned away quickly so that his sudden worry would not show. Although he already knew the answer, he scrabbled on his knees over to the loose plank and peered in the secret cache. "One silverfish and four mites." There had been four silverfish a few days ago, but Ven had needed a wisdom tooth pulled. The pain of it had been driving him crazy.

He sighed. "Tomorrow is Pearl's birthday."

Juss said, "Oh. I didn't know."

Ven was courting the daughter of Stalwart the carter. She had hinted that his attentions were not unpleasing, although her mother certainly disapproved. Juss had mixed feelings about the matter and was rather ashamed of himself in consequence. He certainly wanted his brother to be happy. He could admit now that girls were pleasant company, but they did not promote the same sense of urgency in him that they did in Ven. He understood that he would feel otherwise when he was older. Of course it would be years before Ven could save up enough money to raise the matter of marriage. A birthday gift was a more immediate problem.

"I said I would go out this evening," Ven muttered.

Juss tried not to show his fear. "I will come with you and watch."

"No you won't! I feel distracted if you are around, you know that! Now don't worry and don't get into mischief. I'll be all right." With those words, Ven jumped up and strode quickly out, before Juss could start arguing. Juss was much better at arguing than he was.

They could not live on Ven's daily earnings, not even with what Juss now contributed. They had almost starved when their parents died. All the family possessions had been lost in the fire the authorities had used to cleanse the Godless Quarter of pestilence. In those days Ven had been too young to earn a man's wages, although he had been big for his age. They had survived because Ven could earn money fighting. He had started with boys' matches, the preliminary events to titillate the spectators and start the bets flowing. Now he fought in main events. Sometimes he won as much as two or three silverfish in an evening.

"He has never been seriously hurt yet!" Juss said firmly, knowing that he was speaking to an empty room. But what would happen to the two of them if he ever *was* seriously hurt?

The thought was terrifying. Without that extra money the brothers would be forced to give up their home and move into squalid communal quarters. Without it there could never be little presents for girlfriends or hope of marriage. The only alternative would be crime of some sort—Flower's gang for Juss, worse for Ven. Sadly, an honest living for a laborer in Algazan was not a living.

Men did get seriously hurt at the fights, even died sometimes. Ven himself had once knocked out an opponent's eye and had refused to fight for months after that, although he had been promised real gold if he could manage to do it again.

Already on his knees, Juss spun around to face the box. He touched his head to the floor and said, "Holy Father Kraw, please look after Ven tonight and keep him safe!"

"I cannot."

Juss straightened up slowly. Even more slowly, he looked around the room. What he saw was what he expected to see, and it was more frightening than a gang of the Children of Wuzz would have been. Nobody. Four walls, two mats, one box . . . everything as it should be.

It might be one of his pals in the tenement playing tricks on him, but it had not sounded like a boy's voice.

No, nor even Intrepid's new baritone that he was so proud of when it worked right.

"Who spoke?" Juss quavered.

"I did."

It sounded like a very large voice, a *huge* voice, but a great way off. Juss suppressed a frantic need to race downstairs to the urinals.

"Who a-a-are you?" he asked the empty room.

"I am Kraw, your god."

Juss's forehead hit the floor with an audible bump. His teeth chattered wildly and his skin went cold all over.

"Why are you frightened?" the voice inquired, sounding amused. "I am your god. You are my son. You have nothing to fear from me, nothing at all."

"You . . . You never spoke to me before!"

"You never spoke to me when we were alone, that's why. Besides, now you are old enough to understand. Almost old enough, anyway."

Juss sneaked a look with one eye. The big black tooth was just the same as always. He had half expected to see a misty dragon shape around it, or something, but there was just the tooth. "Why don't you speak to Ven?"

"Because he is not mine," the god said patiently. "You are mine. Only you can worship me and I will speak to no other."

"But Ven is my brother!"

"He is your half brother. You are Sure-justice of Kraw. I am Kraw, the god of your father and his father and very many fathers before them. I suppose I would not be too angry if you referred to yourself once in a while as Sure-justice of Verl, although you had better not make a habit of it. Verl was your mother's god. She has no other children left but you two, so I would not mind sharing you with her. A little of you, that is. Once in a while," the god rumbled, sounding less certain.

A very misty light dawned in the boy's befogged

brain. "Our mother? She was married to another before my father?"

The god sighed. "In a manner of speaking. Your father knew that Cold-vengeance was son—"

"What?"

"Ven, you little goose! His real name is Cold-vengeance. Sea-breaker knew that he was not his father, but he accepted him. I did not, so tell your half brother—"

"Why not?"

The dragon rumbled ferociously. "*Juss!* You do *not* interrupt gods. *Especially* when they are explaining. Gods do not *like* explaining."

Juss had his nose on the floor again.

"Now," said the god, "where was I?"

"You were—"

"Yes, I *know*, Juss! The question was hypothetical. Tell Cold-vengeance that he must not to try to worship me. Tell him gently. He can call himself Cold-vengeance of Verl if he wants."

"But where is his god, Verl, then? Our mother's god?"

"Very far away, but I think safe."

"I don't understand!"

Kraw chuckled. Even at a very great distance, a dragon chuckle was not a laughing matter, and Juss felt a cool breeze chill his skin.

"Bring the book, Sure-justice."

Juss obeyed quickly.

"Turn to the end. Now back up a few pages—until I say to stop . . ."

Juss sat on the floor with the book spread open on his legs, and apparently Kraw could read even from where he was on the box, although the light was fading fast from the little room. The pages of the book were not numbered, but the god told Juss how to find the passage he wanted, and then had him read it, prompting him when he stumbled over a word. The handwriting was

very bad near the end of the book. Juss had avoided it
in the past for that reason, and also because the story
was so sad. It began cheerfully enough, with Morning-
star raising the banner of freedom and chopping off
King Grosail's head on his own throne. Then it grew
darker.

The room grew darker and the story grew darker: the
failure of the revolution, the terrible vengeance of
Vandok, White-thorn . . . Some of the details were gruesome. Ven never let Juss read bits like those.

"That will do," the god said at last. "You have heard
of Morning-star before."

"Yes, Father." Juss slid the heavy book off his shins
with relief.

"And how do the people feel about him?"

A boy who rarely knew a full stomach found political
affairs of faraway lands to be of very marginal importance to his life. He had not listened much. "Some of
them curse him?" he said uncertainly. "Others say we
need another Morning-star to stand up and try again?"

"Very good, Sure-justice! The story in that book is
not complete. Morning-star's daughter escaped."

"Good!" Juss grinned to hear that. The brutality bits
had made him feel queasy.

"She escaped here, to Algazan. But she changed her
name. Why?"

"Um. Because some people didn't approve of what
her father had done? They might have hurt her?"

The god chuckled again, and this time the sound was
less frightening. "Ah, you are a sharp little claw! But
that is what we should expect of a son of White-thorn,
isn't it?"

"White-thorn was . . . But then Morning-star . . . My
grandfather? My *mother*? And Ven's?"

"And Ven's, also. Think, my son! You are clever. You
are more clever than Ven. Think before you ask any
more."

Juss sat back and leaned his chin on his hands for a

while, unconsciously staring at the god in a way no mortal could have endured without squirming, although dragon teeth apparently do not mind. Juss thought things through in his clever, patient way, until eventually he said, "Why did she name him Cold-vengeance?"

"Why do you think, my son?"

"Because he was Morning-star's grandson! So that Ven would lead the next revolution and drive out the Horsefolk and kill King Vandok! Will he?"

"He can try."

And why Sure-justice? Suddenly very excited, Juss scrabbled onto his knees so he could touch his head to the floor again. "Most Holy Father, can I help him try?"

The god sighed. "If you wish to. Frankly, I don't think Ven will get very far without help, and who will help him but you?"

"It is my fight, also, is it not?"

"Yes," the god said. "Yes, it is. Are you ready to start tonight?"

Juss jumped up. His knees trembled but he said, "Yes, Father."

"Then wrap me in your spare cloth and take me with you. You must go and tell all this to a man who may help you. If he doesn't, I don't know who will, and your cause is hopeless."

So Juss wrapped the god up safely and ran down the stairs and out into the city night. He never returned to the Mansion of the Many Gods.

10: The Second Judgment

"**T**hat is ridiculous!" the dowager snapped. "That is only half a story!"

"I promised you a tale of deliverance," I protested. "I cannot tell you what happened next because I don't know. I can guess, roughly, but I never recount mere guesses, only undoubted truth."

"Well, who was the man he went to?"

"Even that I do not know for certain. His real name was not divulged to me, only a nickname, lest it put certain people in danger."

Nine pairs of eyes regarded me skeptically.

"This was two hundred years ago," the minstrel croaked, fear of the uncanny starting to shine in his swollen eyes.

I saw that I had been indiscreet. "Forgive me. I meant that the name was not revealed to the person to whom the story was first told, and hence has not been passed down to us."

"Contemptible!" the merchant growled. The wine had given his flabby face an even ruddier glow than before. "I detest storytellers who leave you dangling over an abyss and demand more money before they will tell you the next episode."

"So do I!" I agreed heartily. "It is very unprofessional behavior. Unscrupulous in the extreme! However, in this case, I had no choice. I do not know the next episode. Does anyone?"

There was a long silence.

I had wagered everything on the hint I detected earlier, in the hope of learning that next episode—I can never resist the opportunity to hear a good tale, and I had been waiting for this one for two . . . too long. But had it been a hint, or merely a slip of the tongue? If the person in question refused to talk, then I had lost my gamble.

The old soldier cleared his throat and straightened himself on the bench. "I may be in possession of some relevant information."

I sighed with relief. "Then I beg you to disclose it. I have wondered about this for a very long time."

"Fah!" the merchant growled. "The wind has dropped. It is time for godly folk to take themselves off to bed—don't you agree, my little lovebird?"

His wife smiled automatically and then stole a worried glance in my direction.

"Take the miscreant, innkeeper," her husband rumbled, heaving himself to his feet with a great effort. "Break every bone in his body for all I care. Come, woman. Duty calls, what?" He chuckled drunkenly.

Fritz smiled hungrily at me and flexed his hands.

"How about a little bedtime story?" I suggested.

The minstrel whistled a few bars of a popular dance tune . . .

"Er, beloved?" the actress said, resisting her husband's urging. "I do so want to hear a few more tales, darling! I mean, if the noble captain has something to tell us, it would only be polite for us to stay and listen, wouldn't it? Just one more? Oh, we haven't finished the wine yet! We mustn't waste it, after you spent so much money on it."

That argument made the fat man pause. With a growl, he sagged back into his chair and reached for the flagon. "A couple of quick nightcaps, then."

The dowager had been frowning at this discussion with rank disapproval. She turned her basilisk stare on the minstrel and then on me . . . and finally on the soldier at her side.

"You wish to engage in this frivolity, Captain? It is hardly the place to reveal anything of a private nature."

There was a hint there, a nuance about as subtle as a rapier through the gizzard. My belief that he was her hired guard had just been confirmed.

The old warrior was not intimidated. He nodded curtly, then swung around to fix me with his raptor eyes. He was old but still dangerous—like his leather jerkin, scuffed and worn but still serviceable. Such a man would not wear a sword were he incapable of wielding it. At last he ran fingers over his close-cut silver hair. "Many ancient legends tell of a vagrant storyteller by the name of Omar, a man who turns up in many places and at many—"

"I have heard them." I gave him my most disarming smile. "Myth begets myth, Captain. Many a rapscallion has taken that name just because of the legends, and thus generated another. I didn't. I was Omar before I was a trader of tales—but mayhap the tradition influenced my choice of career."

"You do not grow old and then young again, to and fro forever?"

"I have heard that part of it. It would be hard to make friends when going the wrong way, no? But you should not take such drivel seriously, Captain. Remember, many stories are more convincing when told in the first person. In his tale, Minstrel Gwill told us of one Omar. White-thorn gave her god into the keeping of a stranger who sounded suspiciously like another, yes? Now, were I less firmly corseted with scruples, I might have related that incident as if I had been there, had actually been that man . . . This is how legends grow, Captain."

He continued to gaze at me as if I were a prospective battlefield.

I began to wilt, although I could not remember the last time a mere stare had discomfited me. "Do I take it that the second round of the contest has been decided in my favor?"

Fritz scowled mightily.

"Apparently no one is ready to deliver you to justice yet," the dowager agreed, glancing around to see if anyone dared to disagree with her.

No one did. Gwill flashed me an approving grin in the midst of his sneezing. The maid studied her hands. The notary seemed close to sleep.

Somewhere outside there was a sudden *crack!*

The actress jumped. "What was that?"

"Frost, ma'am." Fritz glanced at me to make sure I understood the implications. "When the wind drops, the temperature begins to fall. We are very high here. That noise was a tree splitting in the sudden cold."

Marla said, "Oh!" and took a sip of her wine. Her face went rigid with the effort of swallowing the muck.

"It is late!" the dowager announced sternly. "I trust you can be quick, Captain?"

At last he turned his gaze from me, as if satisfied. "I shall be as brief as I can, my lady. I am generally a man of few words, as you know." He reached deep inside his doublet. "All my life, I have been a free sword, a mercenary. I have fought for good causes and bad, although I tried to choose the good whenever circumstances permitted." He produced a small package wrapped in what seemed to be brown silk. "My name is not of consequence . . . No, to be more truthful, my name was once of great consequence. My father abandoned it, lest he bring disrepute upon nobler members of our house. As a youngster taking up the profession of arms, I became known by a foolish nickname, 'Tiger.' I did not disavow it, of course, and it stuck. I am a toothless old pussycat now, I fear, but still remembered as Captain Tiger in some parts.

"Perhaps my constant companion here may have encouraged the practice, although very few persons have ever seen it." He held out his hand with the cloth opened upon it, and upon the cloth lay a small carving, little larger than one of his own big thumbs.

We all leaned forward to peer at this gem. It seemed to be carved from amber, for it glowed in the firelight. It had no stripes, of course, and yet the shape was undoubtedly that of a tiger, prone, but with its head raised as if some noise had just roused it from sleep. The eyes were inset with tiny green gems. In the right market it would have brought a man comfort or even luxury for the rest of his days. I, for one, was seized by a fierce desire to reach out and touch it.

The actress was the first to speak. She seemed awed, and I did not think she was dissembling. "Is that one of these gods we have been hearing about?"

"In these parts I would call him a mascot, my lady. His name is Bargar. He is not the original, of course. When my father, being the youngest of many brothers, set off to find his fortune in far lands, the original Bargar foretold that he would never return to the ancestral hearth, and permitted a copy to be made."

"Does it . . . *talk* to you?"

The leathery old man smiled noncommittally and wrapped the amber tiger away in its cloth. "I have lived a long life for a professional soldier, my lady. My good fortune has been remarked on more than once."

Whatever his merits as a warrior, he certainly had the makings of a teller of tales. Even the fat merchant, sprawled back in his chair like a rolled-up quilt, was blinking attentively.

The tiger was returned to its secret abode. Another tree trunk cracked in the forest like a sharp stroke of thunder, and this time I heard a faint echo from the cliff across the valley. The soldier gestured for Fritz to refill his stein and the innkeeper jumped to obey.

"As to the matter Master Omar was narrating . . . Many years ago, I had occasion to visit my father's homeland, and naturally I called upon the current head of the family to pay my respects. At first I was regarded with some suspicion. When I produced my little Bargar, of course, I was welcomed with joy and great hospitality. I was even presented to the original Bargar—and yes, he spoke to me! It was a very moving experience."

With a superb sense of timing, the soldier paused then to take a swallow of ale. He chuckled. "My so-splendid relations found me a rather rough companion, I fear. I did not fit well into their balls and banquets, and my conversation was more direct than they favored among themselves. But I struck up a friendship with a couple of the younger sons, who took me off hunting. That was more to my taste, and more to my abilities, also. We got along famously then.

"Our journey led us eventually to the ancestral home itself, a moldering old pile now lost in the woods. There, one night, I was shown some rather curious documents."

I sat up straighter.

Captain Tiger noted the movement and smiled drolly. "May I offer you a stein of ale, Master Omar?"

I accepted gratefully. Fritz went to draw it—a rather skimpy measure. Having teased us enough, the old rogue resumed his story.

"One of my . . . cousins, I suppose they were . . . the younger of my new friends, anyway, was indiscreet enough in his cups one night to remark that, for all their airs and graces, for all their titles and orders and ribbons, my grand relations were every one descended from a mere soldier of fortune like myself. He found that fact inexpressibly amusing. At least, that night he did. Eventually he went away to some distant attic and returned with a very decrepit wooden box. It was Algazanian work, ibex and cheetahs . . . no matter.

"Within this box reposed memoirs written by the founder himself. They were incomplete. Many sheets had been lost and many were so faded as to be illegible, but parts were quite detailed. Over the next few days . . . I should mention I had sprained an ankle. Long reading is not my favored occupation, but I was temporarily housebound and so I worked my way through most of the pile. And some of it was certainly interesting stuff.

"It confirmed much of what Master Omar just told us, even in detail. My ancestor's full name, for example, was Great-memory of Bargar, but the exiles in Algazan found these cumbersome names inappropriate and subject to ridicule. They shortened them, as you said. As I am Tiger, he was known as Memo.

"When young, he had fought in Morning-star's failed revolution. He was wounded, although not seriously. He escaped from Kylam in the very same ship as Seabreaker."

The rest of us all looked at the actress. I was surprised to see she had enough shame left to blush. I waited eagerly to hear the true story of White-thorn's escape from Vandok's torments, but it did not come. Either those details had not been included in Captain Tiger's mysterious box, or he was too respectful of the actress's feelings to discuss the subject further.

"So Master Omar left us dangling over the abyss, as His Honor puts it. I have read an eyewitness account of a meeting that transpired that night. I shall report it as well as my memory serves. If you require a title, then I suppose this would be called the Tale of the Improbable Pretender."

11: The Soldier's Tale

At twenty-five, Memo had been a penniless exile on crutches. At fifty he was an honored citizen, famous, wealthy, and miserable. Or if not quite miserable, then discontented. Unsatisfied.

He had been fortunate, perhaps too fortunate. He knew of hundreds who had fled his homeland at the same time as he. They included men of skill and wit, men of courage and character, but very few had prospered as he had. He enjoyed respect and reputation, a luxurious home with many servants. He loved his wife and daughter and received their love in return.

If he had achieved all this by courage, exertion, and endurance—or even by simple fortune, chance flight of arrow or stroke of sword in battle—then he could take some pride in it, but he feared it had all been a blessing from Bargar. If so, then he was grateful, and that was not enough.

Just before Memo had arrived on the island, the Emir had approved an expansion of the Algazanian Foreign Legion. On the strength of his experience fighting the Horsefolk and the wound he had received at Mill Creek, Memo was accepted into the ranks. He proved himself brave, loyal, and obedient, but he also paid heed to his family god, whose warnings frequently steered him aside from death or disaster. In the next twenty years he rose to the uppermost ranks of the Emir's army, leading the Algazanian forces to victory on more than one field.

At some point he found the time to woo and win the

daughter of a prominent merchant. Their marriage was still a joy to them. Memo sometimes wondered if his many long absences had helped there—if the two of them had never been long enough together to grow bored. But at least he had not worn out his wife with childbearing as most men did.

Now he was too old to be a soldier; he had no other skills. Trumpets announced his entry when he chose to visit the Emir's palace, but he detested the intrigues of court. His brothers-in-law ran the family business competently. If they were no more than average honest in their dealings with outsiders, still they did not cheat their sister, so money was no problem.

At fifty Memo could hope for another ten years of life, or even more. What was he to do with it?

Free his homeland, said his conscience. The tales from the Land Between the Seas were heartrending. Vandok the Ruthless ruled it still, striking down any who might ever threaten him—even, it was said, many of his own sons. His killers roamed at will across the country, randomly ravaging and slaying, competing in atrocity. The surest way to the king's favor was to perpetrate some new horror upon the population south of the ranges, or at least stir up a desperate revolt that would provide sport for the army. Month after month, gangs of youths and maidens were led north in chains to be sacrificed to Hool.

The seven cities lay in ruins, the countryside was devastated. Foreign merchants shunned the ports, because the people could offer nothing in trade. The only exceptions were slavers, who had only to open their hatches to have the holds filled with eager volunteers.

The exiles in Algazan provided what help they could, but it was insignificant. Few of them had money to spare. Once in a while they would charter a ship and offer free transportation overseas—not often to Algazan itself, for the Emir reasonably feared the flood that would have ensued had he permitted it. Even this small effort was rarely a kindness. The lot of the emigrants in whatever land they reached was likely to be little better than serfdom. That was well known, and yet vessels had foundered in the harbors under the weight of refugees clambering aboard.

Not everyone had fled or would flee if given the chance. Memo knew of several inhabitants of the Land Between the Seas who were distantly related to him. He had offered them refuge and been declined; he had done what he could to help them, although gold never arrived safely.

Always the exiles talked of gathering an army of liberation and invading the Land to drive out the barbarians, but such a campaign would need far greater resources than they could ever muster. Moreover, no one could seriously believe that the attempt would succeed. Vandok was too expert a tyrant and Hool too strong a god.

Thus, a few days after his fiftieth birthday, Greatmemory of Bargar, known as Memo to his family and friends, to the government as Memo Pasha, was a restless, uneasy man.

Late one night, having bade farewell to the friends he had been entertaining, he paced his house in darkness, unable to rest. His wife had long since gone to bed. As always, the talk that night had been of the sufferings of the Land Between the Seas. As always, the news had been bad. As always, the solutions suggested had been wild-eyed and impracticable. Memo Pasha had seen enough causes in his time to know a hopeless one, and every plan proposed at the table had been more desperate than the one before.

A man could not pace forever. He came at last to his study and the niche where Bargar resided. It was time for bed, and hence time to say his nightly prayer. He sank down to his knees, as he had done so many times before, and he made offering as he had seen his father do, long ago. Where his father had offered copper, Memo now offered gold, adding the coin to seven already lying there before the god's paws. Sometimes the hoard would increase to a score or more, but sooner or later Bargar would speak on the matter, ordering Memo to buy his wife a new coach with it, or impose sudden wealth on a certain beggar, or any one of a dozen inexplicable things. It was the god's gold to do with as he pleased.

When the nightly offering was over, Memo would speak of his gratitude and his unhappiness. Always he would end with the simple prayer: "Tell me how I can help them, Most Holy Father."

Sometimes the god would answer, sometimes he would not—gods and tigers both tend to be unpredictable. When he did reply, the reply would always be much the same: "I am your god, my son, not the god of your people. You I can guard and prosper, they are not my concern. I cannot stand against Hool, for I am only a little god. Small gods should not strive to be great gods—your ancestors discovered the folly of that. Be content with the passing pleasures of life."

That night Memo stubbornly spoke his prayer again: "Tell me how I can help them, Most Holy Father."

That night Bargar said simply, "Go out to your gate and find the boy who is waiting there. Bring him in, hear him, and believe."

He looked about thirteen or fourteen years old—skinny as a fishing pole, not notably clean, but seemingly bright and healthy. He wore a grubby loincloth and clutched a small bundle in his puny arms as if it were more precious than the Emir's crown. His hair hung in tangles around his pinched features, one eye was puffed and discolored from a blow. He stood in the light of Memo's lantern, grinning up at him, gasping huge breaths as if he had been running, but Memo had been observing him for several minutes through the spy hole and knew that the lad had not been running. He had been sitting cross-legged in the dirt as if content to sit there all night. He might have been there for hours.

"Pasha, I was told to come and see you!" He spoke with a childish treble, in the tongue of the Godless.

"Who are you and who told you?"

"I am Juss, Pasha. Sure-justice of Kraw is my real name. And Kraw told me."

Kraw? Memo had a vague remembrance of a god by that name, but could not recall whose he had been. "Then you had best come in, Sure-justice. I am Great-memory of Bargar." Kraw? Kraw?

The youngster had caked blood on his back. He had obviously been in a fight recently. He stank of onions. He knew enough to remove his sandals at the house door, although they could not have been dirtier than his feet.

Viewed under the many lamps of the study, he seemed even bonier and grubbier than before, and the nits in his hair showed. His eyes were huge with wonder as he inspected the furniture, the rugs, the pictures, the drapes. His gaze came to rest on the niche with its amber tiger and its gold. He bowed to it and then shot a worried glance at Memo, wondering if he had offended.

"Bargar, my god," Memo said. "He told me to bring you in and hear what you have to say, Sure-justice."

The gamin grinned with delight, his adult teeth seeming far too large for his emaciated face. "Then perhaps my god has been speaking with your god, Pasha? Holy Kraw never spoke to me before tonight and what—"

"Wait!" Memo laughed. "Serious business takes time. You sit . . ." He chose a plain wooden chair that could be washed later and pulled it forward. ". . . here. Now, may I offer . . ." Wine would knock the kid out cold. Food? Of course food! "I will order something for you to eat. What would you like?"

Already perched on the chair, the boy just gaped at him.

"Come on!" Memo said. "What would you like most?"

Sure-justice of Kraw glanced around the room again and whispered, "Meat?" as if he were asking for the Emir's throne. He licked his lips.

Memo reached for the bell rope. "When was the last time you tasted meat?"

"Don't remember. Had fish last summer, twice!"

"Mm. May I ask what you are carrying?"

"Kraw, Pasha. He said to bring him."

Memo had just settled on a chair—a padded silk one—but he sprang to his feet at that news. To bring two gods into one room was generally regarded as disrespectful at best and unwise at worst, although it seemed that in this case the gods themselves had arranged this meeting. He wondered what correct protocol could be in such a situation. Nobody crowded a tiger.

"Perhaps he should be unwrapped and put in a place of honor. That shelf?"

Nodding eagerly, the boy proceeded to unwrap the cloth and reveal what appeared to be a black rock. "Kraw's a dragon's tooth!" he said proudly. He laid it on the shelf, bowed to it, then hurried back to his seat.

Nobody crowded dragons, either. What a combination!

A suspiciously sleepy-looking servant knelt in the doorway. Memo ordered meat and bread, sweet cakes and fruit—nothing rich, just simple and plentiful, enough for two men. And quickly. Then he sat back and smiled at the bright dark eyes. The boy would burst if he was not allowed to speak soon.

"Now, Sure-justice of Kraw, what did your god instruct you to tell me?"

Words exploded out of the boy, words that in two or three minutes turned his listener's world on its head. *Sea-breaker* of Kraw! Of course!

Memo did not have time to absorb one revelation before another lit the sky. As a boy, he had fought in Sea-breaker's troop at Mill Creek. They had fled into exile on the same ship, but in those days Sea-breaker had been a magistrate's son and Great-memory merely a farmer's. A year or more later, on returning from his first campaign with the Legion, Memo had heard quiet rumors that Morning-star's daughter had escaped and was in Algazan, also. He had even heard her mentioned as one of the casualties in the Great Pestilence, ten years ago. Nothing more, nothing since.

Hear, his god had told him, *and believe.*

"And he said you would help, Pasha!" The tale was ended, the boy staring at Memo with agonies of hope racking his face. Despite the hour, the majordomo himself now stood in the doorway to indicate that the supper was ready.

"Come and eat, Sure-justice, while I think." Memo conducted his young guest through to the dining room. "Sit down. Tell the man what you want to start with. Water the wine well, Mustair. Some of the red for me."

The pasha was famous for his hospitality. When the pasha said "enough for two men," his staff would interpret that to mean that they would be shamed and disgraced if any two men in Algazan, hand-picked for their capacity, could possibly find the offering insufficient. The boy stared in total disbelief at the loaded boards, the golden dishes, then hesitantly pointed at a platter heaped with fat pork. The footman lifted it close, expecting to serve a few slices from it. As soon as it came within reach, Juss scooped up the entire contents with both hands and crammed them into his mouth.

Hear and believe!

Memo had heard. Memo could believe the tale—indeed he was satisfied that traces of Sea-breaker's features showed in that starving ragamuffin. Memo could believe that a war of liberation led by a grandson of Morning-star would have a vastly greater chance of success than just any old uprising. Uprisings were ten a penny under Vandok. He encouraged them. But could Memo believe that it would succeed? Could he believe that it would help the people? Another failure like Morning-star's would turn the land to desert.

The next move, obviously, was to locate the older brother, the unschooled longshoreman who was the designated Liberator. The way Kraw and Bargar seemed to be cooking things up between them, Memo had been granted the job of training this unknown laborer into a patriot hero and war-winning general.

That'll teach me to complain to a tiger!

Memo ordered his coach made ready and his guards alerted. He paid his staff well; if he demanded service in the middle of the night, that was no more than his due.

The boy had reported that the elder brother was prizefighting at the Snakepit, the most notorious dive in the dockside area. Full marks for courage, low marks for brains! Admittedly that was not a sissy's way of spending an evening, but what about leadership, charisma, the totality of the dozen character traits a successful revolutionary must display? A son of Morning-star's daughter could be expected to have courage. In fact White-thorn's legend might be even more of an asset than her father's. And the boy's father, Sea-br—No . . .

Great-memory of Kraw almost dropped his wine goblet.

"*How* old is Ven, did you say?"

Juss gulped down a fistful of something. "Twenty-three, Pasha. He'll be twenty-four in two months."

Servants were rushing in with more dishes. The kid had cleared the first lot completely. He would probably be violently ill in a few minutes, all over the rugs. Memo was feeling almost that way himself, as if a camel had kicked him in the belly.

"Did your god tell you who Ven's father was?"

Still chewing, Juss shook his head, but the frightened expression in his eyes showed that he suspected.

Even a dragon would not want to break that sort of news.

The Snakepit was already emptying, its patrons staggering along the alley in a welter of drunken argument and singing: losers and winners respectively. Memo's guards closed in around their employer and forced a way through the raucous, stinking mob, then convoyed him downstairs to a cellar, almost dark now, suffocatingly opaque with tallow fumes. Not a few bodies lay amid the litter and overturned benches, most of them snoring heavily.

Juss screamed and rushed over to a corner where a group of six or seven men and boys had been laid out to mend. Two or three had recovered enough to sit up. One lay with his head at an impossible angle and would never move again. They had all given their customers good value, and most looked as if they had been marched over by the entire Algazanian army.

By the time Memo arrived, Juss was frantically embracing the largest of them, heedless of what he was doing to his new garments.

That first sight of Cold-vengeance settled any doubts about the older brother's paternity. His fairish hair and reddish beard were unmistakable evidence of Horsefolk blood in his veins, and Vandok was reported to be a very large man. The rest of Cold-vengeance's appearance was distinctly discouraging. He was a dazed and bloody ruin. Breathing obviously hurt him; his face and hands were pulp. Even with help, he had trouble standing. He peered at Juss as if unable to recognize this beaming, happy youth.

Sighing at the thought of the new upholstery he had just had installed in his coach, Memo sent a rider home with orders to find a doctor.

Juss began to explain to his brother. Then he changed

tactics and blatantly ordered the giant to trust him and do as he was told. Ven accepted that insolence meekly—astonishingly so. Even granted that he was not completely conscious, his deference to a slip of a boy hinted that Juss was going to be the brains of the family, if he wasn't already. It was Memo's first inkling that he had been given two pupils, not one.

By the time he had brought his charges home, dawn was breaking and the house was in turmoil. Even his wife was up and dressed and demanding explanations, which he refused to give.

The doctor examined the fighter with distaste. Concussion, extensive bruising, loss of blood, cracked ribs, and broken fingers . . . Ven even had two broken toes, so his opponent had not escaped unscathed.

Memo ordered him washed and deloused, bandaged, fed, and put to bed. Mustair had prepared two rooms for the guests, but Juss insisted on sharing with his brother, and took the family god in with them, also. Memo sent everyone off about his duties, using much the same technique on his wife that the boy had used on his brother. Peace returned.

Then he shut himself in his study and touched his forehead to the floor. "Most Holy Father, is he really the son of Vandok and White-thorn?"

No reply.

"Am I expected to turn that dockside lout into a revolutionary?"

Silence. Gods did not explain.

"Holy Father, the people will never trust him! He does not look like one of us! He can barely speak the language intelligibly. He is uneducated, ignorant, probably simple!"

More silence. Tigers were stubborn.

Desperate now, Memo said, "I grant you, Father, that he is a fighter. I can teach him to use a sword, but what-

ever brains he had to start with have all been knocked
out of him already!"

At that Bargar growled, a blood-chilling sound Memo
had heard only once before in his life. He apologized
abjectly and hurried off to bed.

He left his guests to their own devices for three days.

The doctors had prescribed rest and a light diet for
the invalid. On the first day, Mustair reported that the
two brothers were consuming more food than the entire
staff of the mansion. Memo told him not to skimp, and
include lots of red meat.

On the second day, Mustair passed word that the
older brother was fretting about his sweetheart.

"Tell him to write a note and we shall see it is delivered," Memo said, being fairly sure that neither brother
could write. "Meanwhile, can you lay a little temptation
in his path? Nothing blatant, of course . . . A couple of
youngish . . . Pretty . . . I mean, if they understand that
they will be rewarded . . .?"

Being a perfect majordomo, Mustair frequently knew
his employer's mind before he did. With no change of
expression at all, he said, "As the Pasha has com-
manded, so it is."

Being a perfect majordomo, Mustair also knew the
difference between gossip and relevant information. On
the third day, he reported that the bait had been taken
and the other girl sent back to her normal duties. With
the merest hint of a smile, he added that the man had almost certainly been a virgin.

The note never appeared.

In retrospect, the fighter's injuries were a blessing.
He was incapable of working, which meant that
Memo's miraculous intervention had saved him from
starvation. The brothers might realize that they were effectively in jail, but the alternative was far worse. They
would not have been human had they been able to resist

the sudden luxury, food in an abundance they had never known, respite from labor and worry.

Three days would give Juss time to break the news to his brother that his father had been the monstrous Vandok.

They gave Memo time to plan a war.

To mount an invasion he would need money, weapons, fighters, and ships. An uprising of the population would need money, weapons, and leadership. Both would need superb intelligence and perfect timing, and those in turn required an organized underground in the Land itself. Both! That was where the endless dinner table chatter had gone astray. The would-be plotters had never stood back far enough from the problem to appreciate the sheer size of it, the scale, the time it would take.

Memo had the ear of the Emir, friends in the palace and the army, relatives in the Algazanian mercantile community. If it could be done at all, then he was the one to do it. Most important, he now had the grandsons of Morning-star as figureheads to rally the people.

After three days' hard thought, he decided that it looked possible, from a purely secular point of view. It would take at least five years. Vandok himself was aging and he allowed no obvious successor to thrive, so someday there might be a chance to profit from a disorderly succession. Memo could raise and train an army in exile and a resistance movement in place. He could strike in winter when the passes were closed: Morning-star's primary error had been to underestimate the speed of the Horsefolk's response.

But that was the secular view. Memo could do nothing about Hool, the god of Vandok. History proved that the little gods of the people could not withstand Hool.

Realistically, therefore, the whole thing was impossible.

Memo did not think he could explain that to a tiger.

* * *

On the morning of the fourth day, he summoned the sons of White-thorn to a meeting in his garden, which was private and informal. He ordered that they be clad in the garb of their ancestors, so that he could see how they would look to the people if he did decide to proceed. Knowing that they would feel awkward in it, he dressed the same way himself, although he had not donned motley more than five or six times since he came to Algazan. He discovered that he had either lost the knack or lost a third hand, which seemed to be essential. He had to call on his body servant for assistance. Even then, he had an uneasy feeling that it would all fall off him if he made one rash move.

He had arranged three chairs in a secluded arbor, with refreshments laid out on a table between them and a smaller table placed at the side. He brought Bargar out to lie on that, so the god could listen to the discussion.

Memo rose to his feet as the brothers approached along the path. The boy's sharp eyes noticed the god; he bowed to him first, then to his host. The man copied him, a fraction of a second later each time.

Memo was astonished by the improvement in the boy. Juss had already lost some of his skeletal thinness, and in the clear light of day his quick intelligence was obvious. With the slight frame and dark coloring of his race, Sure-justice was a believable grandson of Morning-star. He was grinning nervously, but he clutched a small bundle that must certainly contain Kraw, his dragon god, so he had foreseen the possibility of being thrown out on his ear at the end of the interview. A realist!

Ven's battered face was halfway back to being human. His hands and right foot were bandaged and more bandages showed through the low neckline of his motley. He was undoubtedly built on a heroic scale, slabbed with muscle, and the stolidity that had seemed like dull wits before now hinted more at steady nerve and courage. In the proper setting he might impress, but he was quite obviously of Horsefolk descent. Why should the people ever trust him?

Memo offered his guests chairs. They sat down diffidently, glancing around with wonder at the flowers and shrubbery. His home must be more luxurious than anything they could ever have imagined, although it was very modest by the standards of the Algazanian nobility.

He bowed to them before taking his own seat. "I honor the grandsons of Morning-star and the sons of White-thorn, his heroic daughter."

The boy grinned. The man said nothing, watching his host with bleary, puffed gray eyes and an air of wary distrust.

Memo poured wine, watering the boy's. "Is there anything you lack? My house is yours." That was a formula that he hoped they would not interpret too literally. "My servants will gladly provide anything you ask."

Juss glanced sideways at his brother and smothered a grin.

"You are most generous, Pasha," the man said.

Small talk was going to be difficult, obviously. Pasha Memo had absolutely nothing in common with these two, nothing to discuss except business.

"I assume that Kraw is in there?" He pointed to the package.

Juss nodded, suddenly worried. He glanced uneasily at the tiger figurine on the side table.

"You are not familiar with these odd costumes? This is what people wear in our homeland, the Land Between the Seas. They use the upper part to carry things, especially their family gods, when they need be transported. That way they are next their hearts, you see."

The boy grinned. He snatched up his bundle and tucked it into his motley. It gave him a notable bosom on one side.

Memo turned to the elder. "I trust you are feeling better, Cold-vengeance?"

"I am very grateful for what you have done, Pasha." The big man spoke in a guttural parody of his forefathers' tongue.

"I am honored to aid the sons of White-thorn."

Juss shot his brother a worried glance.

Something about Ven's face suggested that it might have flushed had there been any of it not covered with beard or bruises. "Even the son that Vandok bred on her by public rape?"

"The guilt is not yours. Tell me how you feel about Vandok."

"I am inclined to kill myself for being his spawn," the big man growled. "He is a monster."

"Given the chance, would you make war on him?"

The big man twisted his swollen lips. "Gladly!"

"Can we?" the boy demanded eagerly.

Memo sighed. "I have thought about nothing else for three days. To be honest, I don't think we can. The barbarians are strong. To raise the people again and fail again would be a terrible crime. To finance and organize a war, if it can be done at all, would take years. I admit, though, that the sons of White-thorn would rally more support than any other leader."

"The son of Vandok?" Ven said contemptuously.

Either the dockside lout was not as stupid as he looked, or his quick-witted brother had coached him. He had certainly gone to the heart of the problem.

Memo sipped his wine. No, the older brother was impossible. Shave off his beard and dye his hair black and he would still look like a Horseman.

What of the younger, then? He was bright and young enough to learn, although the list of things a successful revolutionary must know was mind-boggling: strategy, tactics, ordnance, finance, economics, rhetoric, politics, leadership . . . At the moment the lad would not know what the words meant. He did not even speak the language well.

How long? Juss was barely fourteen. Ten years might do it—but Memo was fifty. He might not have ten years, not ten good years, not in Algazan.

"I asked my god what I could do," he said sadly. "Bargar told me to listen to Juss and believe him. I did believe you, lad! I still do, and I honor my god. But his interest is not the welfare of our people. He is the god of my own family, not anyone else's. He may just be trying to ease my unhappiness by giving me a cause to believe in, and I find that I cannot believe in it. It will fail.

"Much as I would love to throw out the barbarians and restore freedom and democracy, my answer is no."

Two young faces stared at him in horror and disappointment.

"You two are welcome to remain here, in my service. I promise your lives will be much more pleasant than they have been to date."

"But Kraw told Juss . . ."

"With all respect to Holy Kraw, Cold-vengeance, and to my beloved Bargar, also, they are little gods. All the gods of the Land of Many Gods, as it once was, cannot stand against Hool."

Seeming puzzled, the man looked to his brother.

The boy was grinning triumphantly. "You have forgotten the oracle, Pasha?"

Memo's heart skipped a beat. "What oracle?"

"Hool himself!" Juss shouted. "When he ordered Hannail to invade the Land, he promised that his seed would rule it forever, didn't he? Well, then! Why do you think our mother got Vandok to rape her?"

For a long moment, that outrageous question left Memo speechless. Then he said, "Did Kraw tell you this?"

"No," Juss admitted. "I worked it out. It's obvious, isn't it?"

12: Interlude

Another tree cracked open in the forest. The fire still roared, but frost glimmered on the hinges of the shutters and I could feel a steady chill on my back. Had I been in a superstitious mood, I might have taken that for an omen.

"The rest is history," the soldier said. "It took him six years, of course. But the results are well known."

The merchant had fallen asleep with his head on the back of his chair. His snores gurgled disgustingly. The actress was feeling more confident, eyeing me with an intense dislike I had done nothing to earn.

I glanced uneasily around the group. Was the contest still continuing? Could even I top that tale? "Not known to all of us, I'm sure, Captain. The authenticity of your narration is inspiring. Pray tell us of those six years."

"They were missing. The pages may have been lost, or they may have been somewhere else in the box, out of sequence. I did not find them."

"That is indeed a pity."

The old soldier had made his ancestor come to life for me. He had made Great-memory of Bargar seem very much like Captain Tiger. I suspected that Captain Tiger also had found a cause to promote in his declining years. I even thought I knew what it was, but we were not quite ready for that story.

Fritz stretched, smiling sleepily, somewhat like a lion waking to go in search of supper.

The dowager smothered a yawn and replaced her

hand in her muff. "I suppose Master Omar should be given a chance to respond. Can you make it brief, story-teller?"

I could try to make it last until springtime. "Of course, ma'am. Gentle lords, fair ladies, this one is called the Tale of the Homing Pigeon."

13: Omar's Response to the Soldier's Tale

Thirty years after Morning-star's failed revolution, forest had swallowed the ruins of Kylam.

After sacking all seven of the cities of the Land Between the Seas, Vandok returned to the site of his father's murder. He rounded up the surviving natives and set them to collecting fuel—trees, furniture, boats, books, fences, fishing nets, anything that had not already been burned. With all this, he built a pyre on the spot where his father had died and where he had first abused White-thorn. He did not order a halt until the great hall was packed to the roof and not a twig remained within a day's ride.

Then he set fire to it, and it burned for days. The roof collapsed, of course. Much to the king's disappointment, not all the walls did. When the embers were cool enough to approach, he discovered that the stone had fused into a hard green glass that defied all efforts at further destruction. He rode away in disgust, and there is no record that he ever returned to the site.

A small fishing village eventually grew up a few miles farther south, but Kylam itself was abandoned. Trees seeded where it had stood. The ashes within the old hall had made fertile soil, but either it was not deep enough for tree roots, or perhaps the drainage was poor. For whatever reason, the forest shunned the interior of the basilica, leaving it open to the sky, but carpeted with grass and flowers, mostly a form of pale wild rose. This natural garden was walled by grotesque shapes like a frozen dance of giants—ropy, shiny pillars of bizarre form, spikes and fists, on which not even creepers could find purchase. It was a strange, unworldly monument to sad events.

One summer afternoon, two men converged upon this site from opposite directions. Neither knew the forest well, but each knew of the glass garden and contrived to find his way there. They had never met, they had never corresponded, and yet they came somehow to the right place at the right time.

They moved with caution, because the Land Between the Seas was perilous country. When Horsefolk warriors came of age on the grasslands, they were sent south in bands to ravage for a year. They were expected to return with a collection of gruesome relics to show their prowess as killers, plus a gang of youths and maidens to sacrifice to Hool. Then they would settle down to breed more warriors. Every few years, the king himself would lead a larger expedition around to demonstrate what real brutality was.

The native inhabitants were hardly less dangerous, a bitter people. Who could blame them? Anything they created in their lives became automatic hostage to the Horsefolk's spite. Their crops and hovels might be burned without reason, their children carried off. They dwelt in secret places among the hills, cultivating hidden patches within the forests. Many had abandoned civilized life altogether, living like beasts and preying upon anyone weaker than themselves. The travelers' caution was merely prudence.

The first to arrive at the garden was a youngster of around twenty. Specifically, his age was twenty years and one month, give or take a day or two. He was of middle height, slim, sinewy. His hair and close-trimmed beard were black, his eyes dark but bright, and although he had a ready smile, he could be dangerous. He wore the standard motley of the country, but in somber and inconspicuous hues, mainly brown. At this season of high summer, he had left his arms and legs bare. A sword dangled at his side and he could use it.

Having located the ruins, he leaned against the trunk of a beech to study them. He heard birds chirping, insects buzzing. Only when he was completely satisfied that there was nothing more did he approach the walls, moving cautiously to the lowest point he could find. Even that was higher than his head. He clambered some way up an ash tree nearby, being careful not to make it sway. From there he could see the interior. It was deserted. He waited.

The other man, meanwhile, had reached the far side. He took fewer precautions, although he was wary. The two men were of similar type, with much the same trim build and, to casual observation, of much the same age. This one was brown-haired, gray-eyed . . . clean-shaven, as I recall. He, too, wore motley of inconspicuous shades, but in his case mostly greens, and he carried a package or two tucked in the front of it, making the cloth bulge oddly. He was unarmed except for a long staff over his shoulder, from which dangled a wayfarer's bundle.

Green-motley was either more fortunate or better counseled in his choice of approach than Brown-motley, for there was an easy entry on that side. Whether it had originally been a door or a window was impossible to determine. Now it was a blob-shaped hole at waist height on the outside, but slightly higher inside. Having inspected the interior for ambush, the newcomer clambered through and dropped to the ground.

He then advanced cautiously through the flowered shrubs, parting them with the edge of his staff and moving carefully. To the watcher in the ash tree, he seemed to be looking for something. Soon, though, having reached a glassy boulder, he sat down with his back to the entrance. Reaching inside the folds of his motley, he brought out a crusty roll, a hunk of cheese, and two peaches. These he proceeded to eat, while the sun dipped toward the treetops.

Brown-motley climbed down from his perch and set off around the outside of the ruin to take Green from the rear. When he reached the porthole, a quick glance established that his quarry was still sitting on the boulder, apparently lost in thought and unaware of the challenger creeping up behind him. Brown drew his sword and jumped into the aperture. Then things went slightly wrong.

First, the glassy wall was extremely slippery. Second, he had failed to observe that the interior was in shade and the sun was behind him, so his shadow could hardly fail to alert his intended victim. Third, Brown had forgotten that the interior was lower than the ground outside, and he landed roughly. Fourth, he came down in a tangle of wild roses. As far as thorns were concerned, he was wearing nothing between his shoes and his crotch. He stumbled, staggered, and swore luridly. Green's staff cracked down on his arm, sending his sword spinning into the shrubbery.

Brown stood there unarmed, within reach of a second stroke that could split his skull. The two men studied each other for a moment.

Green smiled as if satisfied, lowering his staff. He sat down and gestured at a rock in the sunlight nearby. "Pull up a boulder and make yourself at home."

His attitude was unnervingly confident. Brown glanced around, listening, rubbing his tingling arm, and wondering if he had just walked into a trap. Hearing nothing suspicious, he retrieved his sword and picked his way through the thorns, parting them with his sword just as the first man had done with his staff. He did not go to the indicated seat, though. He approached the other and put the blade close to Green's eyes.

"Who are you?" Brown was young and he had just made a fool of himself. He was annoyed by his own clumsiness and even more annoyed by his opponent's apparent lack of concern.

"I was here first, so you introduce yourself."

"But I have the sword."

Green shrugged. "Again. You display a regrettable lack of manners in the way you keep flaunting it. If I have to disarm you a second time, I am liable to break something. Well, my name will mean nothing to you, but in your dialect you would pronounce it Homer. And yours?"

"I prefer not to give it at the moment."

"Then I will address you as Juss."

Brown flicked his sword angrily. "How do you know that?"

"Rumors swarm over the countryside like ants." Homer was not concealing amusement. "The sons of White-thorn have come to raise the banner of liberty and so on. Juss is the name of the younger brother, short for Sure-justice. You're too young to be the elder."

Juss glared suspiciously.

Homer's eyes twinkled with devilment. "And you don't look the way I expect him to look. Now why don't you sit down and exchange stories in civilized fashion?"

"How do you expect him to look?"

"Sit down."

Juss moved his sword closer. "Answer my questions!"

"Go to Hool."

The sword flicked again, this time opening a tiny slit on Homer's chin. The wound was little more than a shaving nick and hence an impressive display of skill with a yard of steel, but not in the best of taste.

The victim recoiled angrily. "The locals term these bushes white thorn. Did you know that?"

"What of it?"

Pressing the fingers of one hand to his chin, Homer

gestured with the other. "The gods raised this place to her memory. This was where it happened. Right here."

Juss looked around the walled garden and then stared at the other man with disbelief. "How do you know that?"

"Because I saw it. I saw your brother conceived."

"That is impossible! You are far too young!"

"I may be older than I look. Now sit down, stripling."

This time Juss obeyed, taking the other boulder. The sunlight had moved off it. Homer smiled approvingly.

Scowling, Juss sheathed his sword. "Why are you here?"

"Because of a dream. Several dreams. I saw this place, and I saw you. I knew then that it was time."

"Time to do what?"

"First tell me why you are here."

"Because my god told me to come."

The Homer man nodded, seeming pleased. "Then you admit that you are the son of White-thorn? Don't bother to deny it. You look very like your father, Seabreaker. Not as tall."

Brown frowned disbelievingly. "I am Juss. And who are you?"

"A footloose trader of tales, a vagabond. I met her here in this hall, when it was a hall, one morning thirty years ago. She gave me something to look after, and I have guarded it ever since. When she had done that, she went to find her revenge and I watched." He sighed and for a moment the shadows seemed to deepen around him. "Such courage!" he murmured.

"Will you tell me about it, please?"

"I could, but I think another will tell you better. Why did your god order you to come here?"

"He didn't say why. Gods don't explain."

Homer raised his eyebrows. "They can be annoying, can't they! Very well. I have a question. Will you ask it for me and tell me the answer if you get it?"

"What is it?"

"You don't give up easily, do you? White-thorn carried a knife that day, a stiletto. Vandok assumed that she intended to kill him. I think she used the knife as a decoy. I think she expected it to be found. I want to know if she planned all along to bear Vandok's child. I must know! The question has bedeviled me for thirty years."

Juss smiled wryly. "It has bedeviled me for six. If I am told the answer, I shall tell you."

Homer nodded and reached again inside his motley, this time producing a small bundle. "You know what she is?"

"She?"

"I have always thought of her as female. It does not matter with gods. Her name?"

"Verl. But I don't know what she—he—is."

"A dove."

Homer handed over the parcel. Juss took it reverently and unwrapped it. He could not conceal a flicker of surprise, or perhaps disappointment.

"She is nothing much to look at," the trader of tales murmured. "I have sprinkled grain before her once in a while, so she would know she was not forgotten, but of course she will not speak to me. Nor to you while I am here. So why don't I take a stroll while you attend to your prayers?"

Leaving his bundle, the man in green picked his way back to the entrance and clambered out, while the other laid his little god on the rock and knelt before him.

Fifteen or twenty minutes later, Homer scrambled in through the hole again. Juss had wrapped up the god and tucked her away next to his heart. He was smiling, but his eyes were pink and shiny.

"Well?" Homer demanded.

"He says that White-thorn would have killed Vandok if she had the chance, but she did not expect to. She was counting on the oracle."

The storyteller nodded with satisfaction. "That was what I suspected. I hope your brother is worthy?"

"He certainly is!" The young man cleared his throat and held out a hand. "Does this complete our business, Friend Homer?"

"Not at all! I want to hear all the details! How did she escape, and where did she go, and what happened to her, and who organized this revolution?"

Juss glanced up at the darkening sky. "Some of that I do not know. Some I cannot reveal. The rest I will tell you willingly. Verl says you may be trusted."

"I should hope so, after all these years!"

"Then we can go back to our stronghold and I shall introduce you to a few of our locals. Why don't we talk on the way?"

So we did that. This was the beginning of the revolution, the Winter War. Vandok came south just before the passes were closed by the snows, but the countryside rose against him. The Resistance was aided by the little gods, who could pass word of all the tyrant's movements. By spring he was fighting a retreat, and he lost most of his army withdrawing through the mountains. Cold-vengeance was then proclaimed king of the Land Between the Seas, which henceforth was to be known as Verlia, and—

"That is not correct," the notary said.

14: Argument

"*Foul!*" I yelled. "You interrupted me!"

"You were misrepresenting the facts," the clerk retorted, recoiling from my anger.

"You quibbling, bug-infested, ignorant hair-splitter! I will squeeze your grubby little throat until the blackheads pop out of your nose. I was telling a tale on which my life depends and you have the audacity to interpose your ignorant—"

"Gentlemen!" the dowager snapped. "The intrusion was ill-mannered, the response excessive. Continue your improbable fable, Master Omar."

"Improbable fable? What sort of leading remark is that when the matter is still *sub-judice*? You have prejudiced my case, my lady! And how can I possibly recapture the magic, the air of wonder, rebuild the rising mystery, the unmistak—"

"The unmitigated claptrap!" interposed the merchant, who had now wakened and was glowering sourly at me from his chair by the fire. "You were dropping hints that the 'Homer' character was yourself, two hundred years ago. You think us so gullible or superstitious that we can be frightened into saving you from our host's righteous wrath? You remain a dog killer and a would-be horse thief, and all your sly hints of immortality will not keep your backside from freezing out there in the snow. Begging your pardon, ladies."

The actress smirked.

"We have already agreed," I said coldly, "that my

name has been used for centuries as a generic term for storytellers. One such was involved in the events I was attempting to recount."

"You said 'we'!" the actress remarked.

"I may have let myself be carried away by the drama of my own narrative. It happens."

Gwill shot me a worried look, although I had thought him more nearly convinced than any. "I do think we should let Master Omar continue," he croaked.

"I refuse! This round of the contest must be declared null and void."

The old soldier smiled like a cat with an especially obese canary. "How seldom rules are invoked by winners!"

"If Master Omar truly believes in his own immortality," the actress remarked acidly, "then I fail to understand why he is so obviously worried by our host's hostile intentions."

I had never claimed that I did not feel pain. Besides, there is only one way to prove you are mortal, which is why I have never attempted it.

Leering, Fritz rose. "I need go out and fetch more wood, lords and ladies. Do not let the thud of my ax or the howling of wolves disturb your conversation." He took me by the collar of my doublet with one hand and lifted me effortlessly right into the air. "Say good night to the nice people, Omar."

"Just a moment!" The dowager was frowning intently at the notary, her forehead shriveled like a skin on hot milk. "What exactly were you objecting to in Master Omar's wild yarn?"

Wild yarn! Had I been breathing at the moment, I should certainly have objected to that affront.

The clerk pursed his lips. "He omitted certain curious matters that intervened between the military campaign and the establishment of the kingdom of Verlia."

I made a memorably horrible noise.

"Put him down, innkeeper," the dowager said.

Fritz lowered me until my toes touched the floor again.

"I am just coming to that," I wheezed, sounding even worse than the minstrel did.

Fritz raised me again. "No you aren't."

"What do you know about those affairs, master?" The dowager glared at the notary with open suspicion.

His smile was low in humor, high in smugness. "It is a privileged matter, ma'am."

The merchant beamed complacently. "Master Tickenpepper is an authority on the subject. He has been researching it for me."

"Indeed?" The old crone exchanged glances with the soldier. "And you know something of the matter, also, Omar? Omar? Innkeeper, please!"

Once more Fritz lowered me until my toes touched the floor. I managed to nod as I dragged in some air. I had not realized that the notary was associated with the burgomaster and his talented bride, but just then I had more urgent matters to worry about, especially the way Fritz was quietly twisting the collar of his second-best doublet.

The dowager still had control of the room. "Then perhaps you will relate those events to us, Master Tickenpepper? And I suppose we may as well let Omar contribute, just in case he does know anything relevant."

Fritz thumped me back down on the bench like a landed fish. He stalked over to the wood bin and tossed the last couple of logs on the embers. Then he also resumed his seat, scowling promises at me.

I recalled how the beloved Osmosis of Sooth always taught us to love our enemies, but preferably at a safe distance.

The merchant leaned back, stretching out his feet and folding his hands over the gold chain on his paunch. The actress had assumed her most demure expression, which would have uncurdled cheese. As my wits returned, I began to sense a new tension in the room. The soldier was intent; even the lady's maid was clasping her hands so tightly that the knuckles showed white. Like me, they had not associated the notary with the other two until now.

"If my client wishes me to discuss the matter," the clerk said primly, "then I can attempt an exegesis of the salient points. You may find it a bizarre record. The precepts and precedents of foreign jurisprudence can hardly compare with those of civilized realms like the . . ." He coughed faintly. "I must say that the fire has made my throat a trifle dry, Burgomaster."

The merchant nodded grumpily to the innkeeper. As Fritz went to fill the stein, Master Tickenpepper recounted his education and qualifications. He was apparently the leading legal mind of Schlosbelsh, which I found an unnerving revelation. Then he launched into a windy, desiccated account of a great historic catharsis, missing all its pathos and drama.

I hope no storyteller of his caliber ever addresses a court on my behalf—that would guarantee a death penalty, no matter how minor the offense.

Had I been telling the tale, it would have gone more like this.

15: The Tale the Notary Did Not Tell

I caught up with the army again in the valley of the Dubglas, just below Cemetery Pass. With evening falling and the weather throwing a tantrum, the beetling crags ahead beetled unseen. Snow blew in my face, so that I almost walked onto the first sentry's pike. Fortunately I knew a password good enough to get me to his sergeant and a lantern. My credential was signed by Juss himself and validated with some highly ornate seals to impress the illiterate. I don't know if Sergeant Blood-oath could read or not. It didn't matter, because he remembered me from Redberry Pond and Lone Oak Hill. I soon found myself by a campfire with old friends, sharing a stew worth more for heat than meat, but still very welcome.

"Here's trouble!" Private Horse-hater proclaimed. "Any time Homer turns up, you can tell there's going to be trouble."

It was true I often wandered off to more interesting places during the long dull days of waiting that make up most any war. Armies are only part of the story. I could usually count on my knack for timing to bring me back when important things were about to happen, and now felt about right. So Horse had a point.

Nevertheless, I told him he didn't need me to get into trouble. He'd been promoted to sergeant three times in the last half year, hadn't he? And been busted every time?

127

Four times, he admitted, grinning with a mouthful of broken teeth. Twice in one day at Redberry Pond.

Now that had been an interesting day, the others agreed. They could use more days like that one. All those prisoners bound to trees with their own intestines—what more could a man want? Well, plenty. They began to reminisce about what they had done with the next lot, and the ones after, and then moved on to consider techniques for the future. I sat and gathered tales.

Less than a year before, Ven had raised the banner of freedom, promising to restore democracy and overthrow the tyrant. He had launched his war with an elite corps of ex-patriots, Algazanian by birth and training, a professional army. The natives then were raw animals, crushed by lifetime despair into something less than human. But they knew how to hate. Men, boys, even women with babes on their backs, flocked in thousands to join the revolution. The war gave them purpose, skills, respect, and revenge. They had swallowed up the elite, swelling into a huge national uprising, willing to drown the tyrant in their own blood or starve to death trying.

Those men were as tough as any I have ever seen, which is no small commendation. They hated their foes with suicidal intensity. They would follow horsemen into half-frozen rivers—I saw that, more than once. If a dozen freedom fighters must die to kill one of the enemy, two dozen would volunteer on the spot. Vandok could not bring up reinforcements as long as the passes stayed closed; he was outnumbered, running out of fodder and arrows and men. Soon he would be the only one left. For once, a war of attrition had favored the infantry.

Pitting foot soldiers against cavalry is usually a futile business, for neither side is capable of striking a decisive blow. The sloggers can hold a stronghold but not a country. The riders can cut their opponents' supply lines, but rarely do enough damage to drive them away. Neither side can ever win. Eventually one or the other gives up, when there is nothing left to fight over.

In this case the Horsefolk had an enormous advantage because their women and children were safely out of reach beyond the peaks, but they were up against the only army I had ever seen fight cavalry by lying down. No horse will charge over a human carpet. The Horsefolk also ran into trip wires, hidden ditches, and needle-sharp caltrops, which the Algazanians had provided by the shipload. Ven had few cavalry of his own at the beginning, but every captured horse was recruited. I told you what happened to human prisoners.

I have witnessed many savage campaigns, but none more bitter than the Winter War.

After an hour or so, I began to grow fidgety. I rose and wandered off into the camp. Fires glowed blearily through the driving snow. I passed within earshot of oxen, horses, and mules, downwind of the cookhouse and the latrines. Eventually I located the leaders' quarter. I slipped unobserved past a sentry and almost stumbled over a man kneeling in the snow, muttering. I hurried by him, avoided another doing the same, and came upon a third just rising to his feet. As he began to walk, I recognized Juss and called out to him. He spun around, reaching for his sword hilt.

"Homer!" I said quickly.

He relaxed. "Ha! Now I know we have trouble. You always turn up at the critical moments, don't you?" He laughed shrilly.

"What critical moment is this?"

Juss was almost unrecognizable as the pert youth of the previous summer. His beard was wild and bushy, he had added beef to his slight frame, and his eyes were the eyes of a killer. He was swathed in woolen blankets until he looked like a two-legged bullock, caked with snow. To the army he was "General Brains" and his brother was "General Brawn." It was a fair distinction, but Brains was brawnier than before and Brawn had learned a lot.

"Council of War. Come with me, Trader of Tales." He gripped my arm and half dragged me along as he strode through the snow.

"What's the problem?"

"No problem! The war is over for now. Vandok has withdrawn into Cemetery Pass."

"So you have him bottled up? You can starve him out?"

Juss chuckled and pushed me ahead of him into a large tent. There was no table, no stove. One dim lantern hung from the ridgepole and the floor was a mess of trampled mud, snow, and grass. A circle of miscellaneous bundles served as chairs. Ven sat on one, conferring with a couple of his Algazanian advisors. None of them looked up as we entered.

Ven was the only man in the army who shaved his face every day, and he always kept his hat on. Without those precautions, he would have looked so much like one of the enemy that some maniac would have surely killed him. At first I had been inclined to underestimate the big man, with his battered features and slow talk. Like the army, I had assumed that Juss had all the family brains. Now I knew that Ven just liked to think things through at his own pace. He usually arrived safely at the right decision. In battle he did not need to think; with a sword in his hand he moved like sunlight on water.

More men came stumbling into the tent, shaking snow from their robes, wiping it out of their eyes and beards. Shadows flowed over the walls.

Armies are attentive to their gods, always. They carry holy relics, chant hymns, make sacrifice, consult auguries. I once saw a god lead an army in person, but this was the first I had ever met where the gods were almost as numerous as the mortals. How much they had intervened in the actual fighting, I have no way of knowing. I suspect very little. Household deities would be out of their depth in battle, and they may have feared that they would bring down Hool's wrath on themselves if they meddled in great affairs. They certainly gave advice, though, and they passed on valuable military intelligence. Vandok could not brush his teeth without Ven hearing of it. The Council of War had been adjourned so that each member could go off and consult his family god. Now it was about to resume.

"We've won!" Juss said in my ear. There was a squeak of hysteria in his voice. "We can just leave a garrison here and go! Go south, to warm baths and clean clothes! And beds. Food! Oh, my ancestral gods! *Women!* Vandok can't mount another attack. He's beaten."

"You can starve him out?" I asked again. I did not add "Without starving yourselves, as well?" but I was thinking it and Juss knew I was. Only a sizable garrison could be sure of balking an attempt at breakout.

"For certain. We can keep him bottled up at this end."

"Can you really? He has plenty of horseflesh to eat. The weather will break soon, it must. What will a sudden thaw do to the pass?"

Juss's dark eyes blazed at me. Then he pulled a face and sighed in surrender. "Thaw or no thaw, Vandok himself can escape. He will have to abandon his horses and his wounded, but he can cross the pass on foot, back to the steppes."

"And next summer?"

"He'll be back, or we can go to him . . . Homer, we can't go in there after him! The men are dying on their feet! A break will help us as much as Vandok."

Would it? Physically, both sides needed rest and re-groupment. Granted that the two exhausted, starving armies facing off in impossible terrain were equally incapable of fighting anymore, in terms of morale Vandok had far more to gain from a respite. At the moment he was beaten and retreating. He would benefit materially, also, for he could call on a fresh and healthy population, while Ven's land lay in ruins. To withdraw now was to concede both this campaign and the next.

As I thought about the choice, though, I saw what Juss meant. The alternative was worse. Vandok himself was the only one who really mattered, and he would certainly escape. For Ven to try to follow—leading a frozen, starving rabble over the mountains into his enemy's home territory—would be a desperate, suicidal maneuver. He would risk everything on one stroke, and what could he gain except leagues of empty grass? There were no cities there to pillage, no castles to storm. Vandok would vanish over the plains, or circle around and cut the invaders off.

All the seats but one were filled now.

"What does Kraw say?" I demanded.

Juss snorted. "Kraw is a dragon." He stalked away to take his place at his brother's side. I remained standing in the corner, and no one paid me much heed. That was one of the nice things about being friends with a god. Verl had told both Juss and Ven that I could be trusted, so I was trusted. It was her way of thanking me, I suppose. I wondered what advice she had given Ven.

The brothers had divided their two gods between them. Juss was Sure-justice of Kraw, his father's god. Ven was Cold-vengeance of Verl, his mother's. He would not claim his father's, for obvious reasons.

"We will resume," Ven said, and the mutter of conversation died at once. "Bright-hope?"

"Gardilf says we should withdraw," the first man said. Something in the way he said it told me that he did not agree with his god's advice.

"Many-virtues?"

"Lokir says attack," the next man said, even more glumly.

"Straight-blade?"

Ven quizzed every one in turn. The two Algazanian advisors watched with expressions so noncommittal that they spoke volumes. It soon became obvious that the gods were just as divided as the mortals. Finally:

"Sure-justice?"

Juss shrugged. "Kraw says attack, of course! What did Verl say?"

His brother ignored the question for a moment. Ven's thought processes were like ice floes, slow and irresistible. Then he rose to his feet, and of course his size and winter clothing made him loom enormous over everyone else. I guessed what was coming. Men do not stand up to announce withdrawals. Ven was a fighter.

He glowered around with his ugly bruiser's features. "Verl said that the problem is Hool. Hool has not intervened so far. The little gods do not know if he will, or how he will. She said that life-and-death decisions should be made by mortals. You are equally divided and your gods are equally divided. Someone must break the deadlock. Does anyone question my right to do that?"

One man began to speak and quailed under his leader's scowl.

"Very well," Ven concluded. "I say that wars are not won by retreats. We will advance into the pass at dawn. We will continue to engage the enemy as long as there is an enemy. We will fight to the last man, whichever side he may be on."

He did not pause to let them cheer. That was not his style. Nor would he tolerate argument once he had made a decision. He began to talk logistics: priorities in the baggage train, the commissary, tents, and ordnance. I studied the eyes around the circle. I saw little admiration, much fear and doubt and anger. Juss and a few others had crumpled in despair. And these were the senior officers! If Ven could bring his army into battle on the morrow, he would have dragged it there himself, by brute strength of will.

In some ways he took after his father.

The next morning the army of liberation advanced into Cemetery Pass in a blizzard, filling the gorge from wall to wall. Losses on both sides were heavy, but the weather and terrain were impossible for cavalry. The human tide drove the Horsefolk relentlessly before it. By nightfall the barbarians had abandoned their mounts and were fleeing up rocky slopes on hands and knees. Ven led his warriors in pursuit.

The clouds cleared and the battle continued by moonlight, moving even higher up the glacier. The temperature dropped precipitously. Fingers stuck to ice or steel. Men tumbled into crevasses. Many dropped in their tracks and froze to death. There was little real fighting now. The Horsemen fled, the army of liberation pursued, and it gave no quarter.

If there was anything in the melee that could be called a battlefront, it crossed the height of land as the sun rose. The glare brought on snow blindness and triggered avalanches. A human cataract slithered and slid down the incline, fighting when the opportunity presented itself, otherwise merely struggling to survive. There could be no going back now.

As evening fell, the horde spilled into a forest below the snow line. Men lay down in heaps and slept. It hardly seemed to matter, for there was no enemy left. After eighty years of subjugation, the people of the Land Between the Seas had driven the Horsefolk back across the frontier.

So far as was known, Vandok was still alive, although his army had been destroyed. The Horsefolk were certainly capable of raising another, probably very quickly. He might counterattack the invaders; he might break through an easier pass and outflank them.

Even Ven must have wondered what he was going to do next. That problem was in the lap of the gods.

I wish I had been there to witness all that I have just described. I did not arrive until the middle of the following day.

Ven had left Juss in charge of supplies, and he organized a human baggage train more than four thousand strong. It snaked through the pass, over the glaciers, and down the other side like a line of beetles. If you have never crossed a mountain range with a sack of meal on your back, then I strongly recommend that you try it. It is an experience without equal. On the way up I was convinced my heart would burst. At the top I thought my lungs would. By the end, I was certain I should never stand up straight again.

The worst part, though, was arriving too late to see the band of Horsefolk elders that approached under flag of truce and delivered Vandok bound into the hands of his son.

Nor did I see the argument that followed. Ven could never have displayed greater leadership and power of command than he did then, just saving his prisoner from being ripped to shreds. The accounts I was able to gather later were so contradictory that I could make no sense of them. By the time I staggered in with my sack of meal, the principals had all departed for Hool's cave.

I set off at a run. The valley was only a few leagues away and I am happy to report that I caught up with the rearguard after a few hours.

I had a good pair of boots.

The holy valley is a forbidding place, a winding gorge whose sides are steep slopes of rock debris, holding very little vegetation. Above them rise vertical cliffs, sculpted into bizarre shapes and jagged buttresses. I doubt if the sun ever penetrates it, even in summer. At dawn, early in the year, it was a river of cold darkness under a lid of pallid sky. The wind wailed among the high rocks, each successive gust announcing its coming with a chorus of dismal howls that set my teeth on edge.

The mouths of many caves showed as darker patches in the precipices. Hool's cave was the largest, marked by a white apron of bones spilling all the way down to the valley floor. Until Vandok, the Horsefolk had sacrificed only beasts to their god, but for thirty years the offerings had been youths and maidens brought from the Land Between the Seas. Scores of vultures floated overhead or perched on the rocks, waiting for us to depart and let them enjoy their customary feast.

To clamber directly up that hill of skulls and ribs would have been very difficult. It would also have been unpleasant in the extreme, even for the faithful. A path began some distance away along the valley, angling gently up the stony incline to the base of the cliffs and then along to the mouth of the cave. While the army watched from the floor, the leaders began the ascent. Ven went first, followed by a group of his senior officers and one trader of tales. Vandok followed amid his guards, and the elders of the tribes brought up the rear. We were all bundled to the ears in fur and blankets, a procession of trolls. Bitter wind snatched the plumes of steam from our nostrils.

I was surprised to find myself trudging along beside Juss, whom I had believed still back in Cemetery Pass. He looked as if he had not slept since I had, which meant he looked two-thirds dead. He also looked extremely worried.

"What," I puffed, "is Ven planning?"

He scowled at me from red-rimmed eyes. "You tell me. You're the storyteller. I think he's gone crazy."

"What does Kraw say?"

"Kraw thinks he's gone crazy."

Oh? That was not comforting. I panted a few times. "He's been consulting Verl?"

I did not catch what Juss replied, but it sounded a bit like "Bloody pigeon!" Probably not—I can't believe he would have spoken of his mother's god like that.

We came at last to the mouth of the cave. The interior was black. Far below us, the assembled army was a beach of pale faces, staring up. Above us towered a rotting trellis or rock, pitted and weathered. Wind heaved in and out through the aperture, gurgling and sighing like the breath of a great monster. I wished I had not thought of that simile.

Ven sent the Horsefolk elders to the far side. Then he advanced to the center with Vandok.

It was my first clear glimpse of the tyrant since that day in Kylam, thirty years before, when he had publicly assaulted the child of his slain enemy—a disgusting public rape of a helpless woman to herald a generation of abuse of an entire people. Then he had been a striking figure of young manhood—brutal and vindictive, yes, but physically enviable, tall and muscular and exultant. In all his cruelty he had blazed like an evil god. Now he was merely big. Stooped and bloated in winter garments, worn out by years of excess and months of relentless warfare, Vandok walked with a heavy, flat-footed gait. His beard was white. Only the crazy eyes glaring out under the brim of his hat hinted at the sadistic madness that had murdered so many thousands and ground a nation into the mud.

Ven was as tall but not as thick. There was no flame to Ven, and never had been. He was a slogger. He bore a sword in his hand, and another in his scabbard. Seeing that, I guessed what was about to happen.

The wind gurgled and moaned in the dark cave.

"Holy Hool!" Ven cried. "Hear my prayer!"

For a moment there was only the wail of the wind. Then the cavern seemed to draw breath. It roared: "WHOOO—ARE—YOOOO?"

My hair tried to push my hat off. I have heard oracles before, and I had expected no more than an ambiguous wail containing hints of speech that only priests could understand and interpret. Instead, there was no doubt about that terrible voice. I fell to my knees on the stones, and all those about me did the same.

Ven stood his ground, holding his sword aloft. "I am the son of Vandok and White-thorn, bred from rape, raised for vengeance, inspired by hate. Acknowledge me!"

This time the pause was longer. Then the cave sucked in wind and the great voice sobbed again: "YOOOO— ARE—WHO—YOU—SAY—YOU—AAAARE."

Vandok screamed. He tipped forward on his knees and lifted long arms in supplication. "Holy Father! I am Vandok, your son, whom you recognized as the seed of Hannail, your chosen one!"

"YOU—AAARE."

"I have given you sacrifice!" Vandok bellowed, even louder than before. "Every day for a lifetime, I have offered blood to your honor! Do not desert me now!"

The wind moaned, chilling my bones. It fell silent. We waited, until the voice came again, quieter, less certain.

"I am tired of blood. I am sick of blood. GO AWAY! GO AWAAAAY, all of YOOOOO!"

"I also am your son!" Ven declaimed. "Acknowledge me! I claim the Land Between the Seas by your ancient oracle. I claim the kingship of the Horsefolk by right of conquest."

This time the pause was longer still.

Whatever had happened to democracy and freedom?

"Yes, he's completely crazy," Juss muttered. "Kraw defend him! Verl defend him!"

Then a gigantic bellow:

"PROOOOVE it!" the god said.

It was what Ven had hoped for, obviously. He hurled the sword down in front of the tyrant and drew his own.

The spectators in the valley might not have made out the mortals' voices, although I am sure they must have heard Hool. But they could recognize the gesture, and a moan of anger roiled up from the canyon.

Vandok did not rise. He turned his head to grimace at the challenger. "You would kill your own father, upstart?" He did not mention the sons he had slain without mercy.

"I will avenge my mother! I will avenge the thousands you have butchered. Stand up or die on your knees, animal!"

Vandok hurled a human skull at Ven, snatched up the sword, and lurched to his feet. Ven dodged the missile and parried the stroke. The clang of steel echoed from the cave and then, fainter, from the far side of the gorge. By that time another was ringing on its way.

For a moment the duelists exchanged monstrous, two-handed blows, any one of which would have felled an oak. The valley rang like a smithy. Then Ven shifted his stance. His footing failed in the litter of bones. He fell. Vandok swung. Ven rolled, and went on rolling. His father followed him, leaping and plunging down the slope. The wind roared and moaned in the cave, drowning out the cries of the spectators.

Ven stopped and from his prone position swung a scythe-stroke at Vandok's legs. Vandok parried it: *Clang!* He kicked bones down the slope at Ven's face. Ven hurled a pelvis, which struck the older man's head a glancing blow. Then Ven was on his knees, blocking another wild stroke. *Clang!* sang the echoes ... On his feet again, but Vandok still higher ...

Clang! Clang! Clang! Vandok kept striking downward, Ven parried and swung at the other man's legs. Why the impacts did not tear their arms from their sockets, I cannot imagine. Ven edged sideways, Vandok kept blocking him. Slowly, slowly, step by step, the younger challenger drove the old tyrant uphill. Their breath streamed in the wind. I could hear the rasp of their lungs. *Clang! Clang! Clang!* Ven had lost his hat, his hair flew free, and his sweat-soaked face was a mask of hate.

All around me men gabbled prayers, but I did not think the little gods would dare meddle here, not so close to Hool.

The fighters were almost back where they had started. Sinew and muscle could only take such punishment for so long, and inevitably it was the older man who faltered. He misjudged, or else his arms just failed him. The point of Ven's sword glanced off the guard and dug into Vandok's fist. Steel clattered into the rubble of bones and the awful clanging died away in its own echoes.

Even the wind seemed to draw breath then. Clutching the bleeding remains of his hand, Vandok stared at his executioner. Ven's shoulders heaved with his efforts to breathe and he seemed to lack the strength or the will to deliver the final blow. Then he raised his blade.

Vandok spun around and plowed over the bones toward the cave, reeling, staggering, clattering. Ven just stood and watched. The tyrant vanished into the dark abode of his god.

The wind surged. One vast howl exploded out of the cavern and reverberated along the canyon. I think it was Vandok's death cry, magnified by the rocks, but perhaps it was all Hool.

Ven sank to his knees, partly in worship, partly in exhaustion. We onlookers bowed our heads. His opponent did not emerge, and nobody who had heard that dreadful shriek would ever have expected him to.

We stayed where we were, huddled low and shivering until Ven could struggle to his feet again and sheath his sword with shaking hands.

"Father Hool, we leave you in peace!" he cried. "No more will men desecrate your mountain with blood. But one day my son will come and hold you to your promise, and his son after him. My seed will reign over the two lands for all time."

Silence . . . The wind had shifted. And then one last, hollow moan: "so—beee it!"

A roar of triumph rose from the army below and filled the valley, making the echoes ring, on and on. Those men had viewed the drama and heard the god concede. They had not heard Ven proclaim himself their king.

I turned to Juss and we fell into each other's arms. He was laughing and weeping at the same time. So was I. So were all the others.

I was thinking of White-thorn, who had sacrificed herself for this. After thirty years, she had her revenge.

16: Interlude

That was how it should have been told. Instead, the notary quoted interminable legal texts, political commentaries, and religious tracts, with no eyewitness account at all. Any story is improved by the authority of personal testimony. Unethical tellers of tales sometimes stoop to attributing their narratives to fictional onlookers, just to gain that effect. Present company excluded, of course.

My reverie ended. I was back in the dim coolness of the inn, in the flickering firelight. The rafters upstairs clicked and creaked as they adjusted to the plummeting temperatures. And Tickenpepper had not done yet.

"Cold-vengeance united the Seven Cities and the steppes in the Kingdom of Verlia . . ."

How easy the little hack made that seem! It took a lifetime, and it was Juss who did it, not Ven. Juss was the politician of the family. His brother, after all, had promised to restore democracy to the Land Between the Seas and then contrived to have the god proclaim him king. Revolution simmered below the surface for a long time because of that. Juss devised a compromise whereby the monarch ruled with the guidance of elected representatives. The system was cumbersome, but not without merit. The people had someone to cheer in good times and someone else to throw out in bad.

I did not stay to see all that. I watched the king's wedding procession from a distance and heard news of Juss's engagement on the very day I sailed away. Many years later, in a far land, I learned from a chance remark in a spice bazaar that both marriages had been fruitful.

Still the notary droned. "Following the precedent thereby established by Cold-vengeance, his son Brightdawn returned to the cave on his accession, and Hool confirmed him as true heir."

No mention of the rebuilding of the cities, the civilizing of the Horsefolk, the great capital that sprang up at Uthom in the Middle? A lot of that was done by later rulers, of course. It took more than a century.

"The death of True-honor without living issue established two other tenets."

I perked up half an ear.

"The rival claimants were prevailed upon to present themselves together before the god, and he made judgment between them, thus establishing both his willingness to decide such disputes among the direct descendants and the primacy of primogeniture. A further precedent was set at the accession of Fair-pearl, whom the god accepted as queen regnant—'to the surprise of many and the chagrin of her cousins,' as the learned Doctor Forstein put it."

I lost interest again. The fire was smoldering low, starting to smoke and stink up the room. The shutters rattled as if the storm had just been having a rest and was about to return. I considered strategy. Some person in this room knew something I very much wanted to know.

The merchant and his wife seemed extraordinarily smug. If Master Tickenpepper's tedious dissertation was so pleasing to them, his fees must be extremely reasonable.

On the other hand, the dowager's arid visage was all scowl surrounded by the folds of her hat. The maid sat in her usual inhuman rigidity—what was the matter with her? The old soldier wore an expression of dangerous inscrutability, leaning back in his chair with arms folded and his long legs stretched out before him.

The lines had been drawn, the teams were facing off. Only Gwill the minstrel was a bystander, and he had his chin down. His puffy eyelids drooped. Every now and again he made snuffling snoring noises.

"Burgomaster?" the dowager said sharply. "May I ask what your interest is in this?"

The merchant chuckled sepulchrally. "The religious customs of distant peoples have a certain intellectual appeal, my lady, do they not? At least they can inspire in us a sense of relief that we are not expected to follow them. In this case—"

I coughed politely. Uniformly unfriendly eyes turned toward me.

"If my learned friend has completed his address—I mean story—then it must be my turn again, yes?"

"Fiddle!" the old harridan snapped. "The time for trivial diversion is past. This is serious business."

Fritz rubbed his hands together with a gruesome scraping noise. He rose to his feet, huge and ominous.

"Indeed, my lady?" the merchant inquired, lowering his busy brows. "And just what business is that?"

"I thought," I said hastily, "that since I had occasion to visit the fair land of Verlia a few years ago, I might be able to comment on recent conditions."

"Fiddle!" the dowager said again, ignoring me and glowering at her opponent across the fire.

"Omar and I are going out to the woodshed," Fritz remarked, reaching for my collar. "I shall be back shortly."

"Sweet-rose!" I shouted.

All the eyes came back to me again. Even Fritz registered the effect. He paused with his great paw poised over my neck.

It was the old soldier who spoke first.

"When exactly were you in Verlia, Trader of Tales?"

"The last time? Ye gods, Captain! It must be twenty years ago."

There is a certain way men look at you when they

think you are lying. I had met it before, once or twice, and I saw it now in the warrior's narrowed eyes. I did not like the way his fingers drummed on the hilt of his sword, either.

"I was younger then, of course," I said. "Not older, as you suggested earlier. I do not show my years, perhaps. The benefits of virtue and clean living."

His lip curled. Nobody else except young Gwill looked any more convinced than he did. Fritz's thick fingers edged closer to my collar.

"I did meet Lord Ancient-merit of Bargar briefly. He had a slight cast in his left eye."

Captain Tiger's lip straightened again. "You could have seen a portrait," he muttered uncertainly. "What leg did he limp on?"

"Artists are usually more tactful. The noble lord had no limp when I saw him."

The soldier sighed. He turned to the dowager. "Perhaps he is telling the truth this time, my lady. I did not mention that name earlier, did I?"

She was unimpressed. "Not that I recall. But we have some serious matters to discuss." She peered across at the minstrel. "Master Gwill?"

Gwill's head jerked up. He tried to cough and sneeze at the same time, and then spluttered, "My lady?"

"You really ought to be in bed with that cold. Landlord, give him a tankard of that mulled ale. Strong! And Mistress Frieda, I would like some more herb tea. Captain Tiger, don't you think we have tolerated the horse thief long enough? It may be time to let justice take its course."

The tension in the room rose alarmingly. At least, I thought it did. Fritz shot me a gleam of triumph as he went by with the copper jug. All eyes went to the soldier. He was the one with the sword.

He frowned uneasily. Men such as he have strange rules about killing. Steel is permissible, but freezing to death is not. On the other hand, he was beholden to the old crone somehow.

"Just what business do you have in mind, my lady?" Burgomaster Johein was enjoying the play. He had not noticed the worried look in his wife's eyes.

"The Sweet-rose affair, of course."

He leaned back in his chair and folded his plump hands on his corporation. "I cannot see how it concerns you, my lady, but I shall be interested to hear what you have to say."

She pursed her thin lips until they went white. "I cannot see how it concerns *you*! Just why did you retain Master Tickenpepper to review the laws of a faraway land like Verlia?"

Gwill blinked from one to the other, in complete bewilderment. Fritz and Frieda bustled around in the background. The captain was considering me and biting his lip. The lady's maid had her head down as always, gazing at her hands in her lap—how her neck stood it, I could not imagine. Master Tickenpepper was picking his nose.

I directed a meaningful stare at the actress. It was intended to warn her that I would not leave without a few final words on her behalf. The message seemed to be heard.

"Darling," she said reluctantly, "perhaps we should hear what Master Omar has to say before he is ... I mean, why don't we hear what he knows about Sweet-rose?"

The merchant frowned. Possibly he felt the first twinges of suspicion then? Who can say?

"Begging your pardons," Gwill muttered, "but what is sweet rose?"

For a moment there was silence, as if no one wanted to be first to speak. I was about to, for silence always makes me uneasy, but the captain beat me to it.

"The land of Verlia is in a state of anarchy. Civil war may have broken out by now. The dynasty founded by

Cold-vengeance two centuries ago came to an end last year with the death of Just-blade. He left no obvious heir."

The minstrel said, "Oh!" but his face retained its baffled expression.

"There have been claimants, of course," the merchant offered.

"Too many claimants!" the dowager snapped, returning the ball.

He let it go by.

Gwill's hand closed on the tankard Fritz held out to him, but he did not seem to see it. "I thought that the god Hool had decreed that Hannail's line would rule forever?"

"Exactly!" the soldier said. "And delegations went to the sacred cave to consult the god."

Again nobody wanted to reveal any more.

"I'll have some of that brew, also," the captain told Fritz. "Holy Hool was very uncooperative. He would not acknowledge any of the pretenders. When the third delegation arrived, though, he finally told them that they must find the child of Sweet-rose."

Gwill drank, keeping his eyes on Captain Tiger, waiting for more.

"King Just-blade," the notary said, "had a son, Prince Star-seeker. Twenty years ago, he eloped with a lady named Sweet-rose. Nothing has been heard of either of them since."

"The god specified their child," the dowager added, "so we know that Star-seeker himself must be dead. So is Sweet-rose."

"*Ha!*" The merchant sat up straight. "How do you know *that*, my lady?"

"I know! Now tell me why you are troubling yourself with the matter?"

Fritz was hovering dangerously at my back. Frieda had brought the dowager's tea.

Silence. Place your bets, milords. On my left,

Tickenpepper the Terrible, Burgomaster Johein in the elephant class, and his well-known wife. On my right, Captain Tiger of Bargar, a nameless servant serving no obvious purpose, and . . . a certain elderly lady. Nuts! Sweetmeats! Buy your souvenir doublets here . . .

"Perhaps I can cast some light on the matter," I remarked helpfully. "It is my turn to respond to our learned friend's interminable discourse."

"If you are quick." The soldier took a drink.

With an angry growl, Fritz made three long strides to the fireplace. He reached up to the high shelf of bric-a-brac on the chimney and took down a small hourglass. Inverting it, he set it on the hob and went back to his previous place on the bench.

"Fair is fair," I said, rising stiffly. I had walked far during the day and now had been sitting too long. I headed over to the hearth. "The wind blows, the night is not yet done. The matter I shall relate is extremely relevant to your problem. I shall be as terse as I know how, but you must allow me to do it justice."

I laid the hourglass on its side and strolled back again, my heart soaring in triumph. I wasn't going to mention that yet, though.

"I trust that this time I shall not be interrupted! The tale I would tell you is called Virtue Rewarded."

17: Omar's Response to the Notary's Tale

✳

The trade winds brought me from the Misty Isles to Verlia. I disembarked at Myto, a city I had never visited before. Within hours, it had won my heart—a bustling little port of white walls and red-tile roofs. Its crowds were busy and yet good-humored. Men went unarmed, women did not hide their beauty behind veils. The children laughed and even the beggars smiled. It had music and flowers and excellent wine.

I soon found lodging at a dockside tavern and proceeded to earn my board with my tongue, as is my wont. I was minded to spend some time in this restored, prosperous land of Verlia. I would visit all of its seven cities, I decided, and as many of its hamlets as my feet would lead me to.

War and oppression were ancient history. The monarchy was popular, the land at peace. Men and women of obvious Horsefolk extraction walked the streets unheeded, clad in motley like everyone else.

While I rejoiced to see the people flourishing, I felt a tinge of regret that the glory and heroism of the Winter War had been so soon forgot. On my second day in Myto I found a statue of Ven in an overgrown corner of a shady plaza, half buried in ivy. It could never have been a good likeness anyway, and I told the pigeons to continue what they were doing to it.

The next morning, I had a visitor. The tavern was almost empty at that time of day. I sat alone, munching my way through a late breakfast of biscuits, cheese, and

ripe figs, listening in part to the busy clamor of the
docks outside—gulls and pulleys, men shouting, horse
tackle jingling. Mainly, though, my thoughts were on
some inconsequential yarns I had heard the previous
evening. Then two thick and hairy arms laid themselves
on the boards in front of me. Their owner sat down opposite.

"You are Homer, the trader of tales?" He had a deep,
censorious voice. It implied that if I were not who he
said I was, then the fault must be mine.

I confess I blinked a couple of times at him. He was
big and meaty, yet the cloth draped over his left shoulder displayed yellow kittens on a purple-and-emerald
background. On the other he bore violets and daisies in
even gaudier hues. Between them was a forest of black
hair, with a black spade beard above. I found the combination unsettling, although bright color was not
thought effeminate in that country. As it is part of my
craft to be visibly a stranger, I was garbed in drab sailor
clothes, which were screamingly conspicuous in Myto.

I nodded to his question. My nose was telling me
horse, my eyes were saying *road dust*, and both added
sweat, yet his clothes were fresh. He had taken time to
change but not bathe. Urgency? Why?

He announced himself. "True-valor of Galmish. I
have work for you."

His manner nettled me; it implied that the outcome of
our discussion was a foregone conclusion. Granted, he
was capable of carrying me out under one arm, either
kicking and screaming or sleeping peacefully, whichever he preferred. A warrior? Perhaps. A henchman for
somebody, certainly. He was not acting on his own behalf.

"I shall be honored to hear how I may serve you,
True-valor."

He glanced around impatiently, as if hoping his horse
would walk in, ready to leave. "A certain noble wishes

to hear some of your stories. He will pay you well." He laid his big hands flat on the table, as if about to rise.

I tore a mouthful of bread from the loaf. "Speak on," I said, pushing it in my mouth.

He reacted with surprise and then displeasure. "The house in which you will perform is three hard days' ride from here. You are capable of sitting a horse?"

I nodded and continue to chew.

Muscles flexed under his beard. "Well, then? I said you would be well rewarded."

I held out an empty palm.

Glaring, he reached under the violets and daisies and produced a wash-leather bag. After a prudent glance around the room, he tipped a shower of gold coins into his other hand for me to see. Then he replaced them and returned the bag to his motley. "My master is both rich and generous." He folded those arms as if daring me to try to take his expense allowance from him by force.

Apparently that was all the explanation he intended to provide. But no one in Verlia had been expecting me, or even knew of my existence. I had not been ashore long enough for my reputation to travel three days' journey and bring this musclebound flunky rushing to my presence. When the gods have work for me, they usually send word in dreams.

I had thought I was on vacation.

I swallowed half my cud and mumbled around the rest. "Tell me who summons me."

A faint flush crept out of the top of True-valor's beard. "I told you—a noble lord."

"And who told him to?"

Bullyboy laid his arms on the table again and leaned forward threateningly. Obviously he had felt insulted even to be sent on this errand, and to have the object of it talk back to him was close to intolerable. He addressed me as if my wits had worn thin. "My lord takes orders from no one but the king himself. Nor does he answer questions from the likes of you."

"Did he himself instruct you?"

"I will not be interrogated, either! Do you spurn my offer?"

I was tempted to, just to see what would happen. I decided it would hurt.

"Meaning you don't know the answer," I said cheerfully. "I will get it before I sing." I rose and bellowed across to the innkeeper to tell him I was leaving. "What are we waiting for?"

Erect on his hind paws, True-valor of Galmish stood a good head taller than I. The sash binding his outfit together was sea-blue, with an intricate pattern of white gulls and gold dolphins. The jeweled dagger tucked in it must be some sort of insignia. He regarded me with disgust.

"No baggage?"

"Nothing worth going upstairs for," I said. "Pray lead the way, Your Honor."

I could not wait to see him from the rear.

So began a hectic journey across country, through lush green valleys, over rocky upland pastures. Verlia prospered under the rule of its kings, but I hardly had time to notice. I was rushed past vineyards, orchards, olive groves, sunlit hamlets of white and red, all in a blur, mostly at full gallop.

True-valor traveled in style, with four subordinates and two pack horses. His men were all just as dandily dressed as he was, but they set a bone-breaking pace. We thundered over the land like a summer storm, raising dust, scattering peasants and livestock, raining money. At every post my guides demanded the best mounts, regardless of cost, scorning to bargain. By night we dwelt in the best inns, dining like kings, wenching, sleeping on silk sheets. Peacocks my companions might be, but they were a hard-riding, hard-mouthed band. I was pushed to my limits to keep up with them.

Although I had little time or breath for conversation, I soon established what manner of men they were. Despite all the royal edicts forbidding private armies, any landowner of stature kept a few score of tough youngsters on hand and a cache of weapons in the cellar, just in case. Officially I was in the company of a secretary, a flutist, a veneerer, an archivist, and a painter of watercolors. In reality—a captain, a corporal, and three lancers. After the second evening, I would have backed them against a team of Jurgolbian bear wrestlers. The flutist took offense in a bar. The group of them then proceeded to demolish both it and a dozen of its inhabitants. I have rarely witnessed such a detailed annihilation.

Men who ride together can rarely resist the camaraderie of the road for long. I began by regarding my guards as thugs or popinjays, demon-ridden butterflies. They took me for a beggar and resented being required to escort me. A grudging friendship began to arise out of mutual respect. They appreciated my horsemanship and I was impressed by their skills at mayhem. We shared a common interest in wenching.

I learned that their employer was a high lord indeed, Fire-hawk of Kraw, a direct descendant of my old . . . I mean the legendary Sure-justice of Kraw. Juss. Moreover, Fire-hawk claimed descent from his eldest son and was thus titular head of the clan and lord of Still Waters.

Ven's family still held the throne, as Hool had decreed it would, but it had not been especially fruitful. Possibly Verl had restricted the number of progeny to avoid disputes over the succession. The present monarch was King High-honor of Verl—even now, the kings did not name their lineage after Hool except when visiting the northern provinces. High-honor had a reputation as a philanderer, but he acknowledged only two children, both in their teens and both legitimate.

Juss's line, on the other hand, had been prolific beyond reason, scattering sons everywhere. Verlia was widely blessed with his descendants—Lord This of Kraw and Lord That of Kraw, all over the place. I wondered whether they all still worshipped the same dragon's tooth, or if the god had somehow divided himself. How many teeth could a dragon spare? But I was confident then that I knew who had summoned me, and therefore the urgency. Dragons are not known for their patience.

I was wrong. It does happen.

My first inkling that I had jumped to an unwarranted conclusion came on the final day. It was late afternoon, we had been riding hard since dawn, and the sunlight felt like a whip. I was hardly in a mood to appreciate the scenery anymore, although I had registered that we skirted the edge of a large lake, and the shores ahead were heavily wooded.

Suddenly True-valor bellowed a question back to Stern-purpose of Foon, the young artist. I turned in time to see him shield his eyes against the sun. He called out an affirmative.

To my surprise, True-valor at once slackened the pace, announcing that we need not tire the horses. We dropped to a trot. I detected relief all around me.

I edged my mount close to our leader's. "Why this sudden consideration for livestock, Captain?"

"Still Waters." He pointed.

A few spires showed above the trees at the end of the lake. "So it's Still there? Is that surprising?"

True-valor sneered with a trooper's traditional arrogance. "All will be made plain in good time, Master Homer."

So much for our budding friendship! But none of us knew the real reason behind his mission to fetch me, and that was vexing him again, now our destination was in sight.

I turned back to studying the view ahead, to see if I

could discover what had prompted the sudden relaxation. I failed. I was no wiser when we trotted across the bridge into Fire-hawk's palace. Being a foreigner, I did not recognize the royal standard flying from the highest tower.

I have seen my share of palaces, have even owned one or two. I have known some richer than Still Waters—larger, older, more intimidating or impressive—but none more beautiful. It sprawls over a cluster of wooded islands, connected by many bridges. Little of it can ever be seen at one time, but whatever is in sight is invariably eye-catching: trellises of marble against greenery, white arches reflected in jade pools, towers against the sky, balconies floating among branches. For a life amid flowers, birdsong, and fair vistas, Still Waters is unmatched anywhere.

Only a small part of it dates back to the founding of the kingdom, of course, but Juss himself chose the site and began the building. The former errand boy for Gozspin, Purveyor of Fresh and Nutritious Vegetable Materials, had ended his days in splendor. That would have pleased him greatly.

With the sun already sidling down to the hills, I was escorted to somewhat unimpressive quarters and assigned an equally unimpressive flunky as my escort and valet. His name was Towering-oak of Letus. He had as many airs as pimples, a large nose, and an even larger sense of his own importance. He was all arms and legs, bundled in enough spectacular fabric to make birds of paradise look like crows. He did not seem overwhelmed by the honor of serving me.

I washed away the dust of my journey. Towering-oak threw open a chest filled with motley for me to choose from. He offered to assist me in wrapping, if I felt unable to handle the contortions required. I made myself presentable without his help.

Meanwhile, though, I was learning from him that the

royal family was visiting Still Waters: King High-honor, Queen Sea-jewel, Prince Just-blade, and Princess Night-ingale. Lord Fire-hawk and Lady Rose-dawn were understandably honored, my valet confided with a sigh.

And which of these exalted personages had sent for me? I inquired.

He really did not know, he said. He really did not care, he implied. Her ladyship, most likely, he supposed. The king had unexpectedly decided to extend his visit for a second week. Her ladyship had been hard-pressed to find suitable entertainment for the additional evenings, having run out of jugglers, mummers, musicians, and masques. The royal visitors would be departing on the morrow, and then everything could return to normal.

And the trader of tales might be thrown out with the slops, perhaps?

Now I understood the sudden change of heart on the road. All along, True-valor and his band had been worried that they might not deliver me before the king departed.

Even for a man who has seen monarchs without number, there is something special about performing before a court, and I was eager to meet descendants of the legendary sons of White-thorn. My harrowing journey from Myto seemed likely to prove worthwhile.

Yet by now I had realized that the situation was not as simple as it had seemed. Someone must have mentioned my name to Lady Rose-dawn, either her god or a mortal prompted by a god, for no mortal could have known of my presence in the time available. But which mortal, which god? It might not be Kraw, after all.

I was ready. Towering-oak of Letus inquired if I wished to eat, which I did. He led me off across bridges and lawns, from island to island. Dusk was falling, lanterns glowed on the trails. To explore all of Still Waters would take weeks. Even by daylight it is a maze. I was physically battered from my journey and strung tight as a lute at the thought of performing for a god. I did not realize where we were headed until we walked into the heat and din.

"Help yourself," my companion said with a languid wave of overpowering generosity. "Wait here and I'll fetch you if you're wanted."

He turned away as if his work were done. I grabbed his motley and spun him around with a yank that almost unraveled him before the entire kitchen staff of the palace.

"Not so fast, sonny!" I said. "I do not eat in kitchens when I am to speak with kings. Tonight I dine with royalty!"

He squealed. "That is totally impossible!"

"Then I tell no tales."

Seeing that I meant what I said, Towering-oak of Letus did exactly what I expected him to do—flew into a panic. He yelled for the guard. With the palace already in turmoil because of the king's visit, the guards had no interest in one obstinate entertainer, and everyone in authority was engaged elsewhere. They disposed of the problem by throwing me in a cell.

Well, I have seen almost as many jails as palaces, and that one was better than most—four walls of stout timber with a bed, but no chains or bloodstains. Although the window was barred, a nightingale sang outside it. I sat down and prepared to wait on developments, regretting only that I had not filched more than two honey tarts from the kitchen while I had the chance. I had barely finished the second when the lock rattled and the door creaked open.

The man who entered was instantly identifiable, although I had never seen him before. He was of middle years and middle size. He smiled with irresistible politeness. His motley was neither especially gaudy nor especially drab; jade and cobalt, without a fold misplaced, hanging to his ankles and draping his arms to the elbows. He was unremarkable, to a remarkable degree—one of those faceless officials who breed in the crevices of governments everywhere, oiling wheels, greasing palms, making things happen.

"Master Homer? I deeply regret this misunderstanding." The intense sincerity he projected made my skin crawl.

I sat up. "The situation can be corrected, Master . . . ?"

"My name is of no consequence. I am merely a messenger." He glanced out into the corridor and then closed the door and leaned against it. He smiled smoothly, rubbing his hands. "Whatever arrangements you require to aid you in your presentation this evening will be made available. It is our intention to provide the finest entertainment possible for the royal party, and your reputation is our assurance that this final night will be the consummate climax of their stay here."

I felt as if I were being smothered in hot wool. "You serve Lord Fire-hawk?"

"I am of no importance. I am here only to further your art. Your reputation has preceded you, Master Homer. We have all heard wonders of the trader of tales. Just make your wishes known to me, master. Indoors, or outside on the lawns? A large audience, or a small one?"

"Whatever suits." His eagerness to oblige was infectious. "I can perform under almost any conditions."

"And almost any performance by you, Master Homer, would be a triumph for any other storyteller. But we do not seek an average performance, or even an outstanding one. We want Homer's ultimate masterpiece, a telling that will itself be the subject of tellings for generations."

He paused for a moment, appraising me, and I had a sense of something about to pounce.

"Subject to your approval," he continued smoothly, "I have arranged for your narration to take place in the West Portico. It is a sort of veranda, half indoors and half outdoors. We shall hang a single light over you, and leave the rest of the place dark. That will be dramatic, yes? We shall seat the audience among the potted plants and statues and so on, to make the atmosphere as intimate as possible."

Shivers of alarm ran down my backbone.

"I should prefer a small, well-lighted room with the seats close together and as hard as possible, to keep my audience awake!"

His eyes seemed to hood themselves. "Ah? I have been told that the trader of tales can weave a net of words to ensnare the very souls of his listeners. It is said that he will oftentimes entrance his audience, spellbind them so that they become unaware of the passage of time or the worries of the world. Is this indeed possible, master? Can mere words do this?"

If anyone should know the answer, it was he. I felt half mesmerized already, the rabbit before the snake. My wits raced around madly, seeking escape.

"Trancelike states in some listeners have been reported from time to time. Some people are more susceptible than others."

"For how long? An hour? Two?"

I shrugged, my mouth almost too dry to answer. "Not likely two. Not after a heavy meal."

"One, though? You could guarantee one hour?"

He endured my stare with bland confidence. His accent was not True-valor's or Towering-oak's. He came from Uthom. He was one of the court party, a glove over royal fingers. Whose game was he playing? Was the queen trying to cuckold the king, or the prince hastening his own succession? The game was boundless and the opportunity for foul play unquestioned. I suspected, though, that my visitor would not dirty his hands over a mere theft, nor a dalliance. That left assassination.

"Who sent you?"

A smile of deep regret. "That information I cannot give you."

"At least name the one I am supposed to distract! A man? A woman? This will influence my choice of material."

He sighed. "You misunderstand. I seek only to further your art." He slid a hand inside the folds of his motley. "But if you achieve the effect I described . . . one hour . . . Of course at the completion of your tale we expect our host to toss you a purse of gold. That goes without saying. He will be generous. But if you can contrive the sort of spellbinding that I mentioned, then . . ."

He held out a hand. On his palm shone one of the largest jewels I have ever been allowed close to, about the size of a strawberry. Even in the dim little cell, it glowed with a thousand summer rainbows. He moved his hand and myriads of fireflies danced over the walls.

"You are joking!" I gasped. "It is a king's ransom."

He shrugged faintly, as if he agreed with me. "I was instructed to promise you this reward. I admit it seems extravagant, but you have my word on it, by the god of my fathers."

"Riches have little attraction for me," I protested, although I could not tear my eyes from the diamond. "I usually give them away to beggars or pretty wenches."

"One hour," he whispered, tucking the jewel away. He knew he had me hooked.

Conscience told me I should have no truck with this suave scoundrel. Experience told me that he would never deliver the bribe, and it was not the sort of fee that could be obtained by legal action.

Alas! I confess! I found the challenge itself irresistible.

And I was flattered. I am only human, after all.

The best way to deal with temptation, the Blessed Osmosis taught, is to rationalize it into a duty, for there can be no evil in performing a duty. Fire-hawk was head of the senior branch of Sure-justice's clan. This was his home and therefore Kraw's. The dragon was around here somewhere, and nothing was going to happen in Still Waters that he did not want to happen. Anything he did want to happen would. Eventually. No matter what I did or said. Right? Right. So I should perform as requested and do the best I was capable of. That was my obligation to those who had hired me. My duty!

I sighed. "I shall try to earn your bauble, my lord." I hoped that I would not learn of my success from a dying man's scream. I was a lunatic if I thought I would ever see that gem again . . .

The courtier was happy, smiling his sincere smile. "And the staging I mentioned will be satisfactory?"

"It sounds effective." I stood up shakily. "I landed myself in here by demanding that I dine with the king. It helps if I can assess my audience beforehand."

"Alas, the royal party is already at table, Master Omar, and protocol forbids anyone else to be seated now. I can let you view them from a distance, if you wish. I can have you proclaimed by a fanfare of trumpets when you make your entrance later, if it will help."

"Not very much. Show me the victim . . . I mean audience."

I peered out through a marble screen at the royal banquet, the snowy cloths, gold plate, glittering chandeliers. There must have been a hundred people dining in that hall, but only the high table interested me. My mysterious courtier had vanished, doubtless into whatever invisible political crypt he normally inhabited. At my side, a subdued Towering-oak whispered names and titles for me.

The king was obvious. High-honor was then in his early fifties and the sixteenth year of his reign. He was a large man, tending to obesity but still striking. He wore his honey-colored hair long and his slightly reddish beard forked. He was not unlike his ancestor Ven, but the resemblance stemmed mostly from fair Horse-

folk coloring. High-honor's mother had been a north-
erner; his appearance must owe a lot more to her
than to his great-great-great-great-great-great-great-
grandfather. Perhaps to accentuate his fairness, the king
favored motley of dark hues, and that alone made him
stand out amid all the butterflies. He had a loud voice,
a boisterous laugh, a jovial manner. I admired the way
he kept conversation flitting around the table, never mo-
nopolizing attention as monarchs can so easily, keeping
everyone involved. I watched him tease to provoke mer-
riment, and flirt to flatter the ladies, but the victims did
not seem to suffer hurt. Once or twice someone would
aim a barb at the king himself, and his laugh would
boom out as loud as any. Seeing him in the flesh, I understood his popularity. Whatever his policies might be,
High-honor had a great personality, and I did not doubt
that it was genuine. *Likable* is a word rarely applied to
kings, but it suited him.

About Queen Sea-jewel, I was less certain. She, too,
was inclined to plumpness, but her maids had dressed her
well. Her hair was silver, a striking contrast to eyes and
skin darker than most. She was conversing readily
enough, yet I felt that her vivacity was less genuine than
her husband's. She was acting a part, I thought, doing
what queens do in public. In private she might behave
otherwise, but I could not guess how that might be.

Princess Nightingale was of the age at which prin-
cesses are married off. She had her mother's dark coloring. I prefer to describe young ladies as beauties
whenever I can, but I confess that she was too slender
for my taste, too fragile. To my critical eye, her smiles
appeared forced and her movements uncertain. This
public display was a strain for her, although some of
that shyness could be attributed to her youth. She
seemed strangely uninterested in the young men vying
for her attention, which suggested an absent lover, of
course.

Prince Just-blade was a boy barely into his growth

spurt. Although princes are notoriously precocious in matters of the heart, he was too young to be pursuing girls. He was having considerable trouble just staying awake, fighting back yawns. He did not look like a juvenile monster who would plot his father's demise, but that did not mean that someone else might not make such arrangements on his behalf.

So there was the royal family of Verlia.

I turned my attention to the host, Lord Fire-hawk. Again I convinced myself that I could see a resemblance to the legendary ancestor of Liberation days, but I was generalizing. Juss had been a very typical native of the Land Between the Seas, and so was Fire-hawk. He was tall, dark, and sinister. His eyes were never still, the rest of his features immobile. I could read nothing from his face at all. There was too much background noise for me to make out what was being said, so I had to judge the speakers' words by the effects they produced. Fire-hawk rarely seemed to jest, and when he did, I detected false notes in the resulting laughter. I assumed that his wit could bite.

That one, I decided, was dangerous.

His wife, Lady Rose-dawn? Tall, dark, stunning. A year or two past the prime of her beauty, perhaps, but still the most striking woman in a hall that contained more than its share of beauties. The strain of entertaining the royal family for almost two weeks was showing on her, though. She looked jumpy, worried . . . or was that only my overheated imagination at work? To be fair, I doubt if I would have reached that conclusion had I not been searching for suspicious behavior. No one else would have noticed anything amiss.

The two stripling pages serving the royal couple were her sons, so Towering-oak informed me.

I went on to inspect the senior nobles and officials and courtiers present, the young blades and the old foxes. I learned nothing of importance, for I did not know who mattered. I wished I had a better guide. Had

I asked my young companion to name the persons in that hall most likely to be conspiring against the king's life, he would just have stared at me in bewilderment.

Who had arranged for me to be rushed to this place? Who had prompted the nameless bureaucrat to offer me that priceless bribe? By definition, kings have more influence at court than anyone else.

If High-honor was not the intended victim, then he was the most likely conspirator. What could he be up to?

Do you believe in ghosts? I do. I have met them too often to deny their existence, although I grant that they are rare, and usually very shy. I sensed one in Still Waters that night.

The veranda was open on three sides to the gardens, stone arches leading out to lawns and shrubberies and shiny pools, with fountains tinkling and night-blooming flowers scenting the air. It was hard to tell where gardens ended and indoors began. At the far end, this strange chamber flowed back into the palace and became a proper room, furnished with upholstered sofas and rich rugs, but even there it was dark. My audience sat in small groups, spread out amid potted palms and statues and great onyx tubs of roses. I was the only person clearly visible. It was an ideal setting for a murder. Any assassin worth his silken cord could have crept up on anyone there.

No need to consider the tale I should tell. This was Still Waters. I felt a need to pay tribute to its founder.

Silent, I waited for silence, for the last giggling whispers to die away. Then, "Your Majesties," I said softly, "my lords, my ladies . . . I would tell you of an errand boy whom the gods called to greatness." So I began.

Many of the faces were barely visible. I had located the king himself and planned to keep an eye open in his direction, but being under the light myself, with everyone else obscured in the summer night, I had trouble knowing which of the other shadows were audience and which were statuary, or chairs, or plants. Some of my listeners had drunk more than was good for them and at first they tended to murmur comments to their neighbors. They fell silent as my tale progressed, until soon the only sounds were my voice and the fountains, and faint traces of a lute in the far distance.

I thought I started with fourteen listeners, although I might have missed a couple. After a short while, there were only thirteen. Then I felt better. And then twelve. Good! Now I knew the game, I could forget thoughts of assassins without wondering what I should do if I suddenly counted fifteen. One of the departed was the king himself, as I had surmised might be the case. I was too engrossed in my storytelling to work out who else was missing. It was none of my business anyway.

I had promised to give them an hour, and I did. No one noticed their absence. No one so much as coughed.

But as I carried my audience from the slums of Algazan to the rigors of the Winter War, I sensed that another had joined our company. Call it imagination if you like. Put it down to nervous strain on top of three very long days and two very hard nights. I do not claim to have seen a clear vision. Mostly I just felt his presence. Once or twice I thought someone stood in the shadows at the corner of my eye, but when I looked that way, he had moved somewhere else. Can one *feel* laughter? That night I did. I wondered if the dragon god had fetched him—dragons have an odd sense of humor, so they say. I think that Juss heard my tale that night, and I believe that he enjoyed it. I made "General Brains" just a little bigger and braver than he had been. That was only fitting in the house of his line. I was careful not to diminish "General Brawn," of course.

As I described Vandok fleeing into the cave to seek refuge with Hool, I felt somehow that the ghost had left. I drew my tale to a close.

I often see tears in my listeners' eyes at such times. I rarely feel them in my own, also.

There were fourteen people present again, so I had fulfilled my task.

Now my current tale, this tale of a tale, is almost finished, also. Nobility applauded and cheered. Servants rushed in with lights and refreshments and musicians.

At close quarters, the king was as personable as I had expected. He shook my hand, congratulated me, presented me with a ring, made jocular inquiries about hiring me as royal speechwriter.

The queen was perfectly charming, just as she would have been had I bored everyone senseless.

Lord Fire-hawk, coolly grateful, dropped the requisite pouch of gold into my hand for all to see. He made some acidic remarks about my sources of information being more complete than his own records and having one of his archivists interview me in the morning. I did not mention that I knew one of his archivists already and that the lad behaved most royally in the evenings—one learns tact around kings.

Then I was dismissed, like any common lute jockey. It happens.

Usually I frustrate the attempt by extending the conversation until the gentry forget that I am not one of them, but that night I was content to be led off to my room. Feeling I had earned my bed, I threw myself into it with a sigh of relief and a yell of agony. The sharp lump under the sheet was a diamond the size of a strawberry.

Then I knew who had instigated my appearance before the crowned heads of Verlia. Not Kraw, milords! The king must have beseeched his own god, Verl, to aid him in his suit; she had taken the opportunity to reward a certain service I had performed for her many years before. My skills have oftentimes been well rewarded, but never have I received an honorarium to match that jewel. It was a royal reward, and a divine one, also.

I did not meet the nameless courtier again. I did not speak again to any of the royal family. By the time I awoke in the morning, their train was already winding its way up the road, heading back to Uthom.

Nor was there any further talk of archives or archivists. True-valor escorted me to the palace gates. He did offer me a horse, but I declined. I'd had enough of horses for a while.

Who was the lucky lady? Who came slipping back at the same time as the king returned? Aha! A teller of tales is not a tattletale. It was long ago and far away. To reveal her name here and now would do no one harm, but even if I would, I cannot. She was a lady-in-waiting to the princess, and I had paid her no special heed when I inspected the royal party at dinner. I was not presented to her later. I could hardly ask her name in the king's presence. She had the charm of youth, if no wondrous beauty; I confess I felt a little sad that High-honor would pursue one of his own daughter's companions, but he had a reputation as a lady's man, and his people were inclined to turn a blind eye. Good kings are hard to find.

I wish I had known High-honor better. It was only a couple of weeks after the events I have described that the assassins struck him down. Queen Sea-jewel acted as regent until Prince Just-blade came of age.

18: The Fourth Judgment

❊

"**H**ave you quite finished?" the merchant roared.

"I have finished that tale, Your Honor. I have others if—"

"Tarrydiddle! Arrant claptrap! You have wasted our time."

"I thought that was the whole idea? A long winter night to kill—"

"Be silent!" the soldier snapped. He looked just as angry as the burgomaster, and considerably more dangerous. "You said you had relevant information to provide, and you have been spinning moonbeams. First, it is fifty years since the death of High-honor."

"Not quite!" I protested. "Forty-five or forty-six."

"Quiet!" He fingered the hilt of his sword. "And forty-six years ago, you were not conceived."

"First-person narrative—"

"Silence! You are a liar and a common gossip, repeating ancient slanders about your betters."

I glanced around and did not see a friendly face. Even Gwill looked glum, struggling to stay awake after his ale. Fritz bared his teeth hungrily.

"Produce your evidence, Master Omar," the actress said. "Show us the fabulous jewel!"

"Alas, ma'am, it's long gone. I carried it around for months, wondering what to do with it. Then I mislaid it, or perchance a wench went through my pockets while I slept."

"Even if what you said were true," the merchant

growled, "it would all be irrelevant anyway. High-honor is of no interest to us. It's his great-grandson or great-granddaughter we want—child of Star-seeker, the son of Just-blade."

Fritz stood up and flexed his arms. "I must fetch more wood. Have I your leave to take out the garbage at the same time?"

Again all eyes went to Captain Tiger, who shrugged. "Why not? As her ladyship said a few minutes ago, it may be time to let justice take its course. We have tolerated this vagabond long enough."

Fritz began to move . . . I opened my mouth . . .

"Let him be," said a quiet, raspy voice.

We all turned to the dowager. She was staring into the fire, apparently lost in a daydream.

"My lady?" the soldier said. He was not the only one surprised by this sudden change of heart.

"Let him be," she repeated softly, not looking around. "There may well be some truth in what he said."

"Quite impossible, ma'am! I might just accept that he could have been in Verlia as an adolescent twenty years ago, but never forty-five." He was reminding her that his eyesight was much better than hers.

For a moment the room seemed to hold its breath.

She sighed, still studying the embers. "I remember High-honor, and he was much as Master Omar described him. The tale was embellished, no doubt, but these storytellers pass on their yarns to one another, and I daresay that some such event occurred. Let him be."

Tiger shrugged and released his sword.

Gwill looked relieved. "If we are about to judge between Master Tickenpepper's story and Master Omar's, then I do feel that Master Omar's had a more professional polish . . ." He paused to sneeze and did not continue.

No one else was interested.

Fritz snarled like a hungry lion pouncing on a thorn bush by mistake. He went stalking over to the door and

donned a fur cloak that must have been stitched together from the pelts of several bears. Wind howled
joyously around the room for a moment, swirling the
ferns on the floor, and then the great door boomed shut
behind him.

"Rosalind, child," the old woman told the fireplace,
"I think the time has come to tell these people who you
are."

The maid shrank, cowering low on the bench. "Yes,
m-m-m-my l-l-lady." She glanced to and fro in sudden
panic, seeking escape, a hare cornered by a dog pack.

"Why not go fetch the casket?" Still the old woman
had not looked around.

"Yes, m-m-my l-l-lady!" The girl rose and scurried to
the stairs.

Frieda jumped to her feet and grabbed my padded
shoulder. "Quick! Come with me!"

She darted around the counter, grabbing the lantern
on the way, and disappeared into the kitchen. Surprised,
I rose to follow her, shuffling in the cuffs of Fritz's
pants.

The kitchen was much smaller than I had expected,
dominated by a work table, a butcher's block, and a
black iron range, presently cold. Faint odors of fresh
bread still lingered from the day. When Fritz went in
there, he must be constantly banging his head against
the hams and copper pots and nets of onions hanging
from the beams. Three skinned chickens dangled among
them. Two walls were hidden by shelves bearing rows
of jars, crocks, cheeses, but the one opposite the range
held a window. Frieda was wrestling with the bars on
the shutter.

I caught hold of her arm—my hand muffled inside a
sleeve—and I eased her away from it.

"Darling," I said softly, "we do not need to look at
the scenery now. It's never that great in pitch darkness,
anyway."

"Idiot!" she said, pulling free. "He is going to kill you!"

"Many have felt that way. No one has succeeded yet." She was almost as tall as I, but not quite. I could smile down at the anger and fear in her gorgeous blue eyes. I could have stayed there for hours.

"He is not joking, Omar! He loved that monster. You made a fool of him. He really will be revenged on you! I have seen him beat men to dough for much less. After, he will throw you in a snowbank and leave you to die, I know he will!"

"Then give me one precious kiss, my beloved, so that I may go to the gods smiling. Just one kiss, and nothing else that happens in my life will be of any importance whatsoever."

"Oh, be serious, you lummox!" Frieda turned back to the shutter.

I swung her around and wrapped my sleeves around her.

"Do you not realize, my Goddess of Love, that it was your rich lips that brought me back here? The joyful sparkle in your eyes, the bloom on your cheek? Of course I knew that beauty such as yours is always guarded by dragons, but I lost my heart when I saw you in springtime. No threat or danger would keep me from return—"

She began to struggle. I would not have engaged in such tactics had the match not been a fair one. Frieda was a powerful woman, and I only barely maintained my hold as we shimmied and staggered together under the vegetables. I tried in vain to bring my lips to hers.

"I would kiss your toes if we had time for dalliance," I panted.

"Numbskull!" she stormed. "At least he cannot inflict brain damage on you."

"I could spend an hour worshipping your kneecaps and composing sonnets to your elbows."

I might have gone on to become quite lyrical then,

had she not contrived to stamp on my left foot. I clasped it in both sleeves as I hopped up and down on the other, choking back execrations in Drazalian, Jorkobian, and even Wuzzian. When I finally managed to speak civilly, she was again fussing with the shutter—a single-minded woman.

"What," I gasped through my tears, "do you think you are doing?"

"The key to the stable is above the door. Fritz can't see this window from the woodshed. As soon as he comes back in, you must run across and get a horse. You probably won't have time to saddle—"

"Me? Steal a horse? On a night like this? Milady, you cast—"

"That was what you were going to do the last time, wasn't it?" She turned to me with a heart-rending flush on her cheeks.

"I was in a hurry. But you're giving me one now, and that would take all the fun out of it. No, I can never leave without you, my precious mountain blossom."

"Omar!" The catch in her voice was thrilling. "Fritz will kill you!"

"No he won't! By dawn I shall have him kissing my boots."

"Never! They are fine boots, but much too small for him."

"With me in them!"

She snorted in disbelief. "If you think that, then you are too big for them yourself."

I held out my arms to her. "Tell me you return my love. Just so I may die happy?"

"Imbecile! But now you arouse my curiosity."

"I shan't tell you what you are arousing."

She laughed and took my face in both hands. The result was even more inspiring than I had expected. Her kissing was superb, with a fanatical attention to detail. I must have been grinning like a maniac as I limped back into the taproom.

It had been a kind thought, but it wouldn't have worked. If Fritz found me missing when he returned, he would be out to the stable in a flash, long before I could open it and lead out a horse. I didn't have any intention of leaving, anyway.

The maid was creeping downstairs, clutching a small casket. The next tale was about to begin.

The light from the lantern caught her. I saw the thickening under her chin and suddenly some things became obvious.

19: The Maid's Tale

M-m-my name is Rosalind, may it please you, although I am also known as Heidi. I am ... I mean, I was until a few days ago ... a maidservant for the margrave of Kraff. Not in his castle, but in his town house in Gilderburg.

My mom was called Rosalind and named me after her. She always called me Rosie. The cook who came after her had a daughter named Rosalind, too, and I think that was why I came to be called Heidi instead of Rosie, so we wouldn't get mixed up.

My father was a prince and I am rightful queen of Verlia.

I don't remember my father at all. I remember my mom telling me that he was a soldier, a mercenary, and he died of an arrow wound at the siege of Hagenvarch. That was before my mother came to Gilderburg, so nobody else remembers him, either, nobody I know of. I don't know what name he went by when he was a soldier. My mom never said much about him, or I don't remember if she did. I was very little, of course. Not what he looked like or anything. She did tell me he was of noble birth, but not how they met, or anything like that. She used to cry when she spoke of him.

Even here, my memories are patchy. She seemed very pretty to me, but they tell me all little children think their mothers are pretty. She had dark hair and dark eyes. I think she was tall ... I'm not sure. She died of the coughing sickness. I must have still been little, because all I remember is that one day she wasn't there anymore.

The other servants kept me, although I suppose they must have told the margravine about me, and she must have given leave for me to stay. It was kind of her. Not many people would have kept a useless orphan around. I've never seen the castle, not that I recall, but the town house is very big, and the castle is much bigger, so I'm told. I have . . . had . . . a bed up in the attics, but in the winter they let us sleep in the kitchens, for warmth.

As soon as I was old enough, I began to work for my keep. Cleaning pots and scrubbing floors, mostly. I am a good girl. I work hard and try to please. Cook often thanks me for doing a good job, not like some. She trusts me with money to go out and buy things in the market. And I don't let the gardeners and footmen take liberties.

One day in summer, a very strange thing happened. I know you will find it hard to believe, but Captain Tiger and her ladyship have asked me about it, over and over, and they believe me. I'm a good girl. I don't tell lies.

The margrave and margravine had left town and gone to the castle, and we were doing the spring cleaning, which we always do, every year. We do it later than most of the big houses do, but that's because we wait until the margrave isn't in residence anymore. Other houses' staff laugh at us for being always late, but we do as good a job as they do.

So this morning I'm helping Karl and Mistress Muller clean the young master's rooms and she sends me up to the attics with a box of winter quilts to store. This isn't the attics where the servants sleep. That's in the west wing, and this is the south wing, which is just used for storage, and it's all dark and stuffy and I'm frightened of getting cobwebs on my cap. Mistress Muller would scold me. It's full of all sorts of boxes and trunks and things that must have been there for years and years. I finds a place for the box I'd brought, leaving it with the labeled side showing outward as Mistress Muller likes, and I don't waste time and dawdle. I go back to the stairs, and when I'm about halfway down, then a voice speaks to me.

"Heidi!" it says. Plain as sunbeams in a cellar.

I stops with my heart all flittery-fluttery and says, "Who's there?"

"A friend of yours, Heidi," it says, ever so quiet and yet ever so clear. "I have important things to tell you."

I says, "Is that you playing devilment, Rab?" Thinking it was the turnspit, you see. That lad's got more tricks'n a sack of kittens, Cook always says.

The voice says, "No." It says, "Come back tonight when you have time to listen, because I have a lot of important things to tell you."

Well, then I thinks it must be Dirk, the footman, who's got nastier sorts of tricks in mind than Rab, so I says, "You think I'm simple? You come out right now or I'll lock you in!"

But no one came out, so I run down and lock the door, thinking it must be Dirk and that'll serve him right. Then I hears Dirk and Anna sniggering in the laundry corner, so I knows it isn't him, and I sort of forgot all about it all until I goes to bed that night. Then I remembers locking the door and begins to wonder if I've locked young Rab in there. There's no one sleeping in that wing with the family away. I gets to worrying that Rab may be shut in there and shouting his head off and no one'll hear him until next winter. I can't recall if I've seen him around since, or even at supper, and it's not like him to miss his victuals. I learns the next day that Cook caught him into the preserves in the larder and shut him up in the wood cellar with no supper as punishment, but I don't know that then, lying in bed worrying. So eventually I gets so worried that I gets up, ever so softly, without waking Anna who I shares my room with, and I wrap my cloak about me and I go creeping over to the other wing.

It's ever so spooky doing this and I got to be ever so quiet, because if Mistress Muller catches me, she'll think I'm a loose woman carrying on with Dirk or one of the other young men, and I'll be put out in the street like some I could name. But I gets to the attic door and I unlocks it, and then I opens it very quietly, and says, "Rab? You can come out now."

And that strange little voice says, "Heidi, I'm not Rab, and I'm not Dirk, and not any of the footmen or gardeners or stableboys. I have important things to say to you."

I says, "Say them, then, because I'm not coming up those stairs."

"Your real name is Rosalind," the voice says, "and your mother was a princess and your father a prince, and you should be a queen on a throne in a far land."

"Rab," I says, "if you don't come right out here and stop this nonsense right now, I'll lock the door again, so help me."

"You have a birthmark," the voice says, and it says just what the mark is like and where it is, and then I know this isn't Dirk or Rab or any of the others, because I'm a good girl.

I finds it hard to breathe, I'm so taken aback. "How you know all that?" I says.

It says, "Because I am the god of your fathers. I knew your father and his father and all their fathers back for hundreds of years, and they were all kings, and you should be a queen."

Eventually I gets cold standing there, so I do go up to the attic, and wraps myself in one of the quilts I put up there only that same day, and I sit and talk with the voice until I start to go to sleep despite myself and how excited I am. Then the voice sends me back to bed. The next night I goes back again, and the next night, and the voice tells me all sorts of things about me, and about the land I should be queen of.

It says its name is Verl, and on the third night it leads

me to it, and it's just a china dove on a high shelf, ever so small and covered with dust. And it tells me to take it back to my own room, and then I can put it under my pillow and it can talk to me while I'm in bed while Anna's asleep, and then I won't have to spend so much time in the box room. And Verl said it wasn't stealing for me to take it—I mean him, or maybe her, because Verl says it doesn't matter which I call him. Anyway, he had belonged to my mother. Or my mother had belonged to him, since he's a god, but even if people thought she, he, was just an ornament, the ornament had belonged to my mother and my father before her, and was rightfully mine, not the margrave's.

But Verl can't talk with anyone but me to explain this, so she told me how to keep her well hidden by day, in a place I hadn't known about and would never have thought of.

But at night I slips Verl under my pillow and lies still in the moonlight as she tells me about my family.

My father was the son of the king, whose name was Just-blade. My father's name was Star-seeker, and he fell very much in love with my mother, who was a lady and pretty as I'd always thought she was, and whose name was Sweet-rose.

Prince Star-seeker told Sweet-rose he loved her and would marry her. Sweet-rose took awhile to convince, but he wooed her and told her he would love her always and be true until she fell in love, too, and they agreed to be married as soon as possible. The prince went to the king and asked his blessing.

But King Just-blade would not approve. He said that Star-seeker must marry a princess from another land to seal a treaty. He said that the princess was already on her way to Uthom to be betrothed, although she was too young to be married for several years yet, but that did not matter because Star-seeker also was too young to marry. Star-seeker's heart was a stone.

"How can I break this news to Sweet-rose?" he asked

himself, and did not know the answer. So he went to the shrine where his family god was kept, a silver shrine all sparkling with rubies. The god was Verl, of course. The prince knelt down and prayed, telling Verl all his troubles.

"You are right and your father is wrong," Verl said. "Sweet-rose is a fine match for you, and this foreign child-princess is of tainted blood. Bring me the king."

Star-seeker went and told his father that the god wanted him. King Just-blade went and listened to the god, after making her wait a few days. But he refused to change his mind. The betrothal had been agreed to in a treaty, he said, and to break it now would mean war. He also said that family gods should not meddle in politics, which was very disrespectful of him. He ordered Lady Sweet-rose banished from the court, to a lonely castle on the coast, called Zardon.

Prince Star-seeker went back to pray to Verl again. This time Verl was very angry with the king! The god told Star-seeker to take her away from the palace. He mounted his horse and rode out alone, except he took the god with him, 'cos she told him to. She led him to where Lady Sweet-rose was imprisoned. They escaped together. They were married by the god herself. The king ordered a great hunt for them, searching all the ships and posting guards on the mountain passes, but because they had the god with them to help, the lovers fled away without being caught.

They traveled north for a long time, until they arrived in the Volkslander. Star-seeker became a mercenary soldier, and Sweet-rose became a mother, when I was born. After that, when Star-seeker went to fight, he left his god Verl behind to guard his wife and baby, and because he did not have his god with him to protect him at the siege of Hagenvarch, he was struck in the shoulder by an arrow. Wound fever took him.

Then my mother changed her name to Rosalind, because Sweet-rose is not a usual sort of name in our country. She took service with the margravine, as cook.

Foolishly, one summer when I was very small, she left the god Verl back at the town house when we went to the castle. Being away from the god's protection, she caught the coughing sickness and died.

All my life the god had waited on a shelf in the store room, waiting until I was grown up and she could speak to me when I was there alone. And now she told me all this and much more.

She told me, also, that the bad King Just-blade had died and there was no king in Verlia, but I'm rightful queen. She said, too, that an oracle had said that Star-seeker's daughter would be found beyond the Grimm Ranges. She told me that there was a man in Gilderburg looking for me and I must go and tell him that I was the one he wanted.

Well, I was very scared then, and I says I can't do a thing like that, speak to a strange gentleman. Verl say then I must tell Cook or Mistress Muller, so they can speak for me, and I says they won't believe me, and I won't. And every night the god is telling me, and I keeps refusing.

But then the god says that the man will be leaving the next day, and this is my last chance, and it is my duty to go. So I puts on my clothes, all quiet, and my coat, and I puts Verl in my pocket. I creeps down the stairs, feeling like a very bad woman. I never done anything like that before. I unbars the kitchen door, though my hands shake so much I can't hardly manage it. I goes out and creeps through the streets to where Verl tells me, and then she says to wait. There were lights on in the windows still, although it was ever so late.

So I waits in the shadows until a carriage pulls up at the door, and then a gentleman comes out. I never seen him before.

"Now, Rosalind!" Verl says, and I runs forward as he comes down the steps. He looks at me in surprise.

"Captain Tiger!" I says. "I am the queen you are seeking."

And then I faints dead away.

20: Interlude

It was all very horrible. I have left out the awful stuttering, the long pauses, the quiet prompts from the dowager when the speaker mumbled into confused silence. Even had I not glimpsed her goiter earlier, I would have known that the girl was a cretin, or at least a simpleton, just from the way she spoke. We all squirmed with pity as the tale unfolded. The lantern guttered and failed altogether; the fire burned low. A heavy darkness crept in on us.

Rosie seemed to believe her own story. Indeed, she had to believe it, for she lacked the wits to have made it up. I am not without skill or experience in detecting falsehood. I could believe in her. I could not believe the truth of what she said, though. Why did her companions? It was impossible!

The dowager leaned across Captain Tiger and patted Rosie's hand. That was the largest movement she had made all night. It brought tears to my eyes.

For a few moments nobody spoke. Perhaps everyone was trying, as I was, to imagine this pathetic drudge ascending the throne of Verlia. That was impossible, too, unless she was just to be used as a figurehead—married off quickly to some competent young noble who would wield the power and who had no scruples about taking a moron to bed.

Was this the game that Captain Tiger and her ladyship were planning? Had they coached the wretch in that improbable rigmarole in the hope of passing her off as rightful successor so that they could rule through her? I had thought better of both of them. Moreover, this was no ordinary missing-heir problem. How could they ever expect Hool to accredit an imposter?

The notary still sat between me and the girl. He turned to look at me, and I saw my own thoughts mirrored in his eyes. He went up marginally in my esteem. I glanced at the merchant, the actress, the minstrel, and saw the same pity—and the same disgust.

Rosie herself had slumped back into her previous lassitude, the slouch in which she had sat all night. Only the casket at her feet was new, and the tiny porcelain bird on her lap, and its silken wrapping.

The burgomaster spoke first, of course. But he did not spring to attack the girl, who would have been helpless before his bluster. He went straight for the dowager, who must be the prime mover in the conspiracy.

"Perhaps you would explain your part in this, my lady?"

The old woman shrugged and went back to staring at the fire. She would not see eighty again. She must be taxed to her limits by this long night.

"I am from Verlia, as you have guessed," she croaked. "I am pained to see it slithering into civil war . . . the assembly breaking down in riot, cities rebuilding old walls . . . When the news of Hool's oracle arrived, I wondered what I might do to help. I heard of Captain Tiger and hired him to assist me."

"Why you? A woman of your years embarking on such a journey? You carry patriotism to extremes, ma'am."

"My sons were occupied in drilling troops."

He waited, but she added nothing more. His bushy black brows drooped even lower. "If you claim this scullion as your rightful queen, ma'am, then why not dress her as befits her rank?" He oozed disbelief.

The answer came in the same weary whisper. "For her own safety, it seems wiser to pretend that she is my servant, until we reach Verlia and I can assign her greater protection. She agreed to this."

Of course Rosie would agree. She would do anything a "lady" told her to. Even now, she seemed unaware that she was the topic of conversation. But the real reason must be that Rosie was incapable of being anything more than a servant, and to start granting her royal honors would shatter the few wits she had. She would go catatonic.

Burgomaster Johein turned his glower on the soldier. "You accept her tale, Captain?"

"I do."

"A serving girl rushes up to you in the street claiming to be a queen and you believe her? Just like that?" Considering that he was addressing the only armed man in the room, the merchant was drawing close to rashness.

"Not quite like that," Tiger said in a thin voice. "We had her carried back into the armiger's house and revived. She was half frozen and terrified out of . . . alarmed at what she had done. We got her story out of her—not as much as you have heard tonight, but enough to prick our curiosity. We asked her a few questions. The answers surprised us. Next day we asked more. We inquired into her background."

Johein snorted. "But the main witness is that figurine?"

We all looked again at the china bird the girl had produced from the casket. It was a dove, yes—made of porcelain and finely glazed. It did not resemble in the slightest the image of the god Verl that I had . . . that I had described when telling the tale of White-thorn. My word on the matter would carry no weight with this company, of course. And even I could not deny that the god might have changed her icon since those far-off days. The image is not the god, merely a representation, a dwelling, a symbol. An ornament is an ornament.

Tiger spoke again, still softly, but with a hint of danger in his stillness, like a drawn bow. "There have long been rumors that Prince Star-seeker took the royal god with him when he disappeared. That is the commonly accepted explanation of why the king's second marriage proved barren and his sister died childless. Verlians expect their household gods to protect them from harm, but only within reasonable limits. They know that they are mortal. The god's primary responsibility is continuance of the family. Lack of heirs is the fault of the god."

"Of course," the merchant said venomously, "the bird does not talk to anyone but Rosie herself?"

There was a pause. The damp wood that Fritz had brought in earlier fizzed and hissed on the hearth. The hourglass was back on the shelf, forgotten.

The two men stared across at each other in a deepening gloom.

"You are calling me a fool, sir?"

"Not at all."

"A liar, then?"

"I am asking you for an explanation, Captain. I credit you with enough intelligence to want more evidence than we have heard so far."

Tiger nodded, accepting the implied apology but leaving the warning hanging in the smoky air. "Of course I have more. Her ladyship and I had tarried two weeks in Gilderburg. We were intending to move on to your own city of Schlosbelsh the very next day. I had spoken with most of the leading citizens. I had asked a great many questions. Two young men had already come forward claiming to be the missing heir. Another, older man had claimed to be the missing Prince Star-seeker himself. Her ladyship and I discredited all three imposters with no trouble. I had not called upon the margrave of Kraff, as he was not in the city. So if you think that the girl eavesdropped on my conversation, you may discard that theory. It was the first thing that occurred to us."

The merchant opened his mouth, closed it, then said, "Master Tickenpepper?"

The notary coughed. "This is not a conventional legal matter, Burgomaster. Human knowledge has limits. The ultimate judge in the affair will be the god. The precedents ..." Roasted by a glare from his client, he cleared his throat hastily and continued. "But a few points might be clarified. For example ... Captain, you were certainly not the only person running around the Volkslander this summer asking questions. We had several in Schlosbelsh, and the matter was the talk of the town for weeks."

"I expect it was."

That was partly my doing. I had been the first in the field that spring. I had begun telling the tale in Gilderburg the very day I had my argument with Fritz's dog, and I had continued all summer. My labors had borne no fruit at all. I felt irked that Tiger and the old woman had met with more success than I had, especially as they had been working the homes of the nobility. I had concentrated on alehouses and brothels, whose inhabitants are usually much more knowledgeable and entertaining.

Tickenpepper coughed. "In most cities the servants of the noble families behave like a craft guild. They eavesdrop at table and then chatter among themselves—a footman from one house courting a chambermaid in another, for example. Your claimant mentioned that she ran errands for the cook. She could have picked up the story from kitchen gossip, or in the markets."

Staring directly over Rosie's head, Tiger regarded the little man with cold dislike—which I fully shared, as you know by now. Rosie paid no heed.

"You should not be surprised to learn, counsellor, that such a thought had occurred to us. When the girl displayed knowledge of matters I had not mentioned, such as the likelihood that the prince had abducted his father's god, I did consider the possibility that other inquirers might have revealed more than I had. One should never underestimate gossip and rumor, as I am sure you will agree. Soldiers know that as well as lawyers."

Sarcasm was wasted on the little pen pusher. "You questioned the margrave's seneschal?"

"His housekeeper. She confirmed the girl's good character. She also confirmed that the Verlian matter had been discussed in the servants' hall."

Tickenpepper let that answer lie in full view for a moment, as if trying to impress a judge. It was admittedly an important point.

"So the god will not speak to anyone but her?" he went on. "You prepared lists of questions and sent Rosie off alone to put those questions to the god?"

"Of course."

"The replies were convincing?"

The soldier glanced around at the dowager. She had returned to her morose contemplation of the fire, perhaps the only the thing in the room she could see properly. It was puffing eye-watering smoke, which it had not done before.

"In most cases," Tiger said. "There were a few matters the god refused to discuss. There were a couple of odd discrepancies, I admit; but you must realize that the girl's knowledge of the world is limited. She cannot read or write. In some cases she may have misunderstood the question or the god's answer. With those few reservations, she passed our tests with flying colors. She convinced us!"

Almost convinced, I thought. Both he and his employer had doubts they were not admitting.

"May we have an instance?" Tickenpepper inquired mildly.

"We asked her to describe the shrine in which the royal god had lived in the palace at Uthom. She told us: silver and rubies. That is not general information. Only persons very close to the royal family could have known that, but it is correct. That Prince Star-seeker was last reported at Castle Zardon. That, too, is correct, but has never been publicly stated. Did your Schlosbelsh gossip tell of that?"

Tickenpepper glanced across at his client. In the gloom, the merchant was a vague, bloated mass of suspicion. At his side, the actress displayed an expression of polite boredom, but her knuckles showed white in her lap. Gwill was staring stupidly at nothing, almost asleep again. No one spoke.

"We asked her to describe her parents," the soldier continued. "She does not remember them herself. Our inquiries in the household confirmed that she is the daughter of a former cook, a woman who died many years ago, when Rosalind was about four. Few recall her mother and no one admits to knowing anything at all about her father. Rosie asked Verl, and returned with descriptions of Star-seeker and Sweet-rose that we accept as being genuine."

Tickenpepper uttered another little cough, a mannerism that was starting to irritate me. "On what basis? You told us earlier that you were not a native-born Verlian, Captain. May I ask the source of your knowledge of the missing lovers?"

The wind must have shifted. The fire crackled and hissed, and puffed smoke again. Tiger coughed harshly, waving his hand at it.

"Innkeeper! Why cannot we have some light in here? Candles, if you please! I do believe I could use some more mulled ale, too. Perhaps a snack?"

Fritz jumped up like a well-trained dog and headed for the kitchen, bleating apologies.

Frieda rose with more grace. "Bread and cheese, sir?"

Several of us agreed that we were feeling peckish. She followed her brother out.

"Now, Burgomaster," the soldier continued. "I believe it is your turn to answer some questions. What is your interest in the affairs of Verlia?"

"But you did not answer me, Captain. How do you know the truth of the girl's statements?"

"That information is not—"

"Me," the dowager quietly said. "I am Sweet-rose's mother."

The old woman made an effort to rouse herself, peering her filmed eyes across at the merchant with something of her earlier ferocity. "Now do you understand my involvement in this affair? The oracle mentioned a daughter I had given up for dead twenty years ago! Sweet-rose bore a birthmark over her heart, shaped like a rose. That was why she was named Sweet-rose. The god described the mark to Rosalind and she told us. This child is my granddaughter."

That was the most dramatic speech made in that room that night. The merchant went pale in a way I should never have believed possible for one of his florid complexion. So did his wife. I felt as if I had been slugged with a flagstone.

I even wondered, for the first time, if the kitchen maid's story might have some truth in it. But she did not look like Sweet-rose!

No, it was impossible, and the surprising thing was that I thought I could prove it. The audience had come onstage to mingle with the actors. Like an ax turning against its owner, or the bow of Onedar, whose arrows killed the archer, the tale of Verlia had infected its listeners. The old tragedy filled the Hunters' Haunt tonight like the acrid woodsmoke from the fire.

Fritz came hurrying in with two lighted lanterns. The room brightened, revealing bluish haze and watering eyes.

"I think it's time had come to clear the air," I said. "Sweet-rose was a very beautiful and admirable young lady. I find it difficult to imagine her as a cook, although I fancy she would have been capable of doing almost anything to protect a child she loved. What I cannot envision under any circumstances is Star-seeker as a mercenary soldier."

The old woman peered around, trying to make me out. "Master Omar? A while back you claimed to have been in Verlia twenty years ago."

"So I was."

"And were you involved in my daughter's elopement?"

"Yes, ma'am."

"Ha! I might have guessed! Very well. Tell us about it."

"My version of events will not agree with what we have heard already, my lady."

"I don't expect it to. Carry on."

21: Omar's Response to the Maid's Tale

I had not planned to return to Verlia so soon. My intent when I signed on with *Golden Hamster* was to visit the ruins of Algazan, now far fallen from its former glory. But the gods rule the winds, and they sent a truly monstrous storm to fetch me. Tattered and wounded, the bark eventually limped into the harbor of Kylam.

That night, as she lay in safe haven and I in my hammock, I dreamed of Still Waters. In my dream I stood by a ford, where a river ran into Long Lake. I did not know that place, for the road I had traveled with Truevalor of Galmish followed the opposite shore. I had not seen the island palace from that side, but I recognized the towers above the trees, outshining the glory of their fall foliage. I knew then that a god was calling me.

A sailor's life palls quickly, anyway. In the morning, when the water tender came alongside, I slipped aboard unseen and skedaddled.

The season was not yet as advanced as it had been in the dream and subsequent nights brought no recurrence of the message, so I concluded that there was no great urgency. I lingered in Kylam for a few weeks, then set off across country in my usual leisurely fashion. It was harvest time, and there was work to be had when all other sources of sustenance failed.

Times were hard in Verlia. I saw too many shuttered windows, weed-infested vineyards, crops pining for reapers, fruit trees in need of pruning. Offers to drink the king's health met with little enthusiasm, and one mention of taxes was enough to ruin an entire evening.

The trouble was Bunia, a kingdom abutting the steppes of the northern provinces. Attempting to extend his realm, Just-blade had bitten off more than enough to chew him up and swallow him. The resulting war had dragged on for years, draining gold and manhood from all Verlia. The people of the Land Between the Seas had never been much interested in the remote grasslands, and this endless struggle was immensely unpopular. As the Blessed Osmosis told the Soothian princes, wars are like love affairs—easy to start, hard to end, and outrageously expensive.

I shunned places I had visited on my previous visit, and no one peered at me as if my face were familiar.

In time the leaves changed, and I drew close to my objective. The dream began to recur, too. Never was I told what was expected of me. I just saw the lake, the river, a glimpse of the palace in the distance. There were stepping-stones there, signs of hearths. Evidently that grassy spot with its fresh running water was a favorite camp for travelers, but I was not informed who would be there to meet me. I was not told whether to expect comedy or tragedy, epic or romance, for the gods stage all of those and more.

For the last few days, I traveled in the company of a group of merchants and their pack train. I extended cheerful conversation in return for a place at their stewpot and was tolerated with poor grace. The leader of the caravan was a stingy little man named Divine-providence of Nurb—of no consequence now and very little even then. He seemed to believe that the gods had created him for the sole purpose of worrying about the state of his bowels.

It was a sad commentary on King Just-blade's Verlia that so insignificant a party felt the need for a hired guard. He was a foreigner like myself, a professional adventurer, and the only one in the company with any appeal. I could not place his accent, although he called me Omar, not Homer as the natives did. He would admit to no name but Zig, without explaining why his mother would have blighted him so. That he was of high birth was revealed by his skill with horse and sword, his education and manners. He had traveled widely, despite his apparent youth—and who am I to comment on that? He told tales well, laughed readily, and said nothing of his own past, except to drop mocking hints of being banished when he refused the advances of a noble lady.

We reached Long Lake around noon one cool fall day. The hills were glorious in their golden mourning, the water shone as blue as lapis lazuli. I knew by then that Lord Fire-hawk of Kraw had fallen in the war. His sons, whom I had seen playing page for King Highhonor, were grown men who had won renown in battle.

We followed the shore and by evening came in sight of Still Waters, at the place I had been shown in my dreams: ford, stepping-stones, old hearths. It was deserted. I suggested that we pitch camp. Zig glanced around approvingly and agreed. Snarly old Divineprovidence insisted that we push on for another hour. He was a great one for overtaxing the horses, and we should be very lucky indeed to find a site as good as this.

He was leader. Zig shrugged. I sighed. The gods summon me when they wish an event recorded for mortals' benefit. I am a reliable and truthful witness and do not fail them. This was the place. Here I must wait until my services were required.

I could not easily explain all that, though, so I bade Zig farewell, thanking him for his company. Somewhat less sincerely, I also thanked Divine-providence and his companions for their recent hospitality. Then I sat down on my bedroll and glumly watched my evening meal disappear across the meadow and into the trees.

I had barely unsnarled my line and baited my first

hook before I heard hooves returning along the trail,
very fast. I silently congratulated my divine employers
on their excellent timing.

Out of the trees came a runaway horse, complete
with maiden in distress. This is a circumstance that
arises often in romances and sometimes even in the true
tales I tell. The cure is well known—the hero leaps for
the bridle and hauls the brute to a halt. Maiden falls
swooning into hero's arms . . . hand in marriage and
half the kingdom follow in due course.

That's in the romances. In real life, of course, that
prescription is more likely to cause disaster than stop
the horse. The cheekstrap-grabbing maneuver is a great
deal easier to describe than execute. I have seen men
maimed trying it, and riders killed. The prudent course
is to yell at the stupid girl to hang on and let the beast
run itself to a standstill, which it will in a few minutes.
If she can keep her head out of the branches, she will
come to no great harm. Horses are *good* at running,
damn it! Left to itself, a horse will almost never put a
foot wrong.

Having said that, I confess that I jumped to my feet
and began to run like hell to intercept. Call it a reflex.

Out of the trees behind her came Zig, spurring his
mount like a maniac. I remembered that the gods rarely
call me to interfere in events, only to witness, and I
stopped where I was. Unfortunately, as the woman's
horse sensed Zig drawing level with it, it veered in my
direction.

Zig grabbed the distressed maiden from her saddle
and was overbalanced by the weight—even the most
experienced horseman rarely has occasion to practice
such a move. I leaped the wrong way and was struck by
rescuer and rescuee making an unplanned and hasty descent together. The three of us went down in a heap.
One of them, and perhaps both, slammed into my abdo-
men as the ground leaped up beneath me in a bone-
smashing impact.

Zig still had a foot in a stirrup.

Some of the gods' events are very hard to witness clearly. By the time the world had stopped spinning, there were bodies all over the place, including mine.

The girl had risen to her knees. Despite my jangled wits and her bedraggled condition, I registered that I was going to need all my collection of superlatives when I got around to making a story out of this. At that moment I had no breath and suspected I had lost most of my brains, also.

Just call her gorgeous for now.

Zig was also sitting up. Did I mention that he was tall and fair and had muscles in abundance? Broad shoulders, square jaw, et cetera, et cetera?

Verlian national dress is colorful and comfortable, but it does not take well to its wearers being dragged over the grass. The glade was littered with motley.

The two of them stared at each other.

"Are you all right, sir?" she said.

"Aha!" I thought. "A romance!" Then I threw up.

Such was my first sight of Lady Sweet-rose of Kraw. I did not know then who she was, nor the role she was to play in the affairs of Verlia.

Divine-providence of Nurb and his friends arrived on the scene a few minutes later, together with several loudly cursing young men on steaming horses, led by my old friend True-valor of Galmish. He was older, thicker, and pretty much bald when viewed from some angles, but the same imperious True-valor I had known. He was in charge of the lady's escort and spitting fire at having let such a thing happen.

Fortunately I was down at the water, being helped to clean up by some of my merchant friends. I was able to keep myself turned away from True-valor's gaze, and when he sent a trooper to inquire after me, I assured the kid that I had sustained no serious injury and had not been involved in the rescue.

Zig and Lady Sweet-rose had made themselves re-

spectable again, of course. Zig had a broken ankle.
Sweet-rose had a most incredible blush. They could not
take their eyes off each other.

True-valor soon saw them both mounted and borne
off to the palace for proper attention. Divine-providence
decided to pitch camp after all, and I curled up in my
bedroll to nurse my bruises. Next day we were on the
move again, but it was a week before I could stand
straight.

I knew that would not be the end of the affair, but
such things take time. While waiting on the next episode, I decided to visit Uthom in the Middle. During
my previous visit, the capital had been in mourning for
High-honor, so I had avoided it. This time I was resolved to drop in on the royal family.

My methods never fail: a few nights' entertaining in
one of the better hostelries to let my reputation spread,
invitations to perform in private houses, notice from the
nobility ... eventually a royal command.

There was little risk that anyone would remember my
performance at Still Waters. Few had seen me, and aristocrats in general are unwilling to make themselves
seem like greater fools than they already are. "By all
the gods, you look younger than ever, don't you?" No,
it was not likely. If challenged I could have claimed to
be my own son, I suppose, but I make a point of never
speaking anything but the strict truth.

Two months after the runaway horse and three weeks
after I arrived in the capital, I was summoned to court.

The palace was monumental. I have seen masonry
watchtowers smaller than the pillars in the great ball-
rooms. All the doorways were slits, all the staircases
cramped spirals, easy to defend. The contrast between
this fortress and the delicate beauty of Still Waters testified to the difference between the two brothers who

had founded the houses. All his life, Ven had been a fighter.

When I had last seen Just-blade, he had been a sleepy adolescent, stifling yawns. Quarter of a century later, he was a hunted wolf—moody, saturnine, and suspicious. Oh, his manners were impeccable. He behaved exactly as a king should, a gentleman, but a dangerous one. He did not froth and rage and sentence his friends to torture, yet he somehow conveyed the impression that one day he might. In appearance he was tall, lean, and clean-shaven, having driven beards out of fashion by his example. He was reputed to be as fit and active as a man ten years his junior, but he could not hide the darkness in his soul. Too many kings become obsessed with their place in history, and he must have known his reign would not be well remembered. The war was bleeding his people white and would not go away. Reaching for glory, he had grasped frustration.

His wife had died a couple of years before. He was expected to remarry soon, and the court was abuzz with speculation on his choice. His sister acted as his official hostess in the meantime. Princess Nightingale looked even more fragile than she had the first time I saw her—bitter and emaciated. Her marriage had been fruitless. Now her husband lived apart from her, reputedly wenching on his estates and siring progeny like a goat, as if to prove that her barrenness was not his fault. On her I sensed an even darker shadow, and she was to die within the year.

With these two at its head and war seething in the background, the court was a brittle, nerve-wracking carnival—gaiety on the surface and dark currents beneath. You are aware by now that even the most humble peasants in Verlia favor bright colors in their dress. The courtiers blazed like a shower of diamonds in sunlight, gems on black velvet.

At my first appearance in the great hall, I told the tale of the Winter War again, with emphasis on Ven, of course. It went quite well. I received a standing ovation, a sizable bag of gold, and my own quarters in the palace for an extended stay. Noble ladies flocked to invite me to their salons and soirees whenever the king might not have need of me.

I soon tire of aristocrats, for their life lacks reality, but there are times when I tire of poverty, also, and I had resolved to restore my credit rating. The court was depressingly artificial by day, inspiringly promiscuous by night. This was winter, after all, when featherbeds are softer than ditches. For a few days I flourished. All I lacked to amuse me was a source of good stories. From dawn to dusk, I heard nothing but vapid gossip. Then the crown prince returned to court and suddenly the gossip became vicious.

The first time I saw Star-seeker was at a formal ball, where the festive throng glittered brighter than the candles. Music rang back from the high rafters. Youths of all available sexes leaped and whirled in frenzied dance, displaying sprightly limbs through flutters of brilliant motley. I was leaning against one of the huge pillars, gasping for breath after a wild participation in these revelries, and at the same time grasping for metaphors that might do justice to the scene: swarm of dragonflies, school of tropical fish, madhouse of kingfishers? A pot of peacocks ... Bullfinches in a flower shop ...

The music grew even faster, the pace frenetic. More couples reeled to the sidelines, exhausted. Astonishingly, the king was in the midst of the mob, dancing as wildly as any. For a man nearing forty, he was doing most exceedingly well. I chuckled and waited to see how long he could keep it up.

Then I recognized his partner and my holiday had ended.

I turned to my companion—whose name, I am ashamed to confess, completely escapes me, and shouldn't, because ... well, never mind.

"His Majesty has found the second-loveliest lady in the hall, I see."

"Sweet-rose of Kraw," my companion murmured, sliding soft fingers into my motley to tickle my ribs. "Haven't you heard?"

"Heard what?" I retorted, responding in kind—we were reasonably well concealed behind a potted hydrangea.

"The king has made his choice. An announcement is expected momentarily."

Indeed? What about my friend Zig? What about that romance I had detected? I lost interest in ribs while I mulled the possibilities. The gods stage tragedies as well as romances.

The king reached the end of the royal stamina. He stopped abruptly, gasping. Instantly the music stopped, also, of course, and the rest of the dancers. Cheering and laughter and applause . . . The floor began to clear.

I watched as Just-blade offered Sweet-rose his arm and led her off—although I think he was leaning on her, more than she on him. I could not fault his judgment. To have ranked the beauties in that room exactly would have been an impossible task, but she would certainly have been in any man's top four or five. He was older than she, but not impossibly so. When the king of Verlia made his choice, how much choice did his choice have?

The orchestra struck up again. The floor began to fill.

"Ouch!" I said. My companion had just pinched me.

"Pay attention!" she said dangerously.

"I am! I am!" I hauled her away to dance before I got raped in the hydrangea.

But I danced her over toward the royal dais, where Just-blade and his fiancée presumptive were sipping wine. Near them sat Princess Nightingale, looking distinctly unwell. The normally somber monarch was actually smiling. Sweet-rose laughed at something he said.

I could tell nothing at all from her manner. Poised. Gorgeous.

"She must be old Fire-hawk's daughter?" I murmured in my partner's ear—the dance being one of those clingy, swoopy affairs.

"Another word about her," she whispered sweetly, "and I shall scratch your eyes out."

Then . . .

Right across the center of the floor, pushing through the dancers like a badger in tall grass, came a troop of eight or nine young men, marching in unison, all dressed in black. Gaiety collapsed behind them like a startled soufflé.

The sizable but overweight youngster at their head could only be Star-seeker, the crown prince. If his father was a hungry wolf, then he was a starving bear. He had the sort of knothole eyes I can never trust. I thought his face already showed signs of dissolution, but perhaps I had let myself be overly prejudiced by gossip. Even by court standards, his reputation for debauchery was extreme.

The others were his personal cronies. I had heard tell of them, also. Some had even worse reputations than he did—lechers, drunkards, duelists, and plain thugs. They invariably dressed in black. I have nothing against youthful rebellion if it has some moral purpose behind it. Star-seeker's did not, as far as I had been able to discover. He was not antiwar or pro-war, anti or pro anything. He was pro-self and nothing else.

The prince bowed perfunctorily to the king, lifted Sweet-rose's hand as if to kiss her fingers, hauled her from her chair into his arms. Before anyone could speak a word, he whirled her away into the dance. Her crystal goblet shattered on the floor. Nightingale smothered a scream. The king leaped to his feet, his face inflamed with fury. He was too late. They were gone and in any case the prince's henchmen stood across his path—the whole thing had been carefully planned. I

have seldom seen an act so outrageous executed with
greater panache.

The black-garbed men bowed and then dispersed to
steal dance partners of their own. I trod on my companion's feet and stammered an apology.

Needless to say, the court was agog from that moment on. Personally, I would not have been surprised
had Just-blade announced his engagement that very
night without even obtaining the lady's consent. I have
known kings who would have done so, but he did not.
The scandal festered for several days. The king was
fourteen years older than the lady, the prince five years
younger. Which one would she choose? When I asked
why she should necessarily choose either, I received
blank stares for answers.

Rumors bloomed in many hues. The nastier matrons
whispered that the minx was deliberately setting father
against son. From what I had heard of Star-seeker, he
was quite capable of having started the whole affair on
his own, with no encouragement from anyone. Others,
though, suggested that he had been first in the field and
the king was the intruder. The girl's mother was behind
it. Or she had been summoned to court to talk sense
into her daughter, if you preferred that version. The
king had threatened to disinherit the prince. The prince
had threatened a revolution, a theory not too far-
fetched, considering the state of the country.

Next to Sweet-rose herself, the favorite topic for
speculation was the royal god. Any other Verlian family
would certainly seek divine guidance on such a matter
and accept the god's verdict. Royalty was a little different. Ven and all his descendants had been very careful
to distinguish between the household god, Verl, and the
state god, Hool. Hool was mighty and remote; he determined the succession but otherwise never interfered. He
was an exception. Ever since the Hannail disaster, the

people of Verlia had held to a strange belief that gods must not be allowed to meddle in politics.

Which god had jurisdiction here? Did Verl support son or father as future husband of Sweet-rose? Or did Verl have other plans altogether? No one could know the answers except the royal family, and they were certainly not discussing the matter in public.

I dearly wanted a chat with the lady. I was unable to arrange one, for she vanished from view. Her situation was intolerable, yet I was not seriously worried about her, having seen her dragged from a galloping horse to fall bodily on a trader of tales. Any woman who can survive that and then come up asking her rescuer if he is unharmed must be tough as saddle leather. I itched with impatience to find out what was going on behind the scenes, and I was mightily curious to know what had happened to Zig, but I remained confident that I would find out eventually.

I did, of course—even sooner than I expected.

A pall settled over the palace. The king canceled all scheduled balls and banquets and entertainments until further notice. My services as royal storyteller were therefore not in demand, so I was at once showered with invitations to regale the nobility in their own houses. This was winter, remember, and the nights were long. I obliged.

I returned to the palace not long before dawn, and I confess that I was not at my best. I had overindulged in rich food, strong wine, and the attentions of a maiden— well, young lady—by the name of Glorious-virtue of Gnash. She was of very good family, and the most incredible contortionist I have ever met outside a circus. My old friend Galda the Human Python could have learned things from her. Without using her hands she could . . . But I digress. Note that I was very weary and leave it at that.

The palace was in an uproar. Guards were running in

all directions. Normally I should have made it my business to inquire as to the cause of this turmoil, but the steady hammering in my head deterred me. I did notice that I was allowed in without trouble, and that seemed odd. A palace's first reaction to emergency is normally to bar the doors to intruders, yet the watch let me enter without a glance. I climbed wearily up the stairs and staggered along to my door.

I arrived just in time to stop a band of armed men from breaking it down. "What seems to be the trouble?" I inquired in a hoarse whisper.

"Open in the name of the king!" the officer in charge bellowed.

Perhaps he did not bellow, but it felt as if he did.

Being in no mood to argue with such lungs, I fumbled in my motley for my key. I unlocked the door and was thrust aside while the men rushed in. There was nothing there to alarm them. I knew that. I waited until they finished ransacking the place and came stamping out again. Without a word of apology or explanation, they trooped off to the next room.

Morning would be time enough to find out what was going on. Thinking fond thoughts of bed, I tottered inside and locked the door behind me. The lamps were burning bright.

Sweet-rose was sitting on my favorite chair.

I reeled back against the wall and closed my eyes until my insides came to a quivering halt. When I dared another look, she was still there.

"Master Homer?" She spoke softly. She was utterly composed, a vision of female perfection draped in lengths of, I suppose, silk. The colors were dark and rich, deep blues and greens. They clung endearingly to her curves, but it was what they did not cover that took my breath away. The cleavage, the glimpse of flank and thigh! And in my bedroom! The damage Glorious-virtue had done to me was cured instantly. I straightened up, ran a hand through my hair, straightened my motley . . .

Sweet-rose returned my smile uncertainly. It may not have been one of my more reassuring smiles. I registered that her hair was auburn and she had very dark blue eyes. The eyes told me, had I not known already, that this was no simpleton maid to be diverted with a few silver words.

I managed a careful bow. "My lady, your presence does me honor."

"It also puts you in much danger, I'm afraid. Won't you sit down?"

I wavered over to the other chair. She frowned slightly at the unsteadiness of my movements. I eased myself onto the seat and leered at her like an idiot.

Her frown deepened. "We have met before, I believe. I offer my belated thanks to you for your gallantry on that occasion."

"My pleasure entirely, ma'am."

A hint of a smile played over her lips. Oh, those lips!

"Was it? I am afraid I hardly noticed you. I was rather shaken. I should have taken more notice of you at the time and been properly grateful. I only learned of your part in the affair afterward."

"How is Zig?"

Back came the frown. "His ankle should be about healed by now."

I waited. She changed the subject.

"I have come to ask for your assistance again, I fear."

She could walk over me with spiked boots if she wanted. Alas! My cause was hopeless. There were at least three ahead of me in line. That did not matter.

"Name it, ma'am."

"You may have heard—or guessed. I have disappeared. The guard is searching the palace for me."

Six of the guard had just looked for her in this room. It held no hiding places. Secret passages could be ruled out, for the walls and floor were solid granite. I made a desperate effort to gather my wits, although they felt as if they had been scattered by a hurricane.

"You made a noise like a dust bunny and they overlooked you?"

She shook her long hair back over a shoulder. What hair! And what a shoulder . . . "I had protection."

Ah! The fog was lifting. "And how may I serve you?"

"Find a horse for me and bring it to the water gate. I shall swim the river." She studied me, trying to hide her doubts. "You have already proved your courage and gallantry, Master Omar. You tried . . . I mean you rescued me once before. I was told you were a man to take pity on a maiden in distress. Will you do this for me?"

I noticed that a carafe of water stood on the bedside table. I heaved myself upright and headed more or less in its direction.

"For you I will do anything within my powers, my lady. You catch me at a bad moment. Give me a little time to pull myself together. Anything you tell me will of course be in strict confidence. What of my friend Zig?"

I took a drink, not looking at her. A long pause suggested that she might have doubts about trusting an obvious drunk.

"Zig enrolled in our household guard."

"I am sure he is an excellent recruit."

She chuckled and I turned in surprise to see.

"Mother had him posted to Zardon the very same day. Until his ankle completely heals, she says." The dark blue eyes twinkled, but not entirely convincingly.

"Where is Zardon?"

"About as far from Still Waters as you can go in Verlia. Not quite, perhaps, but the farthest estate my family owns. On the western coast."

"And where do you head tonight, ma'am?"

She bit her lip.

Having slaked my thirst and feeling a little better already, I wandered back to my chair. "I can guess, and the rack will not drag it out of me. But why do you need my help at all? You have demonstrated powers of invisibility. Will they not serve you in the stables, also?"

"Probably, but my protection will weaken rapidly beyond the palace itself."

Of course. Verl was only the household god.

"Then I shall be happy to aid you."

Sweet-rose smiled—summer dawn, a chorus of bird-song. "She said you would. I shall be very grateful. So will she, I am sure."

"Your smile is all the reward I ever need—but I confess I am a very inquisitive man."

"Verl warned me about that! But she said I could tell you, for you would be discreet."

"Quiet as the grave!"

Might that be too apt a simile under the circumstances?

She adjusted the fall of her motley, partly blocking the view of her thigh that I was enjoying so much. "The king wants to marry me. The crown prince, also, wants to marry me. The prince would settle for less, although not much less, and certainly more than either his father or I will agree to. Do I make myself plain?"

"I have never met a woman less plain."

She nodded pertly. "Thank you, kind sir!"

"And the man you love?"

"Zig, of course." She pulled a puzzled frown. "I don't know how you knew that. No one else does. Mother believes she got us apart in time. Gods, we'd had two weeks! I never believed in love at first sight before."

I chuckled. "Of course not!"

"Romantic nonsense!"

"Utter rubbish! How long did it take?"

"At least half a second. Just long enough to sit up. I

didn't get a proper look at him before he pulled me off the horse."

"I saw Zig's face. He didn't argue, did he? You know, I've never tried that strong-arm style of wooing. It seems to work faster than my usual technique. We must discuss it on the journey."

"There is no need for you to come! There will be danger, for the king has already ordered a search of the city and—"

"All the king's horses will not stop me from coming, my lady. I will escort you to the man you love or die trying." My tongue does run away with me sometimes.

She hid her eyes under the most perfect lashes I have ever seen. "Thank you. You will make dangerous enemies, you know."

"Which is why Verl chose a foreigner. What does she say to the royal dispute over you?"

"She forbids either match. She is adamant! But I think both of them are past listening to her."

"They are fools, then." Men *can* be driven mad by beauty. I didn't say so.

I was not needed within the palace. Only beyond the water gate might I make a useful contribution. I knew that. Verl knew that. Sweet-rose had known that. They had left the choice up to me. Not that there could be any doubt about my decision. I knew that. Verl knew . . . Oh, never mind.

Being effectively invisible is a very eerie experience. The guards had combed the palace from cellar to battlements without catching one glimpse of their quarry. They went back to the beginning to try again. The king was threatening to have every man jack of them flogged. I knew that because they said so. On the cramped spiral stairs, in the narrow passages, they passed so close to us that we could see the stubble on their chins and the sweat on their brows. They stepped aside to let Sweet-rose pass, as they would for any lady, and yet they never looked at her face or asked her name.

The stables were even stranger. Guards stood around debating where the woman could be hiding. Stablehands played dice. None of them showed any interest as we chose the strongest-seeming mounts we could find and saddled them. One trooper actually opened the door for us as we left, all the while arguing with a companion as to how the fugitive could have escaped.

Similarly, as no one went boating in winter, there was no need to guard the water gate, was there?

I had thought that the weak point in the plan would be persuading the horses that it was a fine night for a swim. Perhaps Verl helped us there, too, but Sweet-rose was a superlatively good rider and may have managed it by herself. My mount followed easily enough. Ugh! It was a very sobering experience.

Moments later we were thundering along the northern highway by the light of a setting moon. Zardon lay four long days' ride away.

Now was when I began to be of some help. Not with any he-man tactics, though—I had not even bothered to find a sword. When you are up against an entire kingdom, one blade is small use. My wits were no faster than my companion's and she was at least my equal in horsemanship. What she lacked was experience on the road. Sweet-rose had no grasp of the value of money, of how to bargain for bed and board without arousing suspicion, of traveling at all without a sizable armed escort. I doubt that she could have made it without my help, and she would have certainly left a trail of puzzled witnesses behind her.

As it was, we arrived at Zardon unchallenged. Traveling in winter is a rough business, grinding down both mind and body. There was no frost, but we met wind and rain aplenty, and mud everlasting, mud that even seemed to settle in the cracks between my teeth. Constant riding, short days, and the unending bleakness of

the countryside are a depressing diet. Sweet-rose withstood it every bit as well as I did, or better. She had her
love for Zig to inspire her.

I was wondering what we were going to do when we
found him, but I brooded on that in silence. I feared the
gods were planning a tragedy.

The whole of the last day we were never far from a
rampart of cliffs, at whose toes the sea frothed and
surged. That area south of Kylam is almost deserted.
Some of the bays hold small fishing villages, but the
cottages are far apart. We escaped detection, sliding by
like ghosts in a soaking gray murk of fog that shrouded
the coast.

As darkness began to fall, we stopped to rest our
mounts and eat a scanty meal. The bread was so stale
that I thought I was making more noise munching at it
than the horses were in the coarse grass. I felt chilled,
weary, and thoroughly depressed.

"We must find shelter soon, lady," I said glumly.
"We shall not see our hands on the reins tonight."

"We are almost there."

I wondered how she could possibly know that. All I
could make out was grass, and little of that. Even the
horses were barely visible, a few paces away.

She must have heard my doubt. "That last stream
was Pil Brook. Many a trout I have caught in that. We
are on my brother's land now."

"Tell me about the castle, then."

"It is not much of one. A blockhouse on a headland.
It was built as a watchtower against pirates. My grandfather turned it into a hunting lodge."

I felt a little better. "How large a garrison?"

"None, in these times. Fighting men are scarce. I
think there will only be Zig and one or two jailers."

Then perhaps there was hope. A man with a broken
ankle is fairly easy to imprison. Put him on a horse, and
Zig would be as mobile as either of us. Would there be
horses there, though? I wished we had thought to ac-

quire a spare, but there seemed small chance of that now.

"Trust in the gods," I muttered, and choked down another mouthful.

Before we reached the castle, we were forced to dismount and follow the track on foot. It wound steadily upward through scanty clumps of trees, emerging eventually on a grassy, stony upland. We spoke only in whispers, but we were not likely to be heard in so much mud, or over the growing rumble of surf. I sensed it with my feet as much as my ears. We were a long way above it. If there were guards posted outside on such a night, then the lodge must be so well garrisoned that our cause was hopeless.

Castle Zardon emerged before us as a square patch of slightly more solid darkness. It was a doll's castle, a box less than ten paces across, no more than two stories high. The track ran right up to an arched doorway, and the gate stood open. I stopped worrying about a garrison and began to wonder what we should do if the place was deserted.

I didn't even know what we were going to do if it wasn't. I had not asked, because I did not wish to hear. Who was I to impede the progress of true love?

I suspected, though, that my strong-willed associate had notions of rushing Zig into matrimony to present her family and her royal suitors with a fait accompli. Then what? Perhaps Sweet-rose was so inexperienced in the ways of royalty that she could not foresee the consequences. I could, only too well. Court gossip listed several persons who had met with violence after annoying the crown prince. The king was certainly capable of throwing Sweet-rose into jail for the rest of her life. What he would do to Zig and myself did not bear contemplation.

Meanwhile, we had tethered the horses to a rail, and

Sweet-rose was heading for the doorway. I caught her arm. "Let's walk all around and look for lights first."

"Try that and you'll make the highest dive on record."

"Oh. Well, explain the floor plan, please."

"Stables, kitchen, guard room on this level. Hall and two bedchambers above. Come on."

We crept through the arch, into total darkness. Sweet-rose took my cold hand with surprisingly warm fingers and found her own way by touch. If there were horses nearby, they were the quietest, most odor-free I had ever encountered. I could smell the sea, mostly, but also traces of woodsmoke. We reached steps and began to climb. Fortunately the stairway was of stone and did not creak. We moved in total silence, broken only by the low growl of the surf and the mad thundering of my heart, which must have been audible in Uthom.

Then we turned a corner and there was light ahead, spilling out from under a door. We sank down on the steps and peered through the slit.

I saw furniture legs and four boots. A fire crackled. Dice clattered on a table. I heard a male voice rumble in disgust.

"Good!" Sweet-rose whispered. "It's True-valor!"

Before I could say a word, she jumped up and opened the door.

I slithered back down the stairs on my hands and knees until I was below the light. I heard cries of astonishment and the sound of two stools falling over. I recognized Zig's voice demanding to know what in the name of all the gods . . . and much the same from another voice I remembered, its arrogance undiminished by the passage of time—True-valor, my long-ago escort, who had whisked me from Myto to Still Waters to entertain the court. Not a dozen people in Verlia could be counted on to remember me from then, but he was one of them.

"I have come to take Zig away," Sweet-rose said.

"You bring your brother's warrant, my lady?"

So he was going to argue, which is what I should have expected of him. I did not trust Sweet-rose's ability to charm that one into disobeying orders, although perhaps she expected that she could. I decided to intervene before the surprise dissipated.

I strode up the stairs and stepped into view at her side. I tried to display my most sinister, cryptic smile, but the effect was probably ruined by the way I had to screw up my eyes against the light of the candles.

The hall did not deserve the name. It was a poky little room, but cozy enough under the circumstances, with a cheerful fire and too many chairs and stools. The walls were lined with bows and fishing rods laid on pegs. Two doors led off it. They remained closed; no reinforcements came bursting out to investigate the newcomers.

Zig was on his feet. He had not moved forward, because there was a chain around his ankle. True-valor was closer, barring Sweet-rose's approach.

"Omar!" Zig shouted.

True-valor made a choking noise, gaping at me.

I told you that Zig was a man after my own heart. The hallmark of an experienced adventurer is that he recognizes opportunity when it presents itself. He snatched the flagon from the table and slammed it down on True-valor's head. The flagon shattered into a shower of wine and potsherds. The big man's knees folded and he hit the floor with a crash that shook the castle.

Sweet-rose rushed into her lover's arms. He was a man after her heart, also.

Ignored, then, I made myself useful. I trussed True-valor's ankles and wrists with portions of his own motley. He was sleeping soundly, but it never hurts to make sure. In the process, I found the key to Zig's fetter, so I unlocked that. I removed True-valor's sword and laid it on the table where Zig could find it when he returned to the real world. I appropriated True-valor's dagger for myself, in the belief that one day it might be useful. It had a lovely hilt of carved amber. Then I selected the most comfortable chair and sat down to appreciate the romance.

Eventually my friends were able to free their mouths for talking.

"Beloved!"

"My true heart!"

And so on. It was ever so sweet.

Meanwhile the entire kingdom was hunting us and the passes were closed for the winter. Who would risk the royal wrath by offering shelter to three fugitives? Where did we go from here?

"Oh, my darling, darling Zig!"

"My sweet, sweet Sweet-rose!"

I can't guess how long they might have gone on like that. They were interrupted by the crown prince and another man. The two of them came stalking into the room together, looking angry and travel-weary. Their black cloaks were spattered gray with mud. Both were armed and dangerous. Being neither, I stayed where I was to watch.

The newcomers glanced around, registering me with gratifying surprise. I raised a languid hand in greeting. I knew the other man, Great-merit of Orgaz. He was the most feared duelist in the court and Star-seeker's closest crony.

Zig and Sweet-rose had sprung apart to face this threat.

The prince wasted no time on pleasantries. "It's time for bed, darling. Who is the peasant?"

"He is my betrothed."

"No, dear. The king is your betrothed. Tonight you sleep with me and tomorrow you go home to Daddy. Everybody's happy, then, if you keep your mouth shut. If you don't, it's your problem. Send the peon away now and no harm will come to him. Show him the door, Merit."

Zig lifted the sword I had left on the table and checked that it moved easily in the scabbard.

The prince sighed. "All right, kill him."

The two men drew simultaneously. Great-merit flashed a contemptuous stroke that he probably expected to cut Zig's throat from ear to ear. It was parried, and he leaped back from a lightning riposte. No peon, sir!

There was far too much furniture around—not to mention True-valor, who had begun to writhe underfoot—for any classic, or even classy, fencing. Whether more space would have made any difference to the outcome, I cannot say. Zig still had a bad limp, which would have been a handicap in courtly swordplay. In the sort of slash-and-bash barroom brawling that was needed, though, footwork was less important and the adventurer outclassed the aristocrat. Swords rang and clattered. Great-merit screamed once and doubled over on the table, scattering dice, goblets, and half the candlesticks. Then he slid back off it like a cloth, crumpling into a heap on the floor. He made some disgusting gurgling noises and could be presumed dead or dying. I crossed my legs and stayed where I was, aware that we were now playing for even larger stakes than before.

Star-seeker was visibly shaken to see his champion so easily dispatched, but he quickly cloaked his alarm in arrogance. "Oh, that was very foolish! Whoever you are, yokel, you have just slain a distinguished member of the aristocracy. Do you know me? Tell him who I am, darling."

"Believe it or not, this is our crown prince."

"To me he's only a witness. Keep out of the way." Zig seemed to have grown. He certainly dominated the room now, blood-streaked sword in hand, the woman he loved at his back, a dead foe at his feet. His pale hair blazed in the candlelight, his blue eyes held no doubts or fear, and he smiled as if he was enjoying himself hugely. I know a hero when I see one.

Star-seeker evidently did not. To my surprise, he held his ground, although there was an open door behind him and probably a gang of thugs waiting downstairs. He had no reputation around court as a fighter. The gossips said he was a pitiful coward when he did not have his bullyboys handy. But now he reached for the hilt of his sword.

"Not only am I crown prince, I am also on a mission of divine retribution! Drop that sword or die, hayseed!"

"Run away while you can, Prince!" Zig lurched forward, stepping around Great-merit's corpse.

Star-seeker noted the limp and pulled out his sword with a chuckle. The move was so awkward that I was certain Zig could have cut him down before he even came to guard. I was surprised he did not. I shot a worried glance at Sweet-rose, hoping that our mutual friend was not going to display any romantic scruples over shedding royal blood. If he expected to give the prince a lesson in tavern swordsmanship, let him off with a minor scar as a diploma, shake hands, and all gallant lads together, the next round's on me . . .

Clang!

Clang! Clang! Clang! Clang-clang-clang . . .

I relaxed. Obviously Zig had refrained from striking an unarmed man, that was all. From the first lunge, it was a match to the death on both sides. Even had Zig wanted it otherwise, he could not play-fight against a man trying to slay him. And why should he, anyway? He had not started the slaughter.

Besides, he was a human being, not a corn mill that will stop when you release the handle. He was fired up with fighting spirit from the first bout. Not one man in a thousand could have stopped there.

The prince had the better of the first exchange. Zig recovered a step. I think he had expected more fancy-dancy courtier fencing and was suspicious of Star-seeker's amateur wood chopping. Zig quickly summed him up, though, and then went for the kill.

He was badly hampered by his game ankle, but he drove Star-seeker away from the door, backed him against a stool in a flurry of steel, and, as he toppled over it, ran him through.

The prince collapsed, screaming horribly. Sweet-rose cried out, moved forward, and then backed away from the shower of gore.

I came at him from the other side—wondering what Verlians regarded as a fitting penalty for high treason. The young lout wasn't dead, but he was as good as. I knelt and pulled him over on his back. Brilliant red blood was pumping out of his belly in a fountain. His eyes were wide with astonishment—none of us ever really expect death.

He gasped one word: "Betrayed!"

I watched as he bled to death. It only took a few seconds.

He was as dead as any corpse I have ever seen. The bleeding stopped, his bowels loosed. I am not mistaken in this. Star-seeker died that night.

I looked up from my knees. The lovers were back in each other's arms again.

"Leave that for later!" I said sharply. "We've just killed the heir apparent. What do we do now?"

Sweet-rose looked up into Zig's eyes. "We leave," she said.

"Exile? Beloved, I am a penniless wanderer!"

"I have no choice, darling! Take me. We shall wander together."

"That's all very well!" I protested before they could start another tongue-wrestling contest. "How do we get out of the country?"

"You're a sailor, aren't you, darling?" Sweet-rose said. "You told me. There are fishermen down in the bay. I have gold. We'll buy a boat."

Zig raised flaxen eyebrows. "An open boat in this weather?"

"If you can, I can, dear. I'll bail."

I shivered at the prospect, but it made sense. "I can handle a sail," I growled. "What do we do with True-valor?"

"You take me with you," True-valor mumbled. "Otherwise I'll be racked and then beheaded."

Zig grinned and poked him with a boot. "You mean that, prisoner?"

"I swear. I heard. You can trust me."

"Not at dice, I don't! Your chances will be better if you stay behind, you know."

"I don't think they will be," I said. "We're going to have divine protection."

I showed them what I had found wrapped in a kerchief, tucked inside in the prince's motley—a small white clay dove. It was not very lifelike or beautiful, just a pottery image of a bird. One eye was a small black stone and the other an empty hole. Its legs and feet were fashioned of twisted wire and it had lost a couple of toes.

That was why the prince had displayed unexpected courage.

That was why he had died saying, "Betrayed!"

In silence, I passed the god to Sweet-rose.

I wiped the royal blood from my hands. I cut True-valor free with his own dagger and returned it to him.

Then I crept downstairs to discover how many men the prince had brought with him. I expected a small army. I found two more horses, tethered to the rail.

That's the true story, my lords and ladies. Sweet-rose eloped, but not with the prince. He died. That I am sure of. Verl the god left the land named after her, and perhaps that does explain why Just-blade never sired another heir.

We rode down to the nearest fisherman's cottage and traded him four horses for a half-rotted hulk of a dory and a few supplies. The boat looked as if it would blow apart in the first breath of wind. Even a surly peasant glower could not quite conceal its former owner's rapture at the exchange, but Sweet-rose gave him coins, as well. Let him enjoy his dream! He would not keep the mounts long when the king's men came around, as soon they must.

The voyage was unpleasant, but not as bad as it might have been. Zig was a competent sailor and there are few rigs I have not handled in my time. Hull and mast and sail all failed us at one time or another, but we improvised and survived. Sweet-rose was a trooper. Trooper True-valor was seasick the whole time.

When we reached Algazan, I was called away to witness a revolution. We split up. I never saw any of them again. Last spring I heard how the oracle had proclaimed a child of Sweet-rose, beyond the Grimm Ranges. Like many others, I came here to find him, or her. I failed.

I can't tell you any more than that.

22: The Fifth Judgment

※

Fritz had done us proud with candles. The taproom was bright for the first time since I arrived, the flames sparkling back from the weapons hung on the chimney, the dusty bric-a-brac on the shelf, even the sad painted clay eyes in the mounted deer heads, every one followed by a shadowy herd of antlers on the stonework. The wind outside wailed louder than ever, moaning under the eaves, sucking in the chimney. Halfway through my narrative, the door had begun rattling like a palsied castanet.

Alas, the only happy face I could see in the midst of all the brightness was Frieda's. She was gazing intently down at her hands, not at me, but dimples had appeared in her cheeks; she was certainly pleased about something. Her brother's vexation had increased in proportion. I could not guess what was annoying Fritz, but I would applaud it heartily, whatever it was.

As for the rest of my audience ... The dowager had apparently gone to sleep. I hoped she was merely brooding, because I was banking heavily on her support.

Rosie had her eyes open, but they did not seem to be seeing anything. The porcelain dove and its wrapping still lay on her lap.

Gwill was barely conscious, probably aware of little more than his own misery. I could hear phlegm rattling in his chest.

Apart from those, the candles revealed only unfriendly glares: the merchant, the actress, the notary, the soldier. Four out of seven—a majority.

"Claptrap!" the merchant grumbled, folding his arms across the dome of his belly. "You might at least have invented a yarn with some plausibility. That one has more holes in it than a laundry-wife's basket. You must think us all simpletons." He coughed harshly. "What's wrong with your chimney, landlord?"

Fritz's fists were clenched into mallets. "The wind has changed, your honor. The chimney smokes sometimes when the wind is from the south." He shot me a glance of hatred.

His sister shot me a wink. "It is good news, sir. Listen!" We listened. Somewhere something was dripping. "The weather here is extremely changeable, but in winter when the south wind blows, it is usually a warm, thawing wind. Our door always rattles then. I won't let Fritz mend it, because I like the sound. It is a promise that spring will return some day, cheerful tidings."

"The road will be clear?"

"The way back down to Gilderburg, certainly," Fritz agreed glumly. "The pass ... possibly. But it is not dawn yet. The north wind may return."

He hoped it would. Even if he turned me out without my boots and cloak, I had a chance now. I should be in the company of other travelers, who might lend me garments for the road. Snow can turn to slush, and then mud, very fast. I smiled blissfully back at him and shook my head to let him know I rested my hopes on more than the temperature. I had no intention of letting the overgrown lout manhandle me or maltreat me any more than he had already.

Meanwhile ...

Meanwhile I regarded the merchant. "Some aspect of my tale distresses you, sir? I swear to the truth of every word."

"You add perjury to your crimes! Counsellor, how would you question such a witness?"

The notary sniggered. "With pleasure, Your Honor!"

"You demolish his fable for us, then, and we shall let our landlord demolish the rest of him." The fat oaf guffawed at his own wit. The actress shrilled agreement. Fritz bared his teeth with joy.

"Very well." The notary turned his ferrety face to mine. "Let us consider the mortals first, Master Omar. What happened to the bodies of the crown prince and his friend?"

I eased back from his rank breath. "I have no idea. We left them lying where they were."

"And yet for twenty years the prince's death has never been reported? Does not that seem a little strange?"

"Perhaps it does, now that you mention it. He should have been found by now."

"And you traded four royal horses for a boat? Why did the king's investigators not find those horses in the area and learn of the fugitives who sailed away?"

"I presume the fisherman was careful not to incriminate himself."

"Would the disappearance of an heir apparent be investigated so perfunctorily?"

"I am not experienced in assassinations, Counsellor. King Just-blade may have been relieved to be rid of such a son." I was enjoying myself. My low opinion of the grubby notary was not being raised by his inept cross-examination.

"Even if he is profoundly grateful for the results, a king does not ignore high treason. Would Just-blade not have ransacked the whole area, using interrogation and torture to establish the facts?"

"You are asking me to draw conclusions. I am a witness, not a theorist."

He pulled a face. "Your description of the god's image does not match the dove that was produced for us tonight."

"I stand by my testimony."

"Indeed? But how can the idol you saw have been the royal god? The prince had brought Verl with him. That makes sense, for it explains how he managed to track you down. But then she let him be killed?"

"I told you. He seemed as surprised by that as you are. Again, I will not speculate—especially about the minds of gods."

"Then you stole the god! You gave him to the woman. How is it possible to steal a family god away from his family?"

"Same answer."

"Bah!" roared the merchant, interrupting this farce. "The whole tale is gibberish. You said that the god told Sweet-rose how to escape from the palace. These family gods of Verlia speak only to members of their families! Is that not the case? Is that not what we have been told many times tonight?"

"It is conventional belief," I said with a shrug. "I merely reported the facts because I was asked to."

We all stole a glance at the dowager, but she had her head down, with her floppy hat hiding her face. She still seemed to be asleep, but I suspected that she was listening. I hoped she was. I was about to need her.

"Not facts!" The big man snorted. "Lies! Lies from start to finish. We have not even mentioned the largest objection of all. If Sweet-rose eloped with a foreigner and not the crown prince, then why has Hool proclaimed her child to be the rightful heir to the throne?"

"I told you," I said. "I do not theorize upon the minds of gods."

"Rubbish! Stable scrapings! Captain Tiger, do you not agree?"

The soldier studied me with eyes like flint. "I find the tale hard to credit, yes. The entire realm has believed for twenty years that Prince Star-seeker eloped with the woman he loved because his father the king planned to marry her against her will. To be told that he

was murdered instead—and the body left lying where it
fell . . . this strains belief."

"Throw the perjurer out! Innkeeper, take him!"

Fritz began to rise.

"Let him be," the dowager croaked, stirring.

"You believe him?" Tiger shouted. Rosie jumped and
looked around nervously.

"Master Omar has told only two lies tonight."

"Two?" I exclaimed over the incredulous murmurs.
"Perhaps one tiny fib. White lies like that do not count,
my lady. They are merely a social grace."

"Two." She peered at me along the row. Her smile
was an unexpected grimace of wrinkles and gums. Her
eyes shone like pearl in the candlelight. "You named
me the greatest beauty in the room."

"That was simple truth."

"It was an outrageous exaggeration, even in those
days. But I am grateful." She chuckled.

"It was true. And the other matter was a trivial gallantry."

The others exchanged puzzled glances. Fritz uttered
an animal growl, as if reaching the end of his self-
control.

"No, it was germane to the matter." The crone's
voice was a crunching of dry leaves. "In gratitude for
that falsehood, I will now rescue you, Master Omar!"

"I shall be in your debt, ma'am."

She nodded, painfully easing herself upright in her
chair. "I do not see faces as well as I once did, but
when I first heard your voice tonight . . . It brought
back memories. Ah, how it brought back memories!
These others may doubt. They squirm and scuttle to
avoid unpalatable truths, but I accept, Master Omar, although I may not understand. Very well, listen, all of
you. I am Rose-dawn of Kraw, and I was the sinner
who caused all the trouble. Long ago, it was . . . yet still
I pay."

23: The Dowager's Tale

What do you know of gods, who were not born in Verlia?

You hanker after great gods, remote gods. You go to grand temples and pray there in your hundreds, each one believing that his own voice will be heard amid so many. You credit your gods with worldwide powers and do not see that you have shackled them with worldwide responsibilities. You expect your prayers to be heard and your sins overlooked. You pray to gods of battle for victory without thinking that your enemies invoke them, also. You deafen your gods with conflicting entreaties and wonder why they fail you.

But we? We are satisfied with little gods, our own family gods. We know that their powers are small, but because we ask little of them, they can help us. Because we, their children, are few, they hear us and help us and keep us true. All my days I have knelt before the same one god, giving him all my love and obedience, safe in the knowledge that I have his love and care always.

Alas that I did not heed his warnings! But that was my folly, not his.

Let me tell you how it is. We honor our gods in our own homes daily, making offerings, praising, worshipping. We live with our gods, and they with us. We ask their advice and seek their blessings on all our undertakings. In Verlia we know more of gods than any of you can ever know. We are brought up with our gods, and by our gods.

Four times in our lives we make special bondings to our gods, four special sacraments. When a child is born, the parents take it to their god in the presence of all the adults of the family, and the god accepts it and names it. "He is mine!" the god will say, or "She is mine!" Verlian men do not worry about their wives' fidelity.

Children grown to adulthood are brought again before the god. They make certain promises and again the god accepts them, speaking to them directly and in their presence for the first time. "You are mine!" Few indeed are those who do not weep when they first hear the voice of their god.

The third sacrament is marriage, when a young man brings his bride, or a young woman her groom, to live in the ancestral home. The god accepts the newcomer, and ever after she or he belongs to that god, also.

And at the end, when the play is done, when we lie a-dying, then our god is brought to us. We Verlians die in the presence of our gods, knowing that thereafter we shall never be parted.

Verlians trust their gods. We trust them especially to ensure we have descendants—to worship them and to remember us.

I am Rose-dawn of Kraw. Even before I was wed, I was Rose-dawn of Kraw. My father was Leaping-spirit of Kraw, a younger son of Kraw's children of Fairglen, a minor branch of the great clan. In truth my father was only a farmer for his uncle, despite the greatness of his god.

When I was twenty, I was deemed a beauty, but what woman of twenty is not? Vanity is a betrayer.

When I was twenty I attracted the notice of Fire-hawk of Kraw, the eldest son of Eagle-soar of Kraw, patriarch of our whole clan. I did not think much of Fire-hawk, even then, but I knew he would inherit Still Waters. His wife would be mistress of the fairest palace in Verlia. The prospect turned my head until I was giddy.

Fire-hawk in due course proposed that our fathers arrange for us to be wed. As I was of noble birth, he found me worthy; as I was of humble station, he expected me to be malleable. Anything else he felt was lust. I already had my heart set on a young man. He was named Honest-labor of Swet, and that sums him up very well. I asked my mother's advice, although I did not expect to heed it. She told me to consult the god, so I did.

I went to the chapel and knelt before the tooth of the dragon. I offered a fine swath of silk I had woven, showing autumn vineyards on the hills. I explained my problem.

"What do you see in Honest-labor?" the god asked.

One does not lie to one's god. "His body," I admitted.

"And what in Fire-hawk?"

"His house."

The dragon sighed. "The body will decay. He will grow fat and bald, and he is so lusty that I will be hard put to limit you to half a dozen sons, each as bovine as his father. Honest-labor is the better man. Fire-hawk is jealous and domineering. His house will endure, but your delight in it will fade with familiarity. Yet what you really seek there is power and respect, and the joy you find in those will grow greater as your own beauty fades. You must choose the sort of happiness you wish."

I chose Fire-hawk. That was the first of my sins. At our wedding, he presented me to his god, and of course it was the same god.

"She is mine," Kraw said, and chuckled. A dragon chuckle sends shivers down the bravest spine. "She was always mine. Do not provoke her too far, my son."

At the time I did not understand, and I don't think my husband ever did.

He found rapture in my embrace, and in time I found

some in his. I bore him two sons, and they have been a credit to their god. But Fire-hawk was as jealous and domineering as the god had foretold. I gave him no cause for his jealousy and I withstood his anger. When he struck me, I struck him back. He threatened to whip me. I told him I would enter a brothel and shame him before the entire kingdom. He tried to limit my power to rule the household, which was my right, and I played upon his jealousy, threatening to bear him a legion of bastards. Our life together was never tranquil, but it was seldom dull, either.

In due course, I became mistress of Still Waters, and no woman could ask for a finer domain.

Thereafter he used mistresses and tried to ignore me. But he had a weakness. He drank too much. When he was in his cups, I would go to him in his room and then he could not resist me. Disgusting, of course, but the price I paid. I used to do it every month or two, just so he could never be certain that any child I might bear was not his. We had the same god, you see. Whosoever might be the father of any child I bore, Kraw would accept it, because I also was his from the beginning. Fire-hawk had not appreciated that problem until after our wedding—I pointed it out to him in one of our first quarrels. The knowledge did nothing to improve his peace of mind, for he was a jealous man.

Yet I remained faithful to him, although he could not believe it.

Until High-honor.

Master Omar described the king for you, and brought him back to life for me. He was everything Fire-hawk was not—jovial, gentle, passionate, good company, forgiving. We were not mad youngsters, but love is not confined to the young. Indeed, true love is a phenomenon of middle age, for only then can one be sure that what one feels is not all lust. Passion is a product of love, not its source. Why do the young never see this?

I fell in love with the king, and he with me. Our af-

fair lasted for years, yet in all that time we were intimate only four times. I remember every minute of those
encounters. Fire-hawk suspected, or just assumed, and
High-honor dared not provoke a man of his power lest
the kingdom be rent by civil war. My husband watched
and pried and guarded. Four times!

High-honor brought his court to call on us, and I was
surrounded by eyes. We could exchange private words,
but only in full view. We were never allowed to be
alone together, to do what we both so desperately
wanted to do.

I went to Kraw in despair.

"An hour!" I begged. "My god, grant me an hour
alone with the man I love."

"I do not grudge you happiness, my child," the
dragon said. "But happiness always has a price. What
price will you pay for it in this case?"

Fool that I was! "Anything! Anything at all!"

"Rash! I do not know the price, Rose-dawn, or I
would tell you. I do know that this time it may be very
high."

"I will pay it!" I cried.

That is the only time I thought I heard my god weep.
"Fire-hawk also is my child, and I will not cuckold him,
much as he deserves it."

"Will you prevent me?"

"No," Kraw said softly. "Listen. There is a man
called Omar, a trader of tales. Send your most trustwor-
thy aide to Myto, to the Sign of the Bronze Anchor, and
he will find him there. Bring him here. Tell High-honor
to offer the man a bribe. It must be princely, for this
tale-teller is contemptuous of wealth. Only a fabulous
gift will impress him. In return for it, he will so bespell
his listeners that the two of you may steal away unseen.
Even Fire-hawk cannot resist that man's tongue. But if
the king stints on the prize, then all will be lost."

What woman could resist such a challenge? I could
require the man I loved to demonstrate how much he

valued me. High-honor rose to the challenge, of course. I felt shamed when I saw the jewel he proposed to squander for my sake.

It was not Verl who organized that deception! Verl was home in Uthom. It was Kraw. Who but the king could have offered Master Omar such a jewel? And who would have required such a price but the mistress of the house herself?

There was Omar's lie. He saw who slipped from the portico that night. High-honor would not have seduced his daughter's companion! Never! It was I, but Omar lied to you tonight to save my shame.

I have never spoken of it before, and now I find I glory in it.

I am eternally grateful to the trader of tales for giving me those precious minutes with the man I loved.

Two weeks later, High-honor died. Nine months later, I bore Sweet-rose.

She was the price, and costly she proved to be.

Oh, how I trembled on her naming day! We could not but invite the senior lords and their ladies from all the innumerable branches of Kraw's family, for such was the custom. They all came, the whole clan. The shrine was so crowded that no one could breathe.

Fire-hawk brought in the babe. He was convinced she was not his. No evidence would have convinced him otherwise, nay, even had he kept me locked in a box to which only he had the key. He laid her before the god.

"She is mine," Kraw said. "She is Sweet-rose of Kraw."

"But is she mine?" my husband screamed in front of his assembled guests, a quarter of all the wealth in the kingdom. Oh, the shame of it!

"You," the dragon said, "are a turd!"

The laughter almost brought down the ceiling. Not another word would the god speak and never was Fire-hawk allowed to forget it. I went no more to his bed again, nor any man's, for my love was dead.

A few years later, Just-blade came to rule in his own right and rashly began the Bunia war. Fire-hawk was slain early, and my heart rejoiced to be rid of him. My son succeeded, but he was unmarried. He went off with his brother to fight, and I ruled Still Waters alone. Those were the happiest years of my life! I could not help what I felt. Am I so wicked to admit it?

I had my daughter, Sweet-rose. She was much younger than my sons, and a great joy to me. Even as a babe she was beautiful, and her beauty waxed every day. She was willful and headstrong. We raged at each other, but it was for love. She knew I loved her, even when we fought.

She must have done.

I am sure she did!

And she loved me. We just did not talk of it; we were too much alike in some ways.

Offers of marriage began coming when she was twelve. I postponed all discussion of the matter until she reached fourteen. When that day came, Sweet-rose herself refused to discuss it. Ten years later, the offers were still coming, and she was still refusing them—refusing even to talk about them! She would not marry while the war was on, she insisted, for she had no wish to be an early widow. All very well, but the promising candidates were falling like icicles in springtime. Better a dead husband than no husband at all.

Half the young men of the kingdom came a-calling at Still Waters. Sweet-rose had a horse she called Tester. Most of the young men ended in a bush after trying out Tester—it favored a small monkey-puzzle near the aviary. Those who survived unscathed she would take canoeing in summer or skating in winter. She drowned them, terrified them, or froze them. Any superman who escaped those perils, she would invite to fencing practice. She had a foil with a trick button . . . One or two almost bled to death. Do you wonder that I was in despair?

Until one day Tester tested her. I don't know what spooked the brute, but I had warned her for years that she was playing with fire when she rode that devil. Skilled as she was, it ran away with her. She was brought home in a very bruised and subdued condition. She remained subdued. It was a month before I realized that we had not had a fight in all that time and therefore she must be avoiding me.

I soon discovered the reason. Master Omar made him out to be a hero, a romantic daredevil. I saw a penniless foreign adventurer who had almost broken my daughter's neck. I did not like him, his accent, his manners, his account of his background, or his obvious hold on my daughter. I disposed of him quite easily, as you heard. With one ankle broken and the other chained, he was not going to be underfoot for a while.

My daughter and I had a fight that was notable even by our standards. I gave her an ultimatum. If she was not betrothed by spring, I would arrange a marriage for her. By law her brother could force the matter, and would if I insisted. Then I packed her off to court. With my sons away and the land in turmoil, I could not leave Still Waters. I told her to write when she had an acceptable offer.

Her letter arrived one bitter winter day. The king or the crown prince, she said. She had not yet decided between them. The king was an old bore and rumored to be impotent, the prince a degenerate lout, but they were both pursuing her night and day, and didn't they both seem eligible enough?

I don't think she had led them on to spite me. Mad as she was at me, she would not have trailed her coat for either of those two, let alone both. I think it just happened. Whether father or son was first, the hatred between them was enough to provoke their rivalry without Sweet-rose having to do anything at all. I am positive she did not know then why either match was out of the question.

I knew, of course. I screamed for my carriage and was on the road for Uthom within the hour. I told the coachman to leave a trail of dead horses if need be, but to get me to the palace within two days. Even in summer, I had never made that journey in less than five.

In considering my daughter's future, I had overlooked the royal family completely. The crown prince was only a boy, five years younger than she. I had forgot that boys grow up. I knew that the king was likely to remarry. Irrelevant!—or so I assumed, because he was her brother. The crown prince was her nephew. But *they* didn't know that! Nobody knew that, just the gods and I. Now I must pay the price that Kraw predicted. I was going to be made to seem an adulteress before the entire nation, a slut who slept with men other than her husband. The fact that it was only four times, only four times and only with the king . . . Well, it didn't happen. I was saved disgrace.

Halfway to Uthom, a courier bound for Still Waters recognized my carriage in passing, ran us down, and delivered a second letter from Sweet-rose. I learned that I was too late.

Star-seeker had accosted my daughter in a corridor of the palace and attempted to fondle her, or worse. Literally fleeing from his unwanted attentions, she took refuge behind a convenient door. It was a room she had never seen before, the royal chapel. I knew it. We children of Kraw always pay our respects to Verl when we visit the palace, although now our descent from Whitethorn is too remote for him to acknowledge us.

The door would not have been locked, of course, despite the richness of the furnishings. No one can steal from a chapel in Verlia.

Sweet-rose knelt and apologized for intruding. Verl replied.

I suppose he began with "You are mine," although all gods have their own liturgy. He told Sweet-rose that he had summoned her. He explained the problem. Both

king and prince had already consulted him about her
and he had forbidden both matches. He had not said
why, because gods never explain. Gods become very
angry if their commands are ignored. Sweet-rose was
one of his, just as much as the men were.

"If a god guards your nasty secret, Mother," she wrote,
"then who am I to expose you?"

I wish I had kept that letter. Some of the things she
wrote were unkind, but they were written in haste. She
also said . . . Well, I did not keep it, and I don't remember. She did say she was going to flee the court. She did
not say where she was going, but I could guess. She
said good-bye.

Fool! She could have kept her penniless foreigner
then! She could have blackmailed me into accepting
him and the assembled children of Kraw would have
rallied to turn aside the king's anger! Why did she not
see that? Why give up so much? Why say good-bye?

Oh, I was a madwoman! My carriage would not manage the byways, so I took off on horseback. Even then
I was old—in my sixties—but in the next two days I
outrode every man of my escort except one boy. Never
say I did not love her! I nearly killed myself on that
ride. An hour from Zardon, my horse went lame. I ordered my last guard to dismount and I went on alone.
Alone!

I could not have missed you by long, Master Omar.
Embers still glowed in the grate. The two bodies were
not yet cold. Two bodies, and only the prince still held
a sword? It did not take much wit to guess that there
had been other people there if there was only one sword
for two dead men. But the crown prince was slain and
all the children of Kraw together could not defend Still
Waters against a charge of high treason.

Boats never entered my mind. An open boat across
the ocean in winter? Ridiculous! Horses and hiding
places were all I considered. The king's officers would
be at my door within days, I thought, and I racked my

brain to recall all the secret rooms and passages. I tried to calculate when Sweet-rose and her adventurer lover would arrive, and by what road ... I was certain she would come home, you see, home to her mother's arms.

I decided I must buy time, muddy the tracks, blur the scent. I dragged the corpses over to the window and let the sea have them. There was too much blood to clean up, so I set the building on fire. Only the roof and the upstairs flooring and the furniture were flammable. The walls remained, and I expect they are there still. The prince's sword was later found among the ashes and identified, but there were no signs of bodies, of course. I never guessed my improvised deception would stand unchallenged for twenty years.

By dawn I was at my manager's door. This was Kraw land, remember, Still Waters land. My men scoured the countryside clean long before the king's ever saw it. We found the horses, Master Tickenpepper! We spirited the old fisherman away, and no one learned of the four fugitives.

Strange how legends grow! Very few people had seen my daughter with Master Omar. More knew of the prince, for he had made himself obnoxious at every stop. The two couples passed by different routes at very similar times. Somehow the reports blended into a myth of two fugitive lovers.

When I learned of the boat, I laughed aloud. I thought it was just a cunning subterfuge to divert pursuit. They would sail along the coast and disembark, would then find fresh horses to bear them to Still Waters. So I thought. I went home, expecting to find them already there. They were not. I waited. As the days passed, I was forced to conclude that they had drowned at sea. My daughter never came back to me. I lost all hope, until earlier this year, when I learned of Hool's oracle.

24: Interlude

The hoarse old voice ground away into silence, and there was not a damp eye in the room. Even Gwill's seemed to have dried up momentarily.

Eventually the actress squirmed and said, "A poignant tale!"

The rest of us made hasty agreeing noises.

"I have suffered much for love," the dowager murmured.

I interpreted Frieda's expression to mean *horrible old bitch!* but it may have lost something in the translation. For once the group seemed close to unanimity.

The merchant cleared his throat. "You appear to have a problem, my lady. Your candidate's story does not agree with your own account of events."

We all looked at Rosie, who did not notice.

The dowager pouted. "Innkeeper? It must be near dawn, is it not?"

Fritz scratched his stubbled chin and heaved himself upright, unfolding his bulk like a horse. "It feels like it, my lady." He stalked over to a window. Leaning into the embrasure, he cupped his hands around a spy hole in the shutter and peered. "There is light in the east, ma'am."

"And still thawing?"

"Yes, ma'am."

"If we are to move on this morning, then we should perhaps catch a little sleep. Rosie!"

Rosie jumped as if someone had dropped hot coals down her neck. "M-m-m-my lady?"

"It is time to go to bed."

"B-b-bed, my lad-d-dy?"

"Upstairs. Take Verl with you, and remember to sleep next the wall, so there will be room for me."

The girl sat for a moment, lips moving, working that out. Then she nodded and quickly stuffed the porcelain pigeon and its wrapping inside the casket. She rose, bobbed a curtsey, and hurried to the stairs.

The minstrel shivered. He stretched, yawning widely. "I think I, too, may . . ."

I caught his eye and shook my head. I suspected I was going to need Gwill quite shortly. Surprised but always willing, he sank back on the bench without another word, staring at me doubtfully and dabbing at his nose with his sleeve.

"What ever do you mean, Burgomaster?" the dowager said sharply, picking up the earlier conversation.

The merchant screwed down his thick brows. "You saw Star-seeker dead, you say. Yet Rosie claims to be his child."

"Posthumous, perhaps?"

"And when did that happen? No, no, ma'am! Her father was a mercenary, who died at the siege of Hagenvarch. Possibly the girl's mother may have romanticized, or the girl herself may, but you quote her as quoting Verl. Your story does not match the god's."

"It really does not matter who her father was. She is High-honor's granddaughter. That is why Hool has proclaimed her child to be rightful ruler—not because of Star-seeker at all."

The fat man's face bulged. "When and where did Star-seeker die? At Zardon or at Hagenvarch? You cannot have it both ways."

The dowager clenched her lips in silence. She was the sort of person who often *did* have it both ways, many ways, believing whatever she chose to believe.

Even yet she would not face the consequences of her adultery. She wanted the world to believe her daughter had eloped with Star-seeker, although she knew he had died. But then she sighed.

"You have a point. I admit there are discrepancies in Rosie's tale. The soldier father sounds more like that Zig boy than Star-seeker. There are also truths! She knew my name, the name of Sweet-rose's mother. That was not public knowledge. She knew the year of her mother's birth. Other things. Perhaps Hool will explain."

The merchant grunted scornfully.

I did not like the way Fritz was hovering in the background, where I could not see what he was up to. I did not like the yawns going around.

"It is not unknown for young women to hear voices," I suggested.

"She is a half-wit!" Johein said, agreeing with me for the first time that night. "She could imagine anything. But how could the voices speak truths?" He glowered at me with a totally unwarranted suspicion.

"Perhaps that pigeon of hers is a demon? If you believe in gods, you must believe in devils, or evil gods."

The audience stirred uneasily at the thought of a demon in the house.

"Just a thought," I added. "She has a terrible stutter, doesn't she?"

"You have another explanation, Master Omar?" the soldier demanded.

My conscience growled at me and I paused to consider the matter. On purely artistic grounds, I was convinced that Rosie was an irrelevancy. She had wandered into the wrong story. The gods may be cruel or capricious, but they usually do have style. Rosie did not belong in the affairs of Verlia. She was a leaf caught up by a storm and blown out to sea.

"I do not think the girl is lying to you, my lady," I said. "But I do not think she is your granddaughter. If

I say anything to shake your belief in that, you will not abandon her?"

The old crone crunched up her wrinkles in a scowl. She was unaccustomed to restraint, unwilling to commit herself to anything, even to bind herself with a promise. "Rosie is a great help to me. She is biddable. I need a handmaid to help me dress. My last absconded in Gilderburg with a dairyman."

When no more came, I said, "Then you will certainly take her back to Still Waters with you, whether she is your granddaughter or not? And even if she is only the deluded simpleton she seems to be, you will see that she finds an honorable living?"

I thought Lady Rose-dawn was about to tell me to mind my own business, but curiosity won out, as it usually does.

"You need have no fear on that score, Master Omar. I look after my retainers, and always have." She probably believed that. "Talk away! We may as well see the sunup now. It is your turn to tell us a tale, anyway."

"I will not presume to try to match your own heart-rending story, my lady! But I do have a parable that may be relevant. You may judge it on its own merits, if you wish."

The merchant groaned and turned his head to inspect his young wife. She smiled at him unconvincingly. Then he seemed to decide against whatever he had been thinking, and he, too, settled into his chair.

"Go on. What flimflam is coming now?"

"The Tale of Agwash the Horsetrader, of course."

Nobody reacted except Gwill the minstrel. He blinked at me in surprise and then smiled wanly.

25: The Tale of Agwash the Horsetrader

In the spring of the year, Agwash the horsetrader went down from Morthlan to the plains, as was his wont, to buy stock for the summer fairs. He came to the village of Vanburth, and there to the house of his old friend Nergol, who was also a man wise in the flesh of horses. Nergol embraced Agwash and seated him under the shade of the fig tree that grew before his house, and called for wine and cakes to be brought for his old friend. Then the two of them discoursed at length upon the mercies of the gods, the follies of men, and the obscene proliferation of taxes.

When Agwash was refreshed, Nergol caused sundry ponies to be led forth and displayed before him, saying, "Oh, Agwash, behold! Observe the straightness of their hocks, the gleam of their coats, the excellence of their respiration!" And Nergol praised the horses in this wise, likening them to legendary steeds of yore.

Agwash turned aside his face and lamented. "Cruel are the gods!" he quoth. "They have brought me to hard times in my old age, when even an honest man may no longer earn his bread by honorable trade. They have reduced the price of horses until they sell for less than pomegranates. But worst of all, they have burdened me with years so that I may observe the friends of my youth decayed and stricken with afflictions of the eyes. Is it that you can yet tell day from night, my old companion?"

Deeming that his friend jested, Nergol slapped his

238

thighs in mirth and then returned to praising the animals he had displayed.

Agwash responded with sadness. "Verily, since coming into the plains, I have not seen a beast worthy to be made into the bindings of books. Every day it grows clearer." Then he pointed out the signs of worms and the prevalence of colic and bog spavin and sundry other drawbacks that the other had missed.

Nergol called upon his menservants to remove the livestock.

Agwash sighed as his heart were breaking. "Because I am a kindly man and Nergol has been my friend for unnumbered years, I will let folly overrule wisdom in this matter. Yes, I will remove the diseased animals from his field to save him the labor of burying them. And, though my wives would berate me if they heard of this, calling me a sentimental old fool, I will leave him four gold pieces so that my friend may start up in goat herding, or some other line of endeavor more suited to his talents."

Then Nergol cried out to the gods to witness that Wernok had offered twenty times that much per head for the whole herd, as he needed to improve his bloodline.

Agwash threw himself in the dust, uttering lamentation that his old friend Nergol had so taken leave of his wits as to believe a single word that had passed through the beard of a notorious liar such as Wernok.

And so it went.

Later, when the shadows began to lengthen, the two of them embraced again tearfully, each vowing that he had beggared himself utterly for the sake of his old friend. Nergol called again for wine for his visitor, and they sat once more under the fig tree and drank toasts to better days ahead.

Then said Nergol, "How sad it is that your business has fallen on such hard times, Agwash! Were you in command of the resources you once had, you might even be able to consider making an offer for Twak, for truly there is no horse under Heaven that can compare with Twak."

Agwash sighed and agreed that the matter was indeed heartbreaking. And although times were hard, he added, it would be a wonderful experience to see a notable horse again, a steed like those they had known in the days of their youth together. He very much doubted that there could be any such horse, though, and he could not imagine what breeder in the district might own it if there was.

Nergol said, "The virtues of Twak are not readily apparent to the eye—or at least not to mine, although I fancy that my sight is still better than yours, as it always was. As to the breeder, the owner of Twak is a man by the name of Pilo, who can commonly be found in the market at this hour of the day. Let us go together, and if you do not agree that Twak is the most remarkable horse that you have ever seen, then I shall deed you back that miserable sack of underweight coins you persuaded me in my folly to accept for my herd. Whereas, if I have spoken truly, then you will double the amount."

Agwash considered the matter for some time, for he was a cautious man, but eventually he agreed to the terms. So the two of them arose and went unto the marketplace. There they found the man Pilo and the horse Twak, within a crowd of onlookers.

Agwash said, "I will admit that I have never seen a horse so spavined and rack-boned, nor one so old and still able to stand up. These, I posit, were not the terms of our wager."

"They were not. Now take heed and watch."

Then Nergol handed a silver coin to the man Pilo, and Pilo gave him in return an oatcake, of the sort that could be purchased in the market at thirteen for a copper farthing.

Nergol addressed the horse, saying, "Twak, this is my old friend Agwash. How many sons does he have?"

Twak began to strike the ground with his hoof, and the man Pilo counted out the strokes. Lo! When the count had come to four, Twak ceased.

Nergol gave Twak the oatcake, saying, "Agwash, you have four sons, and you owe me a bag of gold."

Agwash was much shaken by this, but he was a cautious man, and he pondered the matter for some time, stroking his beard. At last he shook his head in sorrow.

"I would not have believed an old friend would have contrived such a deceit," he said. "Clearly the man Pilo was advised beforetimes of the answer you would seek. He is holding the horse's bridle, and he gave the horse a signal when it was time to cease striking the ground."

The man Pilo brought out another oatcake from the pocket of his robe, saying, "I see you are a stranger. Because you have doubts, I shall tether Twak to this post, and I shall let you ask another question without further payment."

So he tethered Twak and stood back, while Agwash braced himself to speak to a horse before so many onlookers. He said, "Twak, how many horses did I buy from Nergol this day?"

Twak struck the ground with his hoof fourteen times and stopped.

Nergol said, "Agwash, Twak is the most remarkable horse you have ever seen. You bought fourteen head and you owe me a bag of gold."

Then was Agwash sore afraid for his gold. But he considered the matter further, and devised that his old friend Nergol might have guessed what question Agwash would ask of Twak, and might by some means have sent word to the man Pilo beforetimes.

"The man Pilo is a remarkable trainer," he said, reaching for a silver coin. "I shall ask another question, but he must go where the horse cannot see or hear his signal."

He expected the man Pilo to object to this condition, but he did not. He gave Agwash an oatcake in return for the silver coin, and then went and stood behind the tent of Mougour the basket maker, out of sight of Twak. Now Agwash saw that all the spectators were smiling, and he was even more afraid. He determined to ask something that no one in the village except himself could know, so that no accomplice in the crowd might signal the answer to the horse.

"Twak," he said, "I tarried three nights in the town of Pulnk on my way here. How many maidens did I embrace in Pulnk?"

Twak struck the ground four times with his hoof, and all the spectators clapped.

Agwash lamented and tore his beard. "Truly!" he said, "I have never seen so remarkable a horse, and I owe my old friend a bag of gold, may the gods rot his lungs and fill his bowels with worms and sundry arthropods."

Then Nergol took pity on his distress and spoke to him, saying, "Alas that this horse is beyond price, and the man Pilo will not consider any offer for him. But you, my old friend, are as shrewd a judge of the flesh of horses as I have ever had the misfortune to deal with. I will therefore make this offer to you. It may be that the horse is possessed of a demon. Or it may be that the man Pilo has a secret that would bring great profit to any who might share it. Tarry, then, and observe. If in three days you can tell me how Twak works his wonders, then I shall return both bags of gold to you. But if you cannot, then you shall owe me the same."

Agwash was sore distressed at the thought of so much gold, but he agreed to the new wager. Straightaway he began to ply the man Pilo with silver coins for the right to ask questions of the horse, and for oatcakes to reward it.

It came to pass that Twak told Agwash how many brothers he had. Twak told him how many pillars stood in the cloister of the palace in Morthlan, the number of beans in a pot, how many were the taverns of Pulnk and the tables in each. Twak stamped once when the right index finger of Agwash was over the scar on his own left arm, although the arm was hidden by a sleeve. Twak told Agwash the month and the day of the month on which his father's father's brother had been born.

The horse could answer rightly no matter which way it was facing, whether the man Pilo was in sight or not, or even when Twak was inside a tent with no one but Agwash himself.

That was the first day.

On the second day, Agwash spent no more silver coins on oatcakes, but sat on the shady side of the marketplace and watched the horse Twak. Yet there was little to see, because no one in the village would venture to doubt Twak's skill, and therefore only strangers would pander to its expensive taste for oatcakes. One merchant came to ask how many days he must wait to receive a certain important letter he was expecting, but that question Twak refused to answer, so the man Pilo returned the merchant's silver coin and left the oatcake in his own pocket.

On the third day, in the morning, Agwash went again to the marketplace. There he saw a man leading a fine racing mare. Agwash greeted him in his customary fashion, saying, "Stranger, will you sell me that hack, for my dogs are hungry and need meat?"

The man sighed and explained that the mare was all the goods he possessed in the world, and a bosom friend, also, and his only source of income, for it would win any race at any odds, but that he might consider parting with the mare if a man was rich enough to offer a suitable price.

Agwash led the man and the mare over to Twak, and paid the man Pilo a silver coin, and said, "Twak, what is the lowest price this man will take for this mare?"

Twak struck the ground seven times and Agwash said to the man, "I offer you seven gold coins for the mare."

The man laughed at so small an offer and said, "Verily, at twenty gold coins it would be robbery."

"Verily it would," Agwash said, and went away.

Later that day, the man came to where Agwash sat on the shady side of the marketplace and said he would take seventeen coins. Agwash said, "Seven."

At the end of the day, the man came again. Weeping, he took the seven gold coins, giving the mare to Agwash.

Then Agwash arose and went to the shop of the maker of pots and purchased from him two pots of the best sort, one orange and one red, and both having lids. Now the sun was close to setting, and Nergol came unto Agwash, saying, "Old friend, can you now tell me how the horse Twak works its wonders, or do you owe me two more bags of gold?"

Agwash said unto him, "Surely an old horsetrader can outwit an old horse, so that you, old friend, will have to return to me the two bags I have already lost to you through folly and the weakness of my judgment."

Thereupon they went together to the horse Twak and the man Pilo, and Agwash bought two oatcakes. Half the people of the town had come, also, to hear if Agwash the horsetrader could explain how Twak worked his wonders, for he was known as a man wise in the flesh of horses.

Then Agwash showed Twak the orange pot, saying, "Twak, how many beans are there in this pot?"

Twak struck the ground four times as the man Pilo counted, and stopped. Agwash said unto Nergol, "Old friend, do you now look in the orange pot and tell me if this horse has spoken true."

He did and said, "Verily, there are four beans in this pot, neither more nor less."

So Agwash gave Twak the first oatcake. Then Agwash showed Twak the red pot and called upon the horse to tell him how many beans were in that pot, also. Twak struck the ground and struck the ground and struck the ground, and the man Pilo called out the count, and when they had reached a hundred, Agwash said to Nergol, "Old friend, do you now look in the red pot and tell us."

So Nergol looked in the red pot and spoke, saying, "Lo, herein there are but three beans only." Then Twak stopped striking the ground with his hoof, and the man Pilo returned one silver coin to Agwash because the horse had been unable to tell him how many beans there were in the red pot.

At this, Nergol cried out in lamentation and rent his garments, for he thought he would now have to pay his old friend the two bags of gold that had been wagered. He said, "Alas! Now you know how the horse performs his wonders. Tell me then, and I shall deliver unto you the money that was promised, for there is none more honest under Heaven than Nergol."

But Agwash said to him, "Nay, I know not. I go now to my tents to gather together two bags of gold, although it be all I possess in the world and my children shall surely starve thereby, and I shall bring the gold to you, my old friend."

Nergol said, "But you have won the wager."

Agwash said, "Nay, I have lost." And they argued over who owed whom two bags of gold, while all the people looked on in amazement.

Nergol said, "Thou knowest how the horse works his wonders."

Agwash said, "I know not. It is true that I have a theory, but it is a mere guess, a supposition, and I may be wrong. Therefore I have lost and I will pay."

"Tell me your theory," said Nergol to him, "and you need not pay."

Agwash said, "Nay, I will not. I will pay thee, old friend, for I, too, am an honest man."

Nergol tore his beard. "Tell me your theory," he said, "and I will pay you the two bags of gold instead, and take none from you."

"I will not," Agwash said. "I cannot prove that my

theory is the truth, and therefore you would call me a liar. Truly, I will not tell you my theory if you pay me ten bags of gold."

Nergol cried out as if taken by a great pain, and then said, "Five."

Agwash said, "Eight, and no less."

And so on.

Thus it came to pass, later that night, when the old friends were alone at Agwash's tent where no other might see or hear, that Nergol delivered seven bags of gold and three skins of fine wine to Agwash, and Agwash spake to him, saying—

"This be my theory. The horse Twak, I ween, is an old horse, and has been traded many times from owner to owner, and having seen and heard the trading done about it, has learned how to be a horsetrader itself. For when I asked Twak what money a certain man would accept for a mare, the horse Twak began to strike the ground. When it had counted to seven, it stopped, and it came to pass that the man did take seven gold coins for the mare. Now, none knew the truth of that number aforetimes except the man himself, and he did not tell or signal this information to Twak, because that would have been great folly.

"And when you and I, my old friend, were bargaining over the fourteen worthless beasts that I bought from you, I observed that whenever you came to name a sum that you would accept, you paused. You spoke some words, as 'I might settle for . . .' or 'I would take only . . .' and then you would wait until I looked up, yea, until I looked you full in the face, waiting for you to complete the phrase. Now this habit of yours annoyed me greatly, for you learned it from me, myself."

Nergol said, "So it may be, but I had not thought on it before."

"Even in thy youth the stench of thy lies nauseated the gods, and you have not repented in your dotage. The reason for this perversion of yours is that you thereby can clearly view my face when you name the number, and thus judge whether I be pleased by the same."

"The face of Agwash," Nergol proclaimed, "is like unto the Mountain of White Marble, and none may read upon it what is carven thereon. This is well known throughout all the plains, yea, even unto the River of Crocodiles."

These words pleased Agwash, but yet he frowned as if they brought him no happiness. "That may be true for the unwashed mass of the people, but it is not true for a wily and unscrupulous rogue such as thee, my old friend. And I think it is not true of the horse Twak. However much a man may seek to hide his feelings so that they do not show on his face or in his bearing, he may reveal himself in small ways that the shrewd observer will note. It may be that neither is truly aware of these signals, and yet they are both sent and received."

Nergol mused upon this matter and poured more wine for himself and his old friend. "Then explain the two pots that you showed unto Twak, the orange pot that the horse discerned, and the red pot that it could not."

"Verily it is simple. I knew that there were four beans in the orange pot, for I put them there myself. I had contrived that another's hand placed the beans in the red pot and then shut the lid before returning it to me, so thereby I knew not how many beans were within. There being then no one in Twak's sight who knew the answer, the horse observed no signal that it had reached the correct number, and therefore it did not cease from striking the ground.

"Likewise, it could not tell the merchant when he will receive his letter, for no man knoweth the answer."

Nergol said, "Truly, thou art the greatest cheat and villain between the city Morthlan and the River of Crocodiles, and thou hast beggared me in my old age."

The next day Agwash went on his way, taking with him all the horses he had bought and all the gold he had acquired, as well, and was content.

26: The Sixth Judgment

✳

"**R**osie is not a horse!" the dowager barked.

I sighed. The bitter old crone was not going to face the truth, no matter what knots she had to tie her mind in.

"No, my lady. She is a drudge. Do you know what drudgery does to people? I can name many great houses where the horses are better treated than the scullery staff."

The soldier intervened, speaking with quiet authority. It was as if he stepped between two quarreling drunks. "Your parable was amusing, Omar, but how does it fit? What exactly is your argument? The horse you described pawed the ground until it saw that it had pleased the questioner. Then it stopped and received a reward. I have known many very smart horses, but Rosie does not paw the ground."

"She stutters!" I said. "Tell me if this is how it happens? You ask her something—the name of her mother's mother, for example. She goes off to ask Verl, or the image she thinks is Verl. Then she comes back and you repeat the question. She is very nervous, she stutters, gabbles ... In the case of her grandmother's name ... What did the margrave's housekeeper say her mother's name was, by the way?"

He shrugged. "They think it was Marsha, but no one is sure after all these years."

"She believes her own name is Rosalind and her mother's was Sweet-rose, so naturally she might begin with noises like those names. The correct answer is

248

Rose-dawn, so you smile and nod, right? Whenever she makes noises that sound like the answer you want, you show signs of agreement." I looked around for my own signs of encouragement. "All her life, Rosie has been the lowest of the low. She has had to satisfy a dozen people, all at the same time—every one of them shouting at her to do something and all entitled to strike her. Of course she has learned how to please people! I don't think she knows she is doing it."

"Rubbish!" the dowager muttered. No one disagreed. I had not won much support, obviously.

Gwill yawned. The yawn spread around the room. Dawn was here. Tallow fumes from the candles burdened the air. We were all feeling the long night. I sensed that more people were thinking of following Rosie upstairs to bed. If I lost my audience, then I should have Fritz to deal with. But there was another riddle left unsolved, and it should be cleared out of the way first. I looked to the merchant, who was yawning harder than any, stretching his thick arms.

"Well, Burgomaster? Have you no story to tell us, to complete the evening?"

He eyed me sourly and then glanced thoughtfully at his wife. Marla looked brighter than anyone, but of course she must be accustomed to long, hard nights in her line of work.

She glowed a coy smile at him. "It does seem late, Johein darling! Why don't we run upstairs and cuddle into bed, mm?" She fondled the gold chain across his paunch.

He raised his bushy brows in sudden interest. "Sleepy, beloved?"

"Oh, a little. Tired of all this talk." She stroked his cheek.

"Ahem!" the soldier said. "Burgomaster, you never did tell us why you had engaged the services of Master Tickenpepper to advise you on the laws of Verlia."

The merchant pondered a moment, then shrugged his

fat shoulders. "Well, I was planning to keep it as a surprise. My dear wife and I are on our honeymoon, you realize."

Gwill choked. "You take a lawyer along on your honeymoon, sir?"

Fritz and the soldier smothered laughs. Even the dowager made an odd coughing noise.

The fat man glared. "Watch your tongue, minstrel!" He eyed the dowager with equal contempt. "I suppose now is as good a time as any for the truth to come out. I don't know I believe Omar's drivel about the horse, ma'am, but I know that your precious Rosie is not what you think she is."

"Then pray enlighten us!"

"Darling?" said the actress. She leaned over to kiss him. "Don't you love me more than that boring Rosie?"

"Later, beloved."

"Now, darling!"

"Later, I said! I have to tell the seventh story, to solve the mystery."

"Oo!" Marla squealed, in a sudden change of tactics. "Solve the mystery? That is exciting! What is the surprise, my love? A surprise for me?"

He patted her knee. "You will be as surprised as anyone, my little chaffinch." He cleared his throat pompously, frowning around to make sure we were all paying attention. "I am Burgomaster Johein, chief magistrate of Schlosbelsh. By profession, I am an importer. I inherited the business from my father, and built it into one of the largest in the Volkslander. I am rated as the wealthiest man in the city—barring the great landowners, of course, and I know for a fact that not a few of them ... Well, never mind. I have four sons and two daughters still living. My first wife died some years ago. I had been intending to take another, but pressure of business kept me from getting around to it. A serious matter, choosing a wife, you know!"

"My good fortune that you delayed, darling," the actress said, fanning him with her lashes.

I caught Gwill's eye and hastily looked away. I recalled that steamy, scented parlor in the Velvet Stable in Gilderburg, and the girls dancing on the tables. Then I tried to picture the assembled civic fathers of Schlosbelsh being gracious to the burgomaster's new wife. The mind . . .

What exactly is *boggling*, anyway?

27: The Merchant's Tale

My attention was drawn to the Verlia affair some months ago, in early summer. I was in my counting house, busy as usual. Wealth never brings relaxation, you know. We work much harder than the poor. And my civic duties take a lot of my time.

I recall that I was in a testy mood. I forget what exactly had upset me—the continuing stupidity of my clerks, I suppose. Most of them don't have the wits of a chicken, and they're constantly getting sick and expecting time off work. I give them two days off every month! That's time enough to be sick.

Anyway, this particular day, I received a very unusual caller. Most of my visitors are other important merchants and guildmasters, you understand, or often members of the nobility come to borrow money. I like to make 'em wait. When I was informed that there was an elderly nun asking to see me, I was not impressed. I couldn't imagine why a nun would want to see me, other than to beg money for repairs to the nunnery or something. I probably wouldn't have found time for her that day, except there was a weedy young aristocrat in my waiting room, and I knew he was hoping for a sizable loan. I also knew he needed the money very badly. The longer he had to stew about it, the less he would scream when I told him the terms. Besides, if he saw a woman, and a cleric besides, being received ahead of himself, it would make him realize that the sun didn't rise for him alone, just because he had the hereditary right to pee in a silver pot, or something. So I said to send in the nun first.

She came in leaning on a staff. Her habit was a tawdry, threadbare thing, and I didn't recognize her order—she wasn't from Gilderburg. She was old, and frail, so I told her to take a seat, although I didn't intend for her to stay long.

I went on signing letters. "I am pressed for time this morning, Sister," I said. "Come to the point quickly, if you please."

She perched on the extreme edge of the chair and did not seem to know what to do with her stick. She was nervous and twittery. "I apologize for interrupting an important person such as yourself, Burgomaster. I would not impose on you, except the matter is rather urgent. She is due to take her vows in a few weeks."

Obviously she was a confused old bird.

"Who is?" I said.

"Postulant Marla, Your Honor."

"And why should I care?"

"You needn't. I mean, I hope you will. Oh, dear! You see, I think she may be important."

I doubted it at that point, I admit. I decided I would give the hag five minutes to come to the point, or I would toss her out. But as she wandered and maundered, I began to get intrigued. I'm no vagabond yarnspinner like Omar, so I won't try to repeat the story the way she told it. I'll just give you the bare facts.

My visitor said she was Sister Zauch, from some obscure convent in Luzfraul that I'd never heard of. The hills are full of them. It's cheaper to dump unwanted daughters in a house of nuns than give them a dowry when they grow up. The nuns settle for much less—I know!

But this wasn't anything like that. About twenty years ago, one bad winter's night, a woman had come to the convent door. She was sick—dying in fact—and she had a baby girl with her. The mother duly died. The child was kept on in the nunnery. Nothing unusual about that, really. Luzfraul's on the far side of Gilderburg from Schlosbelsh—this side of Gilderburg, that is—and just where someone coming over the Ranges might take a wrong turn . . . I'm getting ahead of myself. At first I was thinking the other way, thinking of going south and finding the passes closed and taking the wrong turn on the way back.

Sister Zauch was already past her five minutes, and I told her to get to the point. She brought out an old letter. Apparently the sisters had made an effort to identify the dying woman, but not much of an effort. The mother superior had written a letter to the margrave of the district, but for some reason it had never been sent. It had been lying in a drawer for twenty years. Nuns are not normally very businesslike people, of course. Sister Zauch herself had found the letter a few weeks before.

Now the girl was grown up and about to take her vows. That would be that, of course. But Zauch herself had been required to come to Schlosbelsh on some family business or other, and had brought the girl along as companion. While she was here, she had decided to consult the authorities. Would I advise her on what ought to be done? If anything.

Me? What did I know or care about lost aristocratic bastards? But I suppose a burgomaster seems much the same as a margrave to a gang of cloistered elderly females.

Well, a letter was better than an ancient nun's confused blathering. It repeated the story of the dying woman, but it quoted a few words she had raved in her delirium. "Prince" was one of them, and that caught my attention, of course. Ravings carry little weight, but there was real evidence, too. The baby had been wrapped in a blanket of very fine woolen cloth, with a coat of arms stitched in the corner. The letter contained a drawing of this, and it certainly had a genuine look to it, although I don't waste my time on heraldic nonsense.

I began to cross-examine old Sister Zauch. She had nothing more to add. The blanket had been lost, the letter had never been sent. She did not want Postulant Marla to hear anything about our conversation unless she did turn out to be of noble blood—it would upset her. That was understandable.

Of course I was skeptical. I promised the old biddy I would investigate the insignia and send word to her as soon as I learned anything. She was changing her lodgings, she said, so she couldn't give me an address. We agreed she would call on me again in a few days, and that was the end of the interview.

I saw her out. I turned my attention to my other visitors, and almost forgot the whole business. But the next day Master Tickenpepper came calling about some important legal business of mine. I noticed the letter, still lying on my desk, and showed it to him. He agreed that it seemed genuine. I told him to look into it, not really expecting anything of interest to emerge.

Well, as you have all guessed by now, the coat of arms turned out to belong to the royal house of Verlia! That was a considerable surprise, because Verlia is not exactly next door. I couldn't imagine how the blanket could have come so far. I decided it probably hadn't. The woman herself had stitched the emblem into it, most likely, to honor her baby.

At that time I had heard of Verlia, but that was about all, and I have traveled widely. Very few men in Schlosbelsh would have even known there was such a place, because most have never been as far as Gilderburg in their lives. In the next few days, some odd rumors began to float around. As burgomaster, I hear the news as soon as anyone does—it is my business to! I stress that point, because it is important. Sister Zauch spoke to me before anyone else in the city had heard about the missing heir!

I set Master Tickenpepper to work finding out the truth of the matter.

When the old woman returned, I told her that the girl might indeed be important. I asked to meet her.

Sister Zauch was unwell and wanted to return to the convent, but she sent the girl to me. That's when I met Marla.

I was bewitched from the moment I set eyes on her! Such innocence, such unconscious beauty—and very possibly daughter of an old and powerful family! I am not by nature a romantic man, but her situation touched me, I admit. Very soon, I stopped caring who her parents had been. I fell in love!

I proposed. She accepted. We were married.

Yes, I knew there was a remote chance that she might turn out to have an aristocratic background, but it was not a factor in my decision. The chances of ever tracking it down seemed very remote, and the odds of ever proving anything conclusive even slighter. Not many lost heiresses have gods waiting to attest to their identity! I love her for herself alone, and would still love her, no matter how humble her birth. I took her as she was, without dowry or credentials.

It was only later, when Tickenpepper came back with his final report, that I realized that I had unwittingly married a queen.

28: Interlude

"**M**e?" Marla screamed. "You mean I'm the rightful queen we've been hearing about all night?" Without giving Johein a chance to reply, she hurled herself on him and kissed him fervently.

There is no fool like an old fool, so they say.

I looked around the room. Stunned disbelief would be an understatement. Frieda's eyes were wide, she had her hands over her mouth. Even Fritz's great jaw hung limply. Captain Tiger's hand had instinctively settled on the hilt of his sword.

Gwill, though, was in the early stages of apoplexy. He and I stared at each other. We knew more than the others. We knew Marla could not possibly be what was being claimed for her . . . didn't we? Lack of sleep was making me groggy. Could an admittedly shrewd businessman like Johein be deceived on anything so vital to his own well-being?

Could Marla be the lost princess, despite the trade she had plied in Gilderburg?

For a moment nobody dared breathe a word. Then the merchant heaved his ecstatic bride off him and looked around proudly to judge our reactions. It was the soldier who spoke first. His tone was dry as salt, giving away nothing.

"My lady, you appear to have discovered a second granddaughter tonight! And a grandson-in-law!"

The merchant flinched. He and the dowager regarded each other bleakly. What a big happy family that would be!

"Indeed, ma'am," he said stiffly. "Behold your true granddaughter, and your queen."

"I don't believe a word of it!"

"I assure you that the facts are incontestable! The dates fit. The mother superior—the previous mother superior, that is—wrote a detailed, if somewhat windy, account of the matter. She quoted the woman's dying words. I have a transcript of the letter upstairs. Would you doubt such a holy lady? I remind you that this came to my attention *before* the story was otherwise known in Schlosbelsh. And who in a backwater like Luzfraul could have known the royal insignia of a land so far away?"

Gwill caught my eye, asking me what we should do. I considered the ethics of the matter. I had no especial reason to spoil Marla's fun, or Johein's, either, for that matter. But I felt I had unmasked Rosie rather brutally. I owed it to her to apply the same standards of strict honesty and integrity to everyone present.

Almost everyone, I mean.

True, Mistress Marla had come to my aid a few times that evening, but not willingly. By way of contrast, her husband's tale of Sister Zauch led to the one person who had never faltered in backing me, one who deserved my support much more than she did.

"My turn again?" I did not wait for argument. "A truly stunning narrative, Your Honor! I gravely feel that I have met my match at last, and in the final round of the contest, too! However, I shall do my best to go down fighting. I can do no better than to recount to you the sad, brief, and salutary tale of Waldgrave Munster."

29: Omar's Response to the Merchant's Tale

I first met Munster six or seven years ago, down in the Winelands. At that time he was a wild, crazy youth. I ran into him again this summer in Gilderburg. He had changed, of course, but not in the way most men do when they reach maturity. Now he is even wilder and crazier.

You must have heard tell of his brother, the margrave. There is no richer landowner in the entire Volkslander. Doubtless you could name several of his royal, saintly, and influential uncles, cousins, and so forth. Their respectability is legendary. Their family tree is primeval, a forest in itself.

Muny is the only black sheep it has ever produced, and he makes up for it being about as black as it is possible to be. He inherited the family good looks, but there the resemblance ends. He commonly begins his day around noon with wine, women, and song, and goes straight downward. His main interests are wenching, dueling, drinking, brawling, cheating at cards, blackening the family name, and soaping staircases, but he dabbles in every other sort of deviltry imaginable, letting no temptation escape.

He is one of the most charming men I have ever met. He flaunts his wealth, dresses superbly, and turns every female eye in the street. I have rarely seen him without a beautiful woman on his arm and a broad grin on his face. He can ride any horse ever foaled. He will drink you under the table and waken you at dawn to propose a steeplechase, being witty and debonair and irresistible. His life is one continuous floating riot.

Let me give you an example. This was when he was in his teens, remember. I was there, but only as a spectator. The hour was late, and all the gold on the table had come to roost in front of Muny, as usual. The rest of the company was drunk and surly, every one of them years older than he and none of them accustomed to losing. He was his invariable jaunty self.

Without warning, he picked out the largest man in the group and openly accused him of cheating. Considering that the man had lost a small fortune in the previous three hours, that was even less probable than it was wise to suggest. He was also a deadly swordsman.

In an instant the man was on his feet, drawing his rapier. "Bloody young coxcomb! You will lose your tongue for those words." Onlookers hastily scattered.

Muny rose deliberately and said, "*En garde*, varlet!"

Then he whipped out his own sword. Where the blade should have been hung a length of silk cord—dangling limply, of course. He stared at it disbelievingly. So did everyone else. The silence was icy.

Then he said, "Damn! I must have been drinking too much." The entire room exploded in thunderclaps of laughter and applause.

Only his opponent chose not to see the joke. He snarled and lunged. Muny parried the rapier with the hilt in his hand and whirled the cord like a whip. It snarled the man's rapier; Muny jerked it out of his grasp. I wouldn't have believed it possible had he been stone sober; he must have practiced for days. Then he planted a fist on the man's chin and laid him cold on the floor. He sat down and picked up his cards without a word.

That was when he was about sixteen.

On my first day in Gilderburg, I wandered into the Margrave's Arms, the most expensive, most respectable establishment in the city. Nowhere are necks stiffer or brows higher. The hall was hushed, a sanctuary of thick carpet and polished paneling. The Margrave's Arms is the sort of place that leaves brass spittoons around, and if you miss one, then a servant rushes forward to clean up—very classy, but somewhat stultifying for my taste. I normally avoid luxury on that scale, but I was weary from my long hike. Having a few thalers in my pocket, I fancied a heated bath and a gourmet meal.

A liveried flunky eyed me scathingly and strolled forward to inquire my needs.

A voice from the top of the stairs bellowed, "Omar!" Muny leaped over the banisters, bounced both feet on a thickly padded sofa, and landed in front of me, steady as a house. The elderly lady who had been sitting on the other end of the sofa was still going up and down in shock. Muny threw his arms around me like a long-lost debtor.

After that, of course, I was perfectly acceptable to the management. Any friend of the margrave's brother was a friend of theirs. Even if Muny later left without paying, his family would cover for him. I was surprised to discover that they had allowed him back across the border. But they had. He ordered the best available room for me, chattered cheerfully at my side all the way there, and demanded wine so we could drink while I soaked in the copper tub.

Later he summoned his current mistress to meet me, sending word that she was to bring along some of his spare clothes. Wrapped in a towel, I was presented to one of the loveliest, most gracious ladies imaginable. I was not surprised. He always had the best. She was being represented as his wife, because the Arms guards its reputation avidly. Even Muny had to observe the proprieties to some extent if he wished to remain there.

Life at once became very hectic for me. I was anxious to track down the missing heir, but Muny's companionship leaves little time for anything else.

About the third day, I came weaving back to my

room from an evening's inquiries in haunts of considerably lower reputation. It was just short of dawn. I was still hauling my clothes off when in floated Muny—fresh-shaven, impeccable, grinning as always.

"Omar!" he proclaimed. "Glad to see you're up already! The river's in spate! I've hired a couple of leaky old tubs for a boat race."

I dived into bed, clutching the covers as he tried to haul them off me. "I have work to do!" I protested.

He smirked. "Then why spend the night carousing?"

"Not carousing. Telling stories, asking questions, listening. Investigating."

"Bah! You're starting at the wrong end! You should speak with priests and nobles, not squelch around in the dregs. Get to them later, if all else fails, if you must. Start with the civic fathers and work down."

"In my experience, the dregs are not only more interesting and better informed, but much more likely to be of assistance. The civic fathers won't give me the polish off their boots." Not without a lot of preparatory work, anyway.

Muny said, "Bah!" again. A familiar and worrying glint shone in his eye. "They will listen to me! If I arrange a meeting with the town notables, will you come along on my boat race?"

I consented, agreeable to anything that would gain me a little peace and quiet. It could not have been two hours later when he tipped a carafe of water over my head and announced that it was time to go, everyone was waiting on me.

We smashed one boat in the first rapids—the one I was in, of course. No one drowned, amazingly enough, although most of us were severely bruised. Muny crammed us all into the other and carried on. That one lasted as far as Thunder Falls. We built a fire to dry out, but the horses arrived earlier than expected. We returned to the Margrave's Arms at a spirited gallop.

I barely had time to make myself presentable. The

civic fathers had begun arriving—merchants, nobles, and priests, led by the burgomaster himself. At least thirty men and a few great ladies assembled in the main hall, sat down, and waited to hear their host's pleasure. It does help to be somebody's brother! The hotel staff were jumping around like frogs.

Muny introduced me and left me to it. Feeling as if I had been beaten by professional torturers for forty days and forty nights without respite, I began to recount the tale of the oracle.

Muny had heard it before, so he wandered off to the side. He was probably itching for some devilment to occupy him for the next hour. If that was his intention, he succeeded admirably. Now I must rely on his own account, told to me later.

An elderly matron came tottering in, carrying an obviously heavy bag. The entire staff, as I said, had been thrown into a panic by the invasion of wealth and power—not a porter in sight.

Drawn by an infallible instinct for trouble, Muny bowed and said, "May I be of assistance, ma'am?"

The old lady hesitated, looked around helplessly, and then muttered something about finding someone to carry her baggage up to her room.

Muny took it from her without a word and offered his arm.

They went up the stairs together.

When they reached her door, she unlocked it and said, "Just lay it on the bed, if you would be so kind, young man."

As Muny was depositing the bundle on the bed, he heard the bolt click. He turned around to see the woman stripping off her clothes. She was then revealed, he assured me, as being at least fifty years younger than he would have thought possible, and a very striking example of nubile female into the bargain.

Ever willing, he bowed. "Is there any other service I may perform for you, lady?"

She was still in front of the door. "I am about to scream," she said calmly. "You forced your way in here and attempted to rape me."

"I don't remember having that intention, ma'am, but now that you suggest it, I will admit that the idea has merit."

Knowing Muny, I am certain he remained quite calm, and I expect that his calmness disconcerted her. She must have known he was a member of a powerful and highly respected family. She must have known that all the civic dignitaries of Gilderburg were assembled downstairs—but she had not carried her research far enough. Scandal was never one of the Waldgrave's worries.

"I shall scream!" she repeated. "Your wife—"

"What wife?" Muny must be one of the fastest men alive. He threw a pillow at her. She deflected it, of course, but then he was on her, muffling her face with another pillow. He dragged her over to the bed and tied her up with strips torn from the sheets. Don't ask me how two hands can achieve that without the victim letting rip. Muny is Muny. Even for him, it must have been quite a tussle.

Whether he did actually carry on and rape her then, he never told me and I did not ask. It would have been no more than her due, but underneath his deviltry, Muny has a curious streak of gallantry. He is wild and violent, but not sadistic. It would have spoiled the joke not to, though, so who knows?

I do know that, down in the hall, I had just reached the climax of my story when Waldgrave Munster came trotting down the stairs with a naked girl over his shoulder, bound and gagged. Lean, elegant, and untroubled, he carried her across the hall to the door, set her down gently on the steps outside, and came back in, wiping his hands.

The assembly of civic notables broke up in a near riot. Muny and his mistress and I were run out of town.

It was weeks before I dared sneak back into Gilderburg to pursue my inquiries in the taverns and brothels.

The last time I saw Waldgrave Munster, he was heading off home to some big family reunion, accompanied by a pet ape he had stolen from a circus.

30: The Last Judgment

"*What are you implying?*" the merchant roared. His face had darkened to about the color of ripe grapes, his knuckles showed white on the arms of his chair. He looked ready to leap at me.

"I'm not implying anything, Your Honor. I report facts and leave implications to my listeners' imaginations. Oh, by the way, Gwill. You mentioned earlier that you were lured into an alley in Gilderburg . . ."

Gwill had already thought of that. He was staring very hard at the actress. By now everyone was, of course, but his stare held dangerous overtones.

Marla was a paradigm of composure, hands crossed demurely on her lap. She endured our suspicion with the bravado of the professional she was. One has to admire brass when it is well polished.

"Your voice!" Gwill said. "Your *voice*! I wondered where I had heard it before! And not just in the Velvet Stable, either!"

"I have no idea what you're talking about, any of you," Marla said sedately. She turned to her husband. "Can we go to bed now, dearest?"

"So there wasn't a gang!" Gwill shouted. "Just you! You had a cane! My father's lute!"

The merchant roared, drowning him out. "You are talking about Gilderburg, not Schlosbelsh, both of you! We don't tolerate women like that in my city!"

"Oh?" I said. "Did I mention that the imposter was run out of town at the same time Muny and I were?"

"Lies and slanders!" He was half out of his chair now, crouched like a human bullfrog about to strike with its killer tongue.

"I admit I didn't get a good look at her face, Your Honor. But I would certainly recognize her tattoos again. I saw them first in the Velvet—"

Johein's face went from purple to pale and then settled into a sickly greenish tinge—an artifact of the candlelight, I suppose. He turned to the actress in sick dismay. *"Tattoos?"*

She shrugged. "I was saving them for a surprise."

"You were Sister Zauch? But the heraldry?"

"I looked it up where Tickenpepper did, I expect—in the town-hall library below your office. You really ought to read more, Johein."

Action! He flailed an arm at her, toppling her back over the bench. She hung on, hauling him with her, chair and all. They hit the floor together in a resounding crash, with roars and screams all round. Vague scraps of insult drifted up from the melee, but I can't recall any that I should care to repeat—Volkslanderian is rich in invective. Marla was certainly winning that part of the battle. Would a burgomaster even know what such words meant? Johein stopped cursing and began screaming.

It took both Captain Tiger and Fritz to separate the loving couple, lifting Johein bodily. Marla climbed to her feet under her own power, looking furious and rubbing her throat. The merchant was in much worse shape, as if she had used a well-placed knee on him in the tussle. She was a pro; Johein was not Muny.

Gwill set the chair upright, Fritz dumped Johein back into it, where he remained, all curled up and whimpering. Marla glanced around to see what the rest of us were planning. Her look at me almost set my hair on fire.

"My father's lute!" Gwill demanded, moving closer.

Marla simpered. "Sue us. Johein's responsible for all my debts. Isn't he, Ticklepopper baby?"

Tickenpepper looked little pleased, doubtless contemplating the loss of an important client. He licked his lips and said nothing.

The actress shrugged. "Besides, minstrel, I gave you a 'specially good time later, didn't I?"

The notary shuddered. Gwill blushed scarlet and turned away.

Johein moaned. I could not feel sorry for him. Whatever he said, I would never believe that his proposal to the sweet little postulant nun had occurred before he received Tickenpepper's report. He had tried to steal a throne and walked straight into a cesspool.

"Well!" the dowager said, conveying volumes. "Very neatly unmasked, Master Omar! Is it dawn, innkeeper?"

Fritz had moved around behind me and now he slammed up the bar on a shutter. It flew open with a blaze of sunlight and a rush of cold morning air—they do have window glass in the Volkslander, but there is no way to convey it to a place like the Hunters' Haunt. Ferns skittered across the floor. The fire's embers smoked, then flamed into life.

The night was over, the tales were told.

Back to reality.

Fritz chuckled throatily. "It is morning! Now I get to settle with Master Omar."

Now I would have to settle with Fritz. I confess I really hated the prospect, milords, but I could see no other way out. I addressed my first remarks to Master Tickenpepper, very respectfully.

"You mentioned wergild last night, Counsellor. The sum of fifty thalers was quoted. Is it necessary to pay in coin, or am I permitted to tender something of equal, or even greater, value?"

He blinked his little rodenty eyes at me. "If the injured party is willing to accept payment in kind, a court will not normally object, subject of course to the sovereign power being able to exercise its right to assess a royalty on such settlements, in jurisdictions where such provision applies."

I decided that meant maybe.

One of Fritz's great paws closed around my neck. His voice rumbled like an approaching avalanche, if an avalanche can sound skeptical. "What exactly are you planning to tender, vagrant?"

As little as possible; as much as needed.

There was no use appealing to the merchant or his wife. Gwill was well disposed, but penniless. Frieda obviously knew better than to intervene.

"Captain Tiger," I said, speaking a little faster, "are you going to stand by and let this overgrown savage indulge his bestial instinct for violence?"

The soldier had remained on his feet by the fire, standing guard over the merchant. He shrugged. "He has justice on his side. You brought your troubles on yourself."

Fritz began to lift. Vertebrae creaked. I grabbed the bench with both hands.

"Lady Rose-dawn! I have performed many not-inconsiderable services for your family over the years. I now find myself temporarily short of ready cash and therefore presume to cast myself—"

"Take him outside, landlord," the old hag croaked. "The sight of blood upsets me. Especially first thing in the morning." She did not even look around. Such ingratitude!

The strain on my neck suggested that Fritz was about to lift me and the bench and Master Tickenpepper all together. I had run out of alternatives.

"Verl!" I squeaked. "Help!"

The pressure eased slightly—or at least stopped increasing—and even the dowager leaned around to peer in my direction.

"You appeal to Rosie's icon?" the soldier growled. "I thought you had discredited that?"

"I appeal to the genuine Verl." I spoke with deep conviction, a full octave lower than my normal tones—I suppose because my neck was significantly longer than usual. "My lady, if I deliver your daughter's god to you, will you buy off this homicidal barbarian?"

Fritz snarled and hoisted me clear into the air, tearing my grip from the bench.

"Wait a minute!" Captain Tiger said. "He has more delays than a child at bedtime! You know where the genuine Verl can be found?"

"Mmm, yeth," I whispered, having trouble being audible. Fritz was now squeezing.

"In a vault in some far-off city, of course? Many months away?"

I tried to shake my head and wriggled like a fish.

The soldier frowned in disbelief. "This is positively your last chance, Omar! Produce the idol. Her ladyship will judge whether it is genuine. If it is, then we shall settle your debt for you. If not, then I shall hold our host's doublet for him."

I croaked and flailed my arms.

"Put him down a moment, Fritz."

My toes touched the floor and I could breathe. "If you will just look behind you, Captain. On that shelf, presently hidden behind the hourglass? You will find a small white clay dove—not very lifelike or beautiful, just a pottery image of a bird. One eye . . . Yes, that one. Blow the dust off. Now if you will just show it to her lady—"

Doglike, Fritz snarled and shook me. "That has been there for as long as—" He fell silent. Frieda had risen and was staring at both of us. Her fair cheeks were considerably paler than usual.

"It is!" the dowager cried, holding the figurine almost at the end of her nose. "Holy Verl!"

Fritz released me and I flopped like a dropped chemise.

"Fifty thalers for your trinket, landlord?" Captain Tiger inquired dryly.

"Captain . . ." Fritz stepped around the bench and went to Frieda, but whether to comfort her, or to be comforted, I could not tell. "It is only an old family keepsake. Of no value at all. Take it and welcome. I don't know what trickery this ragpicker is up to now—"

Alas! I should have left the matter there, but I always take offense at being called a ragpicker.

"It is the genuine Verl, you bone-brained lummox. It proves that Sweet-rose passed this way. Beyond the Grimm Ranges, the oracle said, and this is confirmation. I wish I had known about it this summer, or about the birthmark—"

"Birthmark?" Frieda snapped. "What birthmark?"

Both she and Fritz had been out of the room when that was mentioned. "Heidi has one, but I presume not the correct shape, Captain?"

"No, and totally the wrong location, I understand." The soldier smiled.

"Well, that concludes the night's business," I said cheerfully. "As I am now officially a guest, my good man, you may bring me the breakfast menu right away."

"What birthmark?" Frieda demanded again.

"Also, my own clothes should be dry by now . . ."

Captain Tiger frowned suspiciously in my direction. "Sweet-rose bore a birthmark in the shape of a rose, over her heart."

Oh, how I wished he hadn't mentioned that!

More hindered than helped by his sister's hasty efforts to assist him, Fritz was already unbuttoning his doublet.

31: The Innkeeper's Tale

"**I**t's not as if he was a foundling or something!" Frieda was sitting next to me, apparently unconcerned by my arm around her. "It doesn't make any sense!"

Fritz now occupied the chair to the left of the fireplace, the place of honor. His doublet was still open, the red mark just visible under all the chest hair.

Burgomaster Johein had gone limping up to bed, hunched over in pain, a broken, ruined man. The dowager sniffled into a lace handkerchief, being comforted by Captain Tiger. Marla was still on her feet, hovering in the background. Gwill and Tickenpepper sat in bemused silence.

The candles had blown out. With sunlight streaming in through a single window, the room seemed darker than it had in the night. Shadows lurked everywhere. I had the vaguely dizzy feeling that comes from a night without sleep.

"It makes sense to me," I said. "Although there are a few details missing."

Frieda had described her parents for us. She had even produced a sketch of them, made by some wandering artist in return for a meal. They had been a handsome couple, but solid Volkslander peasant stock, emphatically not Sweet-rose and Zig.

The clay dove lay in Fritz's great hands. He was staring at it in bewilderment, and so far he had not spoken a word since the dowager knelt to him. If I really tried, I thought I could find a resemblance to Zig there

272

somewhere—something about the mouth, perhaps? With a little more effort, I could even see a likeness to Ven, a much younger Ven than I had ever known— Ven's statues, I mean, of course. Ven died almost two hundred years ago, didn't he?

Then Fritz looked up and scowled at me.

"If this is another of your sleazy tricks, storyteller, then I am going to break your neck and stamp you into the slush."

"No tricks. I had no intention of deeding you a kingdom in exchange for your flea-bitten mongrel. Have you never heard voices in this room?"

"No, I have not!" The scowl became a furious glare.

"You don't have to shout about it. Sure? Never wondered who kept your inn safe from brigands? Well, you can find out soon enough. Take Verl off where we can't overhear you. She will speak to you, I promise."

He set his big jaw.

"Humor him," the soldier said. "We all want to know."

He rose reluctantly. "Captain, will you see he doesn't steal anything while I am gone?"

"That I will, lad. Sire, I mean."

Fritz snorted disbelievingly. Still holding the tiny clay bird as if it were an egg, he stamped over to the door. The wind slammed it behind him. His shadow passed the window. For a moment we waited, then we heard his voice rumble in the distance. Nothing else except water dripping from the eaves and the wind in the trees . . . or was there a faint cooing of doves, also?

"Still thawing," I told the silence. "You will try the pass today, Captain?"

"I suppose so. We should leave as soon as possible, as long as the weather holds." The soldier looked to Frieda. "But will your brother consent to leave the inn?"

Now there was a startling thought! Might Fritz refuse the summons?

"Depends what the god is telling him right now," I said. "If you catch a ship from the Winelands ... but you can't get through the passes to Hool before spring, anyway. I don't suppose the kingdom will accept him until he has been authenticated by the oracle."

Tiger glanced at the dowager and then smiled. "Her ladyship's word will carry weight, I imagine."

"Kraw will verify him for the families," she mumbled into her handkerchief.

"That's true, I suppose. And he looks like a king!"

He did? Well, he was certainly big enough—king size.

"He looks marvelous!" the dowager snapped, suddenly more her old self. "A wonderful king, and such a wonderful grandson!"

Poor Fritz.

"But what about the inn?" The soldier turned to Frieda again.

"There's a man in Gilderberg wanted to buy it last year, sir, when our parents ... Master Tickenpepper, could you ... er, are you going on south, sir, or are you going home again?"

The notary mumbled, flustered.

"He's going home," Marla interposed. "I'm sure Johein has lost all interest in visiting Holy Hool." She laughed.

"So am I!" Gwill said, a gleam in his eye. "Going north, I mean. I need an attorney to lay charges of, er, battery and theft, I suppose. Are you still retained by the burgomaster, Notary, or can you take on another client?"

"I shall need to confirm my status with his honor, Master Gwill. If I cannot act on your behalf myself, I can recommend others who can."

"An open-and-shut case?"

"No, I wouldn't say that."

"What he means, Tanglepooper," Marla said, "is that Johein and I will do anything at all to stop him from going to Schlosbelsh and spreading stories. Isn't that right, minstrel?"

"Something along those lines, mistress."

Marla laughed. "How much to shut your mouth?"

"Name a figure."

"That's up to my dear hubby. How about that gold chain he wears?"

Gwill blinked. "I believe that would persuade me to continue my journey south."

"And stay there?"

"Certainly."

"I'll go and talk to old Moneybags, then." She sauntered over to the staircase. "If he proves difficult, I'll show him a tattoo or two." She went up, sniggering at her own wit.

Gwill and I exchanged pleased grins. Even Frieda and the soldier were amused. Our fat friend had married a lot more than he expected, and he was obviously going to stay married.

Then Fritz's shadow passed the window again.

He came in with the air of a man who has just suffered a stunning shock. It takes an outstanding liar to fake pallor. It isn't even easy to make your hands shake convincingly, or shuffle across the floor as if you had an invisible sack of meal on your shoulders. Make that two sacks in his case. Three, maybe. So I don't think he was lying in what followed.

He laid the figurine back on the shelf, hesitated, bowed his head to it for a moment. Then he turned around slowly and looked us over. There were tears in his eyes, but that might have been from the wind. His blond coloring made him seem younger than his years; had he not been so huge, he would have looked like a mere boy.

"Omar . . . We are more than quits. I withdraw all the things I said."

"Don't bother, Sire. Most of them were well deserved."

A satisfying trace of the old Fritzian glare returned. "Very well, I won't. I still want to break your neck, but I'll try not to. She spoke to me."

We waited.

He shrugged. "Frieda ... We're not ... I was adopted. They never told me."

"Or me." She pulled away from my arm and went to him. They hugged. He kept her by him and addressed us again.

"I am the son of Siegfried of Holtzenwold and Lady Sweet-rose of Verl."

"Out with it!" I cried. "What's the story?"

"Sire?" Fritz said menacingly.

"I beg your pardon, your Majesty! Sire, of course."

"Better! She told me this much: They were coming north to the Volkslander. My father had family here. True-valor was still with them—her loyal servant, his friend. Their party was caught in an avalanche. True-valor fought loose, then he and some of the others began digging. They found the baby, me. He decided to go for help and take me with him lest I freeze to death in the storm. He reached this inn."

Frieda: "And Mother took the baby?"

"Yes. And Verl was bundled up with me, of course. There was no help to be had here, no guests in residence. It was the very night you were born. Father would not leave his wife and new child unattended, understandably. True-valor went back alone. He was caught in another avalanche."

For a while there was only the wind in the trees and the drip of water ...

"My daughter died, also?" The dowager's voice was barely a whisper.

Fritz took a moment to answer. "No. She and Siegfried were dug out and went south again with the others. In the spring, they came north by another pass, having given me up for lost."

"She is still alive?"

"Verl told me to tell you that Sweet-rose found happiness and you are to search no more."

Holtzenwold was one place I had missed in the summer. I wondered why.

"She had more sons? Daughters?"

"That is all I am permitted to say, my lady!"

Obviously the god had told Fritz more, much more. He spoke softly, but already he seemed to have taken on some royal authority. The old woman shrank back in her chair and was silent. If Fritz's mother was still alive, with a husband and near-grown children, she would have little desire to drag herself back to the land of her birth. Sweet-rose had always known her own mind, and I could assume that her god knew it equally well.

"I was told to accompany you to Verlia and promised that in the spring, Hool will acknowledge me as rightful king of the realm." Fritz looked down at his adoptive sister in wonder. "We must just abandon the inn, dear, I suppose. It seems wrong, but we have a kingdom now."

"Oh, no!" Frieda pulled free from his arm. "Mother and Father would not approve of that! And besides, suppose Hool rejects you? I shall wait here until I receive an official summons to your coronation."

"I can't leave you alone here!"

She laughed shakily. "It's my inn, not yours! Your kingdom, not mine."

"You will always be welcome, and you will always be my sister. Lady Frieda! I shall deed you a royal estate!"

"No, you won't! I shall stay in the background and choose a suitable wife for you. I shall stop you being pestered by all the beautiful gold-digging palace ladies."

He chuckled. "We'll see about that! Meanwhile, we

are still dutiful hosts. We must offer our guests breakfast."

"Kings don't wait on people!" Frieda said sharply.
"You go and pack. Omar will help me, won't you,
Omar?"

I felt a twinge of delight. "I should love to assist you,
beloved! My specialty is sautéed haunch of camel with
damsons."

"Can you fry eggs? Come along. Go and pack, your
Majesty!"

"What do I have worth packing?" he asked, smiling.
The smile was thin, though. Either the sky and all the
stars had just fallen on the innkeeper, or he had just em-
barked on a very large deception.

Later I watched them all depart, standing at the door
with my arm around lovely Frieda. I had promised to
remain and help her run the inn until we heard from
Verlia. Snowy peaks towered over the forested valley,
gleaming under a blue sky. But mountain weather can
change in minutes. With any luck, we should be storm-
bound for weeks at a time, just the two of us. I was
looking forward to that.

Burgomaster Johein and Mistress Marla rode away to
the north, with Master Tickenpepper following at a respectful distance on his palfrey. I heard Marla's voice
lecturing until they were mere specks on the scenery.

Captain Tiger drove the carriage off along the south-
ward trail, bearing Lady Rose-dawn and Rosalind, her
maid. With them, also, went a certain clay pigeon and
Minstrel Gwill, resplendently bedecked in a chain of
solid gold links, plus Fritz of Verl, rightwise born king
of Verlia.

When silence returned to the valley, I planted a kiss
on Frieda's fair cheek.

"Just think," I said. "His descendants will rule forever! An awesome conception!"

"And I suppose you will drop in on them in future centuries and tell them tales of their forbears?"

I frowned at the unseemly shadow of doubt on her lovely face. "Just because I have been around a long time does not mean I shall be around forever."

"And we have only your word for how long you have been around, haven't we? Do I really want to be friends with a man who is thousands of years old?"

"There is no substitute for experience. Shall I demonstrate?"

"Not just now." She tried to pull free of my arm, without success.

I nibbled her ear. "I hope Fritz keeps a proper respect for the bird. She is a hard deity to serve. His ancestors, Juss and Ven, learned that, and their mother Whitethorn, also. His uncle Star-seeker discovered the truth the hard way. She is a dangerous dove."

"Apparently. Why would the god have brought such disaster on the royal family?"

"I told you I never speculate on the minds of gods. But perhaps she had made a mistake. Sea-jewel, for example. Her son Just-blade was a poor king, and Starseeker seemed fated to be worse. So Verl may have wanted to introduce new blood. Or perhaps she had grown bored, after a century shut up in a palace, and wanted to go adventuring again, as she had with me. She must have enjoyed her vacation in the Hunters' Haunt."

Frieda snorted, a very unattractive sound. "You have answers for everything, don't you?"

Again I was piqued. "What does that mean?"

"I realize that the dove was hidden behind the hourglass. You didn't by any chance go snooping this spring, did you? And find it then?"

"Lady Rose-dawn identified her as the genuine Verl," I protested, hurt by this lack of confidence. "Do you think I would have wasted my entire summer skulking around the northern marches had I known that what I sought was here at the inn? And there is the birthmark."

"When you broke into the stable and Fritz caught you at it—he had his shirt off, as I recall?"

"I did not know that birthmarks were important then! I remind you that it was Lady Rose-dawn who brought up the subject of birthmarks. She identified that, too."

"That old witch can't see her hand in front of her nose."

"Frieda, my love!" I wailed. "Are you saying that your brother is an imposter? That he was lying when he said the god spoke to him? How can he possibly hope to deceive Holy Hool?"

She sighed. "I don't know! Hool may decide to make the best of it. Even gods have to improvise sometimes, I suppose. Given such an opportunity, Fritz would be a fool not to try it, wouldn't he?"

I sighed at her lack of trust—it was very unbecoming in one so young and innocent. "It has been a very long night, my delicious edelweiss blossom! Why don't we creep upstairs to bed?"

"Bed!?"

"Why not? The saintly Osmosis of Sooth taught the faithful that there are many kinds of love, and you should always take what you can get."

"Sisterly affection is my specialty. Omar, the cows have to be milked right away, and you must fetch water from the well so I can do the dishes. There is wood to be chopped, floors to clean, butter to churn, meal to grind, stables to muck out, a pig to be slaughtered, skinned, and dressed, bacon to smoke, chickens to feed, horses to groom, and malt to brew. I need wood and water brought to the copper and the laundry must be hung out."

I howled until the echoes howled in sympathy. "But by the time I have done a tenth of that, then there will be more guests arriving!"

"A hotelier's work is never done. Why do you think

my parents never had time to produce more than one child? Start with the cows."

There's the story, milords!—the innkeeper's tale. Not an untrue word. That's how I came to the Hunters' Haunt. I pray you to observe that our tariff is still quoted in Gilderburg thalers. Now, may I pour you some more of our celebrated mulled ale?

POSTSCRIPT

The tale of the wonder horse Twak is based on the story of Clever Hans, a horse in Germany who exhibited the same abilities. I wouldn't want you to think I made it up.

About the Author

Dave Duncan was born in Scotland in 1933 and educated at Dundee High School and the University of St. Andrews. He moved to Canada in 1955 and has lived in Calgary ever since. He is married and has three grown children.

After a thirty-year career as a petroleum geologist, he discovered that it was much easier (and more fun) to invent his own worlds than try to make sense of the real one.

Coming soon from Del Rey Books ...

Dave Duncan
THE CURSED

In the beginning were the fates, dispensing unto mankind in equal measure their light and their darkness, their joy and sorrow, their blessing and their curse ...

More excerpts from current and upcoming Del Rey books are available online!

Via gopher: gopher.panix.com, Del Rey Books subdirectory

Via fileserver: send "help" e-mail to delrey@tachyon.com for instructions

SHOOL is Time, the Slow One, stealer of youth, guardian of what has been and what is to be, maker of ends and beginnings

IVIEL is Health, Star of Evening, bringer of wounds and sickness, Star of Morning, the healer, the comforter

MUOL is Passion, the Red One, bringer of love and hatred, maker and destroyer

AWAIL is Change, the Inconstant One, the fickle one, ruler of the night

OGOAL is Chance, the Swift One, the joker, spinner of fortune

JAUL is Thought, who is Reason, the Bright One, dispenser of truth and falsehood, maker and breaker of law and justice

POUL is Destiny, the Great One, giver of life and death, the mover, queen of days

1

In Tolamin, it began with a runaway wagon. Two horses came careering down the narrow street in panic, trying to escape from the terrible racketing monster pursuing them. Its load of pottery ewers clattered and rolled; every few seconds, another would bounce right out to explode on the stones and splatter contents everywhere. Bystanders leaped for the safety of doorways or pressed back against walls. There was no sign of the driver.

A child stood directly in the wagon's path, thumb in mouth, an infant clad only in a wisp of cloth, staring blankly at the doom hurtling down upon him.

The boy's mother rushed out to snatch him away to safety, but her foot slipped and the two of them sprawled headlong together, directly under the plunging hooves. Horses and wagon flashed over them and continued their headlong progress to certain destruction at the river. The woman scrambled to her feet, clutching her child. Apparently neither had suffered as much as a bruise.

"There!" Jasbur screeched. "You see that?"

"Lucky," Ordur muttered.

"Lucky? You call that lucky? I say it's impossible. I say somebody is *influencing*."

Ordur scratched his head and thought about it. He wasn't thinking too clearly these days. "Suppose it could be."

"Suppose? Hah! You're even stupider than you look, you know that?"

"You, too!"

"You look like a moron, but you're not that smart. You don't have the brains of a lettuce."

"You, too!"

That was the best Ordur could manage in repartee these days. He knew he was slow. It wasn't fair of Jasbur to call him ugly, though. Maybe he was ugly, but this time Jasbur was just as bad—short and bent, almost a hunchback. His face was a grayish, swarthy shade as if it had not been washed for years, and gruesomely wrinkled. The whites of his eyes were yellow; he slavered all the time. Although the fringe of hair around his head was silver, its roots were dark. There were patches of shadowy dark stubble on his cheeks and more on his bald pate. His teeth were nastily prominent, his clothes tattered and filthy.

The wagon had reached the dock. The horses veered to right and left; trappings broke miraculously to free them. The wagon sailed on by itself, passing narrowly between two moored barges and vanishing into the water. Jasbur crowed witlessly at this further evidence of fatalist *influence* upsetting the normal probabilities of the world.

But talk of lettuce had reminded Ordur that his belly ached. He peered up the long street, then down it. There were a lot of people standing around, mostly staring after the wagon. An excited group had gathered around the woman and her child, babbling about their miraculous escape.

"I'm hungry. Haven't eaten all day!"

Jasbur shrieked in derision. "All day? It's barely dawn! You mean you didn't eat all day yesterday!"

"And I'm still hungry."

"Whose fault is that? You're supposed to be a beggar, but you look so bad you give children hysterics. Women set their dogs on us because of your ugly face."

"You, too!"

"Half the people in this town don't eat. It was your idea to come to Tolamin and it was a stupid idea."

Ordur didn't think it had been his idea, but he wasn't going to argue with Jasbur today. Maybe tomorrow would be better. "You eaten today?"

"No, nor yesterday neither!"

"Don't like this town," Ordur announced. "It smells."

"Curd brain! It's all the burned buildings. It was sacked, you numskull."

As if to emphasize the point, a ruined shell of a house farther up the hill collapsed out into the street in a cascade of bricks and charred timbers. Dust flew up in black clouds. People screamed.

"There!" Jasbur cackled. "Months it's been standing, and now it falls down. I tell you, there's somebody *influencing!*"

"Who?"

"How should I know?"

Lightning flashed, and thunder cracked almost overhead. Ordur jumped. "Oughta get out of here!"

"Naw. Thunder at this time of day? How often d'you see that?"

"Don't *see* thunder, Jasbur. See lightning. Hear thunder."

"Bah! There's an Ogoalscath around here somewhere. Let's find him." Jasbur hobbled off down the hill on bandy legs.

Ordur strode after him. "Why? How'd you know he's this way?"

"I don't, but he will be, you'll see."

Surely wise people would go away from an Ogoalscath, not toward him? But if Jasbur said to go this way, then Ordur would have to. Jasbur wasn't being very nice to him just now, but he did seem to be the smart one. He said he was, so it must be true.

Lightning flashed again, thunder rumbled, rain began to fall in grape-size drops.

2

In Tharn Valley, it began with a bad tooth. Bulion Tharn was no stranger to having teeth pulled. Any man who lived long enough to outlast his teeth had been blessed by the fates—that was how he liked to look on the matter. He had been fortunate in having Glothion around. Glothion was the blacksmith, the largest of his sons, with limbs like an oak. Old teeth tended to shatter when gripped with pliers, but Glothion could pull them with his bare fingers. It felt as if he were about to snap the jawbone, and the way he steadied his victim's head under his arm would surely crush some unfortunate's skull one day, but nine times out of ten he could yank a tooth cleanly out.

This time had been one of the other times. Bulion should have stood the pain a week or two longer, perhaps, to let the rotting molar rot some more. He hadn't. He'd been in too much of a hurry, and Glothion had pulled the crown off.

That meant real bloodshed. Wosion had insisted they wait three days, until the fates were propitious, and by then Bulion had been almost out of his mind with the pain. It had taken Glothion and Brankion and Zanion to hold their father down while Wosion himself tried to cut out the roots with a dagger.

He hadn't found all of them, obviously. Now, two days later, Bulion's face was swollen like a pumpkin and nigh hot enough to set his beard on fire. He was running a fever. The pain was a constant throb of lightning all through his head.

He was very likely going to die of this.

There were surgeons in Daling. The odds that he could survive the two-day ride there were slim. The odds that any leech or sawbones could help him now were even slimmer.

It seemed the fates were ready to close the book on Bulion Tharn.

In Daling, it began when Tibal Frainith came to Phoenix Street.

Gwin was helping Tob the stable boy replace the wheat sheaf over the door. She was needed only when a cart came along and threatened to sweep ladder and Tob and wheat sheaf all away together, but her presence discouraged passing urchins from attempting the same feat. Meanwhile, she could clean off the road with a broom—not just because it made the entrance more appealing, but because it meant less dirt to be tracked inside. She could have sent a servant to do all that, but then it would have taken twice as long. She welcomed an excuse just to go outside. It seemed she did not leave the hostel for weeks at a time nowadays.

Meanwhile, the staff indoors were probably sitting around eating and talking when they should be working. Morning was busy time. The last guests had just left. There was a stable to be shoveled out, water to carry, beds to make, bread to bake, bedding to air, and all the interminable cleaning. The Flamingo Room needed fumigating again, having still not recovered from the sailors who had infested it with bedbugs the previous week.

Morning sunlight brightened the narrow streets of Daling as gladly as a baby's smile. Stonework shone in the color of beechwood. The cobbles were polished little islands, each one set off by dark mire in the crevices between them, giving the roadway a texture of coarse cloth, a cobble carpet, dipping here and there into noxious puddles, although even they reflected the sun. Exterior windows were rare, but a few bronze grilles gleamed joyously; and all the doors were limed to a brilliant white.

Phoenix Street was occupied by pedestrians and horsemen and much idle gossip. Every few minutes, an oxcart would come clattering and rattling along, usually being chased by small children trying to cadge a ride, and being shouted away by the carter. Strolling hawkers called their wares, stopping to talk with the women at the doorways.

The old wheat sheaf hit the cobbles, disintegrating into a cloud of dust and a mess of rotted straw where Gwin had just swept. She clucked annoyance, and hastened to pass up the replacement bundle to Tob. He took it without a word. Not even his own mother could call him swift. The only good thing about Tob was that he was too stupid to be dishonest.

She laid into the straw with her broom, spreading it out for hooves and wheels to crumble. She tried not to remember that selfsame sheaf being hung—thirty-six weeks ago, a day as hot as this one promised to be. She had been helper then, too, but it had not been a half-wit stable boy up the ladder. It had been Carp himself. Now Carp was rotting in an unmarked grave somewhere near Tolamin. Karn and Naln had followed their father. She was the only one left now—widow, bereaved mother, innkeeper, Gwin Nien Solith.

"Gwin!"

She spun around, blinking into the sun.

The speaker was tall, lean, and clean-shaven. He bore a bulky pack sack on his shoulders. His smock and breeches had never been dyed and now were a nondescript gray. They were ordinary Kuolian garb, yet of an unfamiliar cut, as if they had traveled far from the loom that birthed them. He had steady gray eyes, and brown tangled hair, worn shorter than was normal for men in Daling. Bone and sinew lay close under his skin. Yes, tall. He was smiling at her as if the two of them were old friends, close friends. She had never seen him before in her life.

"I don't . . ."

He started. "Sorry! I am Tibal Ambor Frainith." He bowed.

"Most honored, Tibal *Saj*. I am Gwin Nien Solith."

"Yes. I mean I am honored, Gwin *Saj*." He was blushing.

Blushing?

Pause.

The expectant look remained in his eyes. She could not recall being thrown off balance like this for years. She did not forget faces. He was at least as old as she was, so why were his cheeks flaming red like that?

A stranger in town would seek out a hostelry. Carp Solith had won a good reputation for the Phoenix Street Hostel; his widow had sustained it so far. Most of her business came from repeats, established customers—merchants, farmers, ship captains—but first-timers were not rare.

So why was she gazing tongue-tied at this man? Why was he staring down at her with that blush on his cheeks and that wistful, disbelieving expression in his gray eyes? There was something strange about his gaze that she could not place.

"The Phoenix Street Hostel," he said in his unfamiliar accent. "Everyone will ... Everyone told me that it's the best hostelry in the city, Gwin *Saj*." He spoke too softly, stood a little too close.

A lead pair of oxen emerged from Sailors' Alley, with another following.

"They spoke no less than the truth, Tibal *Saj*."

"I need a room, Gwin." He still seemed mildly amused that she had not recognized him. He was a little too quick dropping the honorific.

"Rooms are my business, Tibal *Saj*." Why else display a wheat sheaf above the door?

Tob was still up the ladder, tying the sheaf to the bracket. The oxcart was advancing along the road. Tibal backed into its path, holding up a hand to stop it, all without ever taking his eyes off Gwin.

"You came by way of Tolamin?" she said. He must have, to be arriving in the city so early in the day.

He hesitated and then nodded. The wagoner howled curses at him.

"How is it?" she asked.

Tibal blinked and frowned. "Much the same," he said vaguely.

Whatever did that mean? The Wesnarians had sacked it in the fall.

The teamster hauled on the traces and brought his rig to a clattering halt with the lead pair's steaming muzzles not an ell from the lanky stranger—who still ignored it all, still stared at Gwin.

Tob came slithering down the ladder, leering with pride at having completed an unfamiliar task. "All done, Gwin *Saj*."

"Take the ladder down, Tob."

"Oh. Yes." The lout moved the ladder. Tibal stepped out of the way so the team could proceed.

"You almost got yourself jellied there," she said.

"What?" He glanced at the cart and its furious driver as if he had been unaware of their existence until she spoke. He shrugged. "No."

There was something definitely odd about Tibal Frainith, but he raised no sense of alarm in her. Almost the reverse—he seemed to be signaling friendship. Not asking for it, just assuming it. Curiously reassuring, somehow . . . clothes neither rich nor poor . . . carried his own pack. Not a rich man, therefore. Soft-spoken. Not a soldier. Not a merchant. A wandering scholar, perhaps? At least he wasn't proposing marriage yet. Lately she spent half her days fighting off suitors who wanted to marry a hostel, and she was going to lose the battle.

She opened the door, setting the bell jangling. "I'll show you the rooms we have available." They were all available, but she would not admit to that.

He stepped past her. As she was about to follow him inside, a voice said, *It has begun.*

Startled, she jumped and looked around. There was no one there. Tob was just disappearing into the alley with the ladder, heading around to the back. The wagon had gone. The voice had not come from Tibal Frainith.

294

So who had spoken? Her nerves must be snapping if she was starting to hear voices. With a shiver of fear, she followed her guest inside, shutting the door harder than necessary.

And so it begins ...

Dave Duncan
THE CURSED

Coming soon from Del Rey Books!